Threads of Infinity
7th Book in The Dimensional Alliance series

By: Bonnie K.T. Dillabough

Cover Art: Rick McKenzie and Delia Michael
Copyright: Infinite Publishing Alliance 2023

Acknowledgments

Thanks to all of those who make these books possible, starting with all my amazing fans. Every time one of you tells me how much you enjoy the books, it fires my desire to make these more interesting and fun for each of you.

Second, thanks to my amazing copyeditor, Lynette Smith, and all my beta readers, and a special shout out to some of my first enthusiastic fans, Cassidy McQuain, Carolyn Greiner, Delia Michael, Jeremiah Maluse, Margo Stepp, and, of course, my dear hubby, George C. Dillabough. Thanks once again to my amazing cover artist, Rick McKenzie and his helper this time out, Delia D. Michael.

To my mother, who introduced me to the magic of books and libraries, and to all my librarian friends who contributed to my love of books back in the days when I was the school "library nerd," long before there was such a thing as a computer nerd.

Table of Contents

Prologue

"*Y*ou *are approved for duty, Gatekeeper,*" Ulla sent, raising one cautionary finger. "*However, I still want to see you in six weeks and ask you to come in at any time you experience unusually strong headaches or dizziness. Agreed?*"

Jenny Scout nodded, looking over at Burt, a big smile on her face. "*I promise, healer, that my husband will be relentless to require me to follow your instructions. He has a vested interest in keeping me healthy, after all.*"

Ulla smiled and nodded at Burt. "*I'll hold you both to that. Now off with you both. I have other patients to attend to.*"

Jenny hopped down from the exam table, taking Burt's offered hand. Chidwi chirruped happily and leapt up onto her usual perch on Jenny's shoulder, her tail delightedly curled around Jenny's neck like a fuzzy chartreuse necklace.

"So, what's next on the agenda?" she asked her smiling husband, nearly bouncing on her toes in excitement. "I know we aren't supposed to spend much time at headquarters these days for security's sake, but should we stop in at the council chambers before we head home?"

"I think they're all actually waiting for you," Burt said, his grin deepening as if he knew something he wasn't telling.

"Oh? What's this? You wouldn't be keeping a secret from your wife, would you? After all, you know how much I like surprises…"

His imitation of a mad scientist's laugh was answer enough.

As they entered the chamber, all three councilors were waiting for them, not on the dais, but standing just in front of a row of chairs. On one side, three people were seated seemingly engaged in mindspeech, gesturing and nodding. Liliath, the Chief Councilor, stood foremost and gestured Jenny and Burt forward.

Jenny immediately recognized the three seated on that front row as her "girls," the bodyguards assigned to her since before that incredible last attack by Sam, aka Engoza. Not only had they been by her side ever since, even staying at the dimensional barracks in the gateroom of her house while she had been in recuperation, but they had been lifesavers on more than one occasion.

They looked up when they noticed Liliath's gesture, and all stood immediately, going to parade rest, all three sets of eyes attentively riveted on Jenny.

"Welcome, Gatekeeper," Liliath intoned in mindspeech. *"I hear you have been cleared for duty by healer Ulla."*

"I have, Liliath. And will you please ask my guards not to do that? Attention to my safety is one thing, but these formalities just feel like it calls attention to me in ways that make me uncomfortable."

Liliath nodded at the three women, and they sheepishly relaxed and then sat back down.

"Thank you." Jenny sent to both Liliath and the girls with a sigh of relief. *"Liliath, I know you would prefer I not stay in headquarters any longer than necessary. Is there anything I should know before I head back to my gate?"*

"Not anything in particular. I understand you spent your recuperation time reading Lizzie's journals. I hope it was time well spent?" Liliath cocked her huge head, one eyebrow raised ironically.

"I have to honestly say that it was an educational experience. I now understand a lot more about what it means to be a guardian and gatekeeper and the sacrifices that have gone before me by those who have tended my gate in the past. I would rather not have had to be out of ac-

tion for several weeks, but I think I will serve the Alliance better because of it."

Liliath nodded. *"This is good, since things are about to get, shall we say, interesting? From here on out you will continue to have training mixed in with your other duties. I suggest you take every opportunity to get rest when you can. When you get home, consult your tablet and you will begin to understand why I suggest this to you. You will be making weekly trips to Amenia to continue to hone your mental skills. As you know, based on what you have read of your aunt, you are only beginning to see the full implications of those gifts."*

Jenny nodded, humbly and a little bit alarmed. She knew from prior experience that Liliath was a master of understatement and knew how to get every last scrap of energy out of a training session.

"Then we will bid you farewell. Your guards will once again be staying with you day and night. You will be doing some traveling, as you will notice on your schedule, and they will go with you wherever you go. I leave you in the hands of The Creator of All Things, my dear Jenny. You are the linchpin of our effort to conquer the machinations of the Inseni. Stay true and stay safe."

Liliath stepped forward and hugged Jenny, her huge arms and wings enfolding her and a squeaking Chidwi. Dragon hugs! Of all of the things Jenny had experienced since she first turned the key at the house on Infinity Loop, this had to be one of the strangest and curiously the most satisfying things she had ever imagined possible.

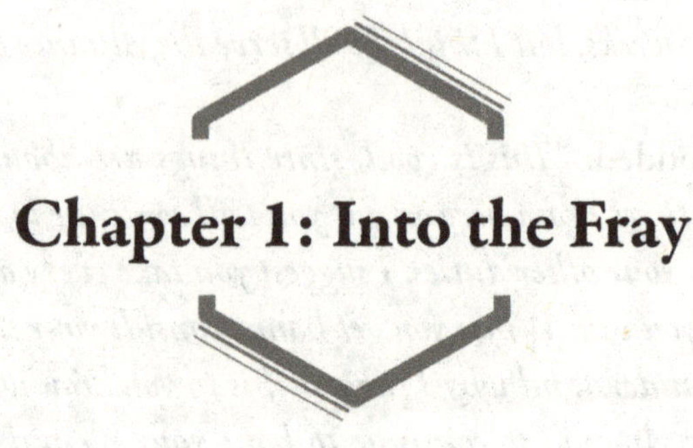

Chapter 1: Into the Fray

I t didn't seem possible that it had been less than two years since Jenny first opened the door to something so much more than a lovely little house from an aunt she had only met twice in her life.

Over that time, she had experienced life-threatening situations, heartbreaks and met the love of her life, not to mention hanging out with dragons and with scientists from other dimensions, visited many different planets in faraway universes, and successfully defended herself in face-to-face combat with alien beings.

Now, as she entered her house through the hallway door from her gate office, it felt good to be home. Not that she ever seemed to get much time there. Probably the longest she had ever spent any significant amount of time at home had been during her convalescence after administering "the shout" to the Inseni army she had faced on the Groga planet. It seemed like both ages ago and just yesterday.

The time she had spent in Lizzie's journals had been so engrossing and epic that she was still having a bit of trouble adjusting to the present and her role in the ongoing struggle between the Alliance and the Inseni. She had been living in her aunt Lizzie's head without many breaks over the past three weeks, and now she knew it would take some time for her to fully absorb the impact of what she had learned.

What was ahead for her? As the Gatekeeper, she was the protector and director of all gate activities in the Alliance. She had a long list of not only the usual responsibilities of that position, but she was still in training. This included the addition of the huge task of helping coordinate all of the communications and interactions among the Alliance during the conflict with the Inseni, to ensure the privacy of all of those communications via her mental ability to traverse the dimensions. This all weighed strongly upon her.

It had been intimated by Amenia and Liliath that perhaps others could now be trained to help her. Once that happened, she would be intensely grateful, but for now even part of her sleep time would be taken up with these additional duties.

Chidwi leapt from Jenny's shoulder and padded over to the French doors in the dining room. Opening the doors, she scampered happily out to the little Yew tree, clambering up its trunk and lighting joyfully into the crook of a branch where she could observe the koi.

Based on what they had learned in Lizzie's journals, the yew tree was named Windsong and was capable of mindspeech, something Jenny had yet to explore in her mental ability training. She hoped to find the leisure to learn this new skill, as she already felt kind feelings for the tree and how it had been such an important element in Lizzie's story.

Burt trailed behind her into the hallway, looking contented. He walked up behind her and put one arm around her shoulders.

"Well, Wifie-poo, what do you think? Shall we order in some Chinese food and hang out for a bit? I get to play hubby for a couple days while you get settled into your new routine. Do your girls eat Chinese food?"

"We sure do," piped up Nona. "Extra eggrolls, please."

The girls gathered in the living room for only a moment. Then, with a nod from Nona, each went to a different part of the house to inspect for any potential dangers. This kind of gave Jenny a shiver, recognizing that it wasn't without reason.

Even though every layer of security that the Alliance could muster was in place at her house, these three women weren't taking any chances; and woe to the bully who ever took for granted that just because they were nice looking "young ladies" it would be a good idea to challenge them.

Tidbit would be back in the morning. Currently he was home with Amenia, for which Jenny was grateful. She knew he didn't get to spend as much time as he would like with his family, especially Amenia. She knew she would be seeing Amenia again soon, as Tarafau and Amenia were as much a part of her family as her own parents here on Earth, and she would soon be doing regular training sessions with Amenia in their home.

For now, however, it was finally time to get back to work. As of tomorrow morning, she would be getting back into her regular routines of physical and mental conditioning. And as of right this minute, she was back on duty as the official Gatekeeper of the Dimensional Alliance. She settled herself in her cushy chair in the living room while Burt and the girls bustled around, he making arrangements for supper and the girls now checking the back and front yards and verifying the functionality of the surveillance equipment installed on the property.

Bob had notified her the day before she went in for her checkup that they had added some new functions to the various gizmos stationed around her house and that there were few places more secure in the multiverse, as far as they could tell. Her upgrades included all of those recently installed at Alliance headquarters, so she felt like she could truly focus on the tasks at hand.

In addition, they had used "dastardly alien tech" to add an inside entrance from between Jenny and Burt's bedroom and the guest room into the garage. Gaston, who had owned the house prior to Lizzie, had installed an upstairs apartment in the garage for his live-in maid, Nita.

"The girls" were going to move in there under the pretense they were college students renting the space from Jenny. Later today they would be moving into the space which had also been rigged with some serious security features. All Jenny would have to do is to send out a mental call and they would all be there on the spot for whatever she needed.

They had already created an around-the-clock schedule for one of them to be with Jenny at all times and to also keep watch at night from the living room any time Burt was not in the house.

Jenny extracted her tablet from her MDP and opened the communications app. There at the top of the page was the document alluded to by Liliath. The schedule had been converted into Earth times and her usual 24-hour day. Because she was who she was and did what she did, this literally meant that she was working long hours, as even a portion of her sleep time was taken up with interdimensional communications with the scientists, military leaders, gate guardians and various members of the Alliance council.

Her job was to coordinate sensitive communications, as, to the best of their knowledge, her mindspeech interactions were the only secure method they could count on. As far as any of them knew, it wasn't possible for anyone to eavesdrop in on a private mindspeech conversation, which would be a definite advantage in the upcoming conflict.

The schedule on her tablet, for instance, had been uploaded in person by Liliath while Jenny had been in the infirmary for her checkup, as they didn't trust sending the information via the Alliance communication network.

Although Sam's retribution on Gall and the Inseni who had murdered her family and destroyed her entire kingdom had coincidentally combined with a coordinated attack by Alliance troops on key planets and had disrupted the Inseni government on a massive scale, the Alliance council were pretty sure this would still give them only a short time to assemble a plan to free the various populations enslaved by the Inseni during Gall's rule. Hundreds of planets in different dimensions continued to be terrorized by the Inseni troops and their leaders who had invaded their planets under that now-defunct government.

It had occurred to Jenny that this may have actually made the Inseni more dangerous to the native populations, as, because of the disruption of the Inseni's central government, there was no oversight or direction coming to them, so they could do whatever they wanted.

Over the past three weeks of Jenny's recovery, the Alliance had continued to create strategies to methodically identify the affected planets and to develop plans of how best to locate the ones they could reach via dimensional gateways attached to the Alliance network and how to puzzle out how to reach those that were attached only to the Inseni gates.

One thing the "wizards," aka the scientists rescued from the Inseni, had made clear was that the known Inseni dimensional portals had still been found mostly by accident. Although the technology to reach these gates employed a completely different frequency than Alliance gateways, the Inseni had never developed technology to connect them into any kind of organized network.

Realistically, they probably would never find all of them, but for now, the Alliance had their hands full just reaching the gates that were known to the Inseni. Once they had done all they could to rescue the endangered populations of those enslaved on Inseni controlled planets, they would try to find a way to shut down the gates permanently.

But for now, the first step was to organize as quickly as possible, before the Inseni could reunite to go against them in force.

Jenny repressed a sigh of resignation. She needed to "fish or cut bait," as her dad would have said. Therefore, she was deep into her long list of to-dos when the doorbell rang and Burt retrieved the bags of food that emitted those tantalizing aromas. He called out to the girls and thanked Lizziebot for setting the table out on the patio.

"Figured you needed some outside time before you get back to work," he explained with a grin as he escorted her out to the patio and gestured with a wink and a formal bow to her seat at the patio table.

Lyra, Nona and Mynn gathered at once around the table, having done their thorough inspection of the grounds. Although none of them were "from around here," they could have mostly passed for earthlings. Nona's brilliant aquamarine eyes shone brightly from her rich dark skin, nearly a blue black. She was careful whenever they were out and about, to wear brown contact lenses to avoid any special notice, but Jenny thought she was gorgeous as is. Short little Lyra, with her short bouncy blonde curls, could have been any girl from the states, and Mynn looked like your average nerd from L.A. with her spiky brown hair and brown eyes.

Jenny had learned to love these three for their diligent care of her, having saved her life more than once. They were fun to be around, and she knew she could count on them to stay on top of things. She hoped at some point to visit their home dimensions and meet their families, as she definitely wanted them to know how very carefully the girls had taken care of her since they had been given the assignment to watch over Jenny.

Anyone looking in at this scene would have simply seen the newlyweds entertaining some dear friends out on the patio that day. Peering through the special filters surrounding the house, Chidwi would have seemed to be a very tame squirrel frolicking in the yew tree and eating from the offerings of the picnickers.

At any time that Jenny left the house with her guards in tow, it would have just seemed like a girl's day out. "The girls," as they were often called by other Alliance agents and guardians, were careful to dress in current Earth styles and went out of their way to not stand out in any way. They really enjoyed their outings with Jenny to purchase appropriate clothing, one of the things they did from time to time to bolster Jenny's cover story.

They ate and laughed and joked and teased and simply enjoyed being out in the sunshine in a beautiful backyard with some great food.

Burt and the girls cleared away the leftovers and shooed Jenny back into the house to finish up doing the clerical part of her job in preparation for the virtual meeting they were all to attend in the gate office later that afternoon.

She knew she would have to get used to a certain amount of pampering, but something inside her head was somewhat rebellious at the thought. She had been extremely independent since leaving home for college and she liked it that way. But adjustments had to be made; and hard or not, Jenny wasn't going to give anyone any reason to regret the choice Miriha had made in choosing her as the Gatekeeper.

As had been repeatedly explained to her by various members of the Alliance, every general or head of state had people they relied on for the mundane tasks related to their position so they could focus on the crucial parts of their mission.

"Okay, missy," Bob said, startling Jenny by abruptly showing up from the hall door of the gate office. "We have work to do. I want to do a pre-briefing before the council briefing later today. Do you want to do it outside in your extremely high security backyard, or would you prefer to go into the gate office?"

"We can do it outside if you'd like. The new neighbors haven't moved into Elias's house yet, and Lacey is out on another one of her lecture tours, not to mention the sound barrier and the visual filter completely around the yard. Too bad you missed lunch. Burt ordered in Chinese, and we and the girls just finished up. You might find there are a few leftovers if you're hungry."

"Nah, I'm good. Okay, the backyard it is. Burt and the girls probably will want to listen in as well. Cornelium and Merv send their regards, by the way."

They went back out into the yard, where Burt and the girls were discussing the koi in the little pond that always so fascinated Tidbit and Chidwi. Chidwi was keeping up her end of the mindspeech conversation and was evidently entertaining them with her own observations of the situation.

While they had been in the house, evidently Tidbit had reappeared and was gazing thoughtfully into the koi pond.

"Have a nice visit at home?" Jenny asked the cat, who looked lazily up at her.

"All is well with Amenia. She looks forward to seeing you now that you are back on active duty," he replied, his tail twitching contentedly.

"Break time is over!" Bob called out with a loud clap of his square palms, gesturing with a grin at the little convention. "We have things to discuss before we get into what the Alliance has for us. Let's get settled and call Lizziebot, please. This will be recorded for use of the Alliance scientists, the Sanglarka bunch, and the Council."

Lizziebot was already on her way out of the open French doors, obviously having heard her name. Bob invoked Fidget out of his MDP, and the two bots stood silently looking on as the humans got themselves organized once again around the clean patio table.

"Okay, folks, here's the scoop. Our Mookookie friends, the Nanoites, and Fidget have been hard at work under the eye of Cornelium, Merv, and yours truly on some interesting insights regarding the potential use of our MDPs in future endeavors.

"They have found they can work well together, and a few of the Nanoites have volunteered to transfer to the newest bot at the Swedish observatory gate to aid our compatriots there in their own research.

"The first interesting news is that the Nanoites have a unique ability to detect differing DNA patterns in pretty high definition, compared to most of the technology on Earth and even in the Alliance. Minute differentiations even between what we might consider identical twins are discernable via their programming. This means we can up our security in some new and interesting ways, as they are also capable of triggering programming in other bots and computers.

"There are so many potential uses for this ability that my mind is blown every time I spend any time thinking about it. It could allow us to automate many of the strategies we are creating for eliminating the Inseni threat. This means potentially saving lives on both sides of the conflict.

"We are still exploring the possibilities, but I will keep you informed as we move forward.

"Second, you probably haven't noticed it yet, as there has been no need to tell you, but Lizziebot continues to get ongoing upgrades in her programming, something that Liliath will be discussing with you privately, Jenny, in your ongoing expansion of your mental gifts. Yes, it involves incorporating some of the things you can do and more, so be prepared. I know you have been craving more training and understanding, and even with everything else you have on your plate, we will be fitting it all in.

"Third, we will be instituting some advanced training for several likely candidates regarding trying to give you some help. One of the things you and Liliath and Amenia will be undertaking is the training of more interdimensional communicators via mindspeech.

"This is the baseline. There will be more, but we don't want to overload you. Your guards, Lizziebot, and Burt, when we can spare him, will be insuring you get the space and help you need to accomplish these things.

"Next week you will be doing some traveling, which is all I can tell you right now. We are still figuring out the logistics of how to give you what you need and keep tight security on your movements. I know this is a lot to be dumping on you so soon after completing your recuperation, but time is not our friend right now."

Bob took a deep breath, and the last was said almost apologetically.

Jenny nodded. Taking a deep breath herself, she said, "Well, I was anxious to get back into the action. But I'll admit, even if it takes some extra time and a little less sleep, I will be happy if we can extend the mental communication network and organize it so it can all be done in shifts."

Burt cut in a bit curtly, his usually cocky grin now turned serious, his eyes narrowed. "How much extra time is this going to take? It isn't like she has even been inactive during her 'light' duty. How can we make sure she doesn't have a relapse? Seriously, Bob, aren't we asking an awful lot here?"

Bob held up his hand. "We're taking into account that we may have to use some less secure channels of communication at some point to ease the stress so we can put this plan into operation. Please don't think that we're going to push Jenny beyond her ability to cope. Liliath has given us some very strict guidelines and will be checking in with Jenny on a precise schedule to be sure she doesn't get more than she can handle. After all, we know Jenny is pretty good at hiding her stress, and we don't want any further incidents..." and he trailed off with a significant look into Jenny's blue eyes.

"Please don't talk about me like I'm not here," Jenny interjected with a sigh. "Seriously. Let's just do what needs to be done. I pinkie swear that I won't overextend myself. If things get to be too much, I promise to ask for help or for a break. Fair enough?" As she said this, she looked directly into Burt's expressive eyes, seeing there all of the love and care he had for her.

He just nodded and held out his pinkie, linking it with hers, then smiled and bent forward to kiss her hand.

"Okay, you two," Bob said with a wicked grin, "None of that. Just because you're newlyweds who hardly ever see each other..."

The girls all laughed at the joke and the mood lightened.

Bob looked at his watch. "Okay, bots, recording off. It's time to retire to the gate office for some more show and tell."

With a scraping of chairs, they all stood, and Burt offered his arm to Jenny with a gallant flourish. They trooped back into the house and through the gate office door, silently followed by both bots. Evidently Bob had already set up all of the chairs in the office facing the large "air screen," as Jenny called it. Currently it displayed the words, "Conference Pending," with a countdown of three minutes.

"Get comfy, everyone," Burt said. "These things usually start on time, but you never know. You won't have to take notes, as the entire transcript as recorded by our friendly bots will be added to your tablets at the end of the meeting."

So they all sat, Burt slouching in his usual casual manner, Bob leaning his elbow on the chair arm, his hand propping his chin. Jenny simply relaxed. She had been in too many virtual conferences with clients before she joined the Alliance to be at all nervous about this, notwithstanding that she knew Bob's bombshells wouldn't be the only ones today. The girls sat erect and alert, even with the gate office door closed behind them.

Anyone coming into the house at this point would see only a blank wall unless they were authorized otherwise by the Alliance as a guardian or agent, so Jenny would have hoped the girls could have relaxed at least a little, but she didn't chide them for doing their job.

The screen went alight with the video feed precisely as the numbers on the screen went to zero. The screen took in the three councilors and Gariel, the leader of the military forces Jenny and her companions had worked with previously. His often-squirmy beard was quiescent, and his face was calm. Jenny wasn't sure if this meant he was working hard to control it or if he was actually as laid back as he appeared to be. She knew, due to her time with Lizzie's journals, that all Alliance agents who went through the training learned to control their outward emotions when necessary.

Liliath appeared to be looking directly at Jenny. Jenny knew this was a trick of the screen technology. She had learned that each person, no matter what angle they were viewing from, would see the dragon in the same way. Her coloration was the blue and green tones that would usually indicate a state of calm. Whenever she was angry or frustrated, she would begin to turn shades of red and purple, and tendrils of smoke would begin to float up from her nostrils.

It was hard to tell anything from Liliath's first and second councilors' expressions, as Jenny had only just met them before everything had kind of flown apart, and just before she participated in the conflict that ended with her using "the shout."

They were an odd pair, to be sure. Rilian reminded Jenny of nothing more than a very large otter. When Jenny had met her before, she had noticed that Rilian had been nearly a foot taller than she was. Balth, on the other hand was slightly shorter than Jenny and round bodied, and reminded her a lot of the munchkins of Oz, although he generally wore subdued colors and dressed plainly in a long tunic, breeches, and boots. Regardless, Jenny knew them to be not only competent but fair and truthful, something Liliath obviously valued in her councilors.

The tech that allowed all of them to communicate in mindspeech through the network interface was very similar to the tech that allowed Bob's bots to use mindspeech. Jenny continued to be in awe of all of the intricacies of the technology available to the Alliance. And yet, what impressed her even more were the great minds and hearts that made the Alliance such a force to be reckoned with. Liliath began.

"Thank you, each of you, for taking the time to meet with us today. I know you would have preferred to meet in person, but for now, for good

reason, we are taking the utmost precautions to see to the safety and security of the Gatekeeper and her staff. That is one of the reasons we needed to meet today.

"Jenny, you should know that we are also connected to Cornelium, Merv, and Anela, as well as the entire Earth guardian council. Other than this very carefully monitored circle, none of the information disseminated in this meeting is to be revealed to anyone not vetted specifically by this council.

"Those engaged in this conference are your core team. Everyone else in the Alliance is strictly on a 'need to know' status. Please be sure to clear it with the council if you feel like you need to give anyone else access to the information revealed here today."

Jenny nodded, noting that every head in the room had duplicated the action, somberly. Liliath smiled her intimidating draconic smile in acknowledgment.

"Then let us proceed. We have a number of issues that need resolving as quickly and as effectively as possible. Currently, the lab on my planet, directed by Merv, Cornelium, and Bob, is working on some projects that seem to have conspicuous import for the coming conflict.

"It is our hope that they will be able to, while working with the science teams both on Earth and here at Alliance headquarters, give us some edge that will not only decrease casualties on both sides and move us forward on more precise control of the Alliance gate network but also potentially either control or shut down the portals being used by the Inseni to terrorize and subdue dimensions we are not currently connected to.

"In the final analysis, one of the priorities in this regard will be to first gain access to that portal system, if a system it can be called. Initial research tells us that although there is a technology that allows them access to these portals, there is no actual organized network such as exists in the Alliance.

"Such access may allow us to use the tech we are working on to cut the Inseni off from their conquests while removing them permanently from any further temptation in that regard. We are doing everything we can to not have to kill even the Inseni soldiers and leaders, but to simply isolate them in a way that will eliminate the threat to the rest of the multiverse.

"We have no illusions that this will solve every problem, nor will it mean that we can relax our vigilant protection of the gate system. However, we will do our best to see to it that we save as many dimensions from this threat as is possible."

Jenny noticed Gariel nodding soberly, and that his beard had begun to twitch gently. Liliath's councilors betrayed no clues as to their own thoughts, but Jenny felt the slight edge to Liliath's voice.

Jenny spoke up in the pause. *"So, what is the role of the Gatekeeper in all of this? And how can I best use my resources of staff and tech?"*

"A valid question, Gatekeeper," Liliath sent in approval. *"First, remember that you do have staff and technological resources you may not even realize yet. It would be arrogant for you to try to take on every task yourself and completely inefficient in the long run. Asking questions, requesting assistance, and being open to alternative solutions doesn't often come naturally to such a strong personality as yourself. Like your Aunt Lizzie, you are an intelligent, strong, independent person; and, like her, you tend to want to protect others around you from harm.*

"You need to recognize that we are all in danger here, and we have all chosen to take the risks and responsibilities of our various callings within the Alliance structure. Of course, we don't want to take unnecessary risks; but even then, we will not win the day without some unavoidable albeit unfortunate losses."

Jenny could feel Liliath's draconic eyes drilling into hers and knew she was, at that moment, the focus of every other eye in the conference.

"Do I have your agreement that you will not take matters into your own hands without counseling with your advisors and staff, and that you will organize your tasks and responsibilities in such a way that you don't have an inordinate amount of those responsibilities on your own shoulders?"

Jenny sighed but answered, *"Yes, Liliath. I promise all of you to learn how to be a better leader and to keep to my own part of the work ahead of us. I know I have been impulsive in the past, and I can see where it got me. Thank you, one and all, for your patience as I grow into this assignment."*

Liliath smiled her somewhat intimidating draconic smile, fangs glistening and the tips of her forked tong apparent. *"I have seen so much growth in you. You are both similar and different from your aunt in so many ways. Let's just move forward with the understanding that you will do your best, which is all anyone can ever expect of anyone else.*

"You and your team have a lot ahead of you, but for now there are a few things we need you to focus on. First on your plate, Jenny, will be the twofold task of continuing with your relays of sensitive communication using your unique talent and helping us select and potentially train those who may be able to learn to do the same.

"Second, you need to begin to consider a replacement for you. Although, as you know, we have a replacement in an emergency, we also may decide to train another in advance. This may or may not be someone from Earth, although we have discovered that Earthlings are gifted in many ways we find unexpected and previously unknown to anyone in the Alliance.

"Third, you will be heading up the Sanglarka council teams. You won't be directing them so much as simply being an access point for keeping them organized and focused on their various objectives. There are many creative minds engaged in the current projects, and it would be unusual for them to not find distractions as they make new discoveries and find new solutions for the current challenges.

"And lastly, you will be taking on new training for your own abilities, to potentially expand the boundaries of your talents. That seems enough to be going on with, do you agree?"

Jenny repressed a sigh. *"Definitely. I guess I'll have to put off learning how to play Cubes for now,"* she remarked, recalling the game from her aunt's journals.

"Maybe Burt can teach you during your midnight chats," Liliath returned slyly.

Jenny blushed, realizing that the two of them had not kept their nightly rendezvous a secret and wondering what they all might have thought went on during those times at the side of the Merced River at the little eddy pool.

Burt jumped into the pause. *"What do we know about the current state of affairs where the Inseni are concerned?"*

Jenny wasn't sure if Liliath even heard the question, as Liliath's eyes went wide, her reptilian eyes slitted. She began to transform from her usually relaxed blue and green to deep red and purple and a thin tendril of smoke issued from opened nostrils. With a mental growl she erupted with a single word, *"YOU!"* and the air screen went dark.

Chapter 2: Relatively Speaking

In the Alliance private council chamber, it was as if they had all been turned to statues. Gariel had leapt to his feet, one hand on his blaster, Liliath's two councilors were rigid, not sure what was happening, and Liliath's only motion was the flexing of her claws as she sat disbelieving, seeing the one being before her she had never expected to see in the private council chamber of the Dimensional Alliance.

He stood, filling the doorway, his bronze scales gleaming in the artificial light of the chamber. *"Hello, Big Sister. Did you miss me?"* he sent as a broadcast to be sure that all the rest in the chamber could hear his question.

For a stunned moment Liliath simply narrowed her eyes, then she shook her head in disbelief.

"What are you doing here, Gighin? Who let you in?" she finally demanded when he didn't continue.

"Now, now, Liliath, my dear sibling. Is that any way to greet your little brother?"

"I ask you again... why are you here?"

"I have news and I am sure you want to hear it. Besides, the home council has elected me as the liaison during these troubled times. You are looking at the battle coordinator for the supreme force of the Alani. Can we now at least be civil?" His chin, bearded with a gold fringe, was raised, his neck bowed behind him in a challenging rigidity.

The smoke dissipated from Liliath's nostrils in a final wisp and her color gradually started to shift back into the cooler tones she usually exhibited in her calm state. She nodded curtly and settled back onto her chaise on the dais. Her companions also relaxed and regained their former seats surrounding her.

Gighin edged closer into the room, eyes fixed on Liliath. *"I have a missive from the Alani council regarding future participation in the Alliance's continued confrontation with the Inseni. There is some concern that this may not have a foreseeable end, and many wonder if it is wise to pursue the rescue of the unknown unfortunates who are trapped on Inseni governed worlds. While it is true, we have pledged to eliminate the Inseni threat where it menaces the gate system, do we have the resources or any hope of actually freeing all of the potential wretches who have been conquered by the Inseni?"*

"The Alliance is pursuing many potential solutions, Gighin. We have, for security purposes, as you may understand, not yet revealed all potential strategies or approaches to the problem at this point," Liliath responded, her cool composure now restored. All could hear the mental tone of strained patience in her response, and Gighin grinned a satisfied smile.

"A very diplomatic answer, my sister, that tells me absolutely nothing. We are secluded here, are we not? We are secure in our communications? Like it or not, I am the liaison between the Alliance and the Alani, and answers are needed. Just when can I expect an answer that will satisfy my superiors? Come now, Liliath. Are we or are we not, allies?"

"At this time, Gighin, we are keeping our counsels close. In a very short time, we will be bringing all of our allies into our confidences as we put important security measures into place. We will in no way keep the Alani or any of our other significant confederates out of the planning, but we are also very aware that we have underestimated our enemies in the past, an error we can no longer afford, as the dimensional gate sys-

tem is at risk of compromise at this point more than we ever imagined possible.

"Please relay our desires to your superiors and let them know that we will be notifying them very soon about an important meeting to reveal our plans. The Gatekeeper of the Alliance will be intrinsically involved in assuring the safety and security of all future communications."

It was clear that Liliath intended this as a dismissal, but Gighin continued to stand resolutely before her, looking her directly in the eyes. There might have been no one else in the room, for the intensity of his gaze.

"Very well, sister mine. Do you have accommodations for me and my retinue? We have instructions to stay at headquarters for the duration. There are three of us and a humanoid servant each."

Liliath exhaled in what could have only been a draconic sigh. *"If that is your wish. On the same floor as my apartments, we have five suites that are meant to house the Alani. The receptionist will be happy to show you to your quarters. As it is, I have to get back to my meetings. Perhaps we can dine together this evening."*

Gighin nodded curtly and turned and exited the room as quietly as he had entered. Liliath sent orders to the receptionist and gestured for Gariel to close the door behind her brother as his tail swept through into the reception area.

She looked from side to side at Gariel and her councilors. *"Resume the broadcast, please. I am sure we left our compatriots in disarray. Jenny contacted me and I told her to let the others know we would finish in a few minutes. She assured me that they will try to wait patiently."*

The screen once again popped into being above them, and soon they could see all three groups represented virtually before them.

"Where were we?" Liliath sent, trying not to show her agitation over the interruption. *"Evidently some of the members of the alliance are beginning to get a bit impatient with our process. All the more reason to get on with our plans. Jenny, over the next few weeks we will be*

introducing you to some significant contact points to add to your own personal mental communication network.

In a couple of weeks, we will be holding a much larger conference that will potentially strain your personal resources, but it will be necessary to succeed in this, as the standard methods of virtual conferencing may not be secure enough for what will be said there. yet another reason for you to spend some significant time with Amenia at this point.

"Bob, you, Cornelium, Merv, and your team will be working on upping both bot production and your continued upgrades of the entire bot network, your ongoing work with the Nanoites, as well as staying in touch with the Sweden gate team who are working with our Mookookie partners. We foresee some significant correlations of the two projects in the near future.

"Sanglarka, your ongoing focus will be security of the Earth network. The portal in South America is still an issue that needs addressing, and the potential threat of an undiscovered alien portal is still problematic. Earth will also be getting new gate guardians for both the India and the Australia gates, so continued training on your part will be essential.

"It was truly unforeseen that Earth would play such a large role in the upcoming struggle, especially since Earth is still not an official member of the Alliance."

Liliath paused, looking deep into the eyes of each of the participants. Even from eons away her stare was penetrating, as each one of them felt the deep commitment and courageous intent of this amazing being.

"So," she finally continued, *"if there are any questions or concerns, please submit them and any reports via your team leaders through Jenny. That will be all. We are by necessity, for best security, keeping this short and to the point.*

"Please do not send any questions or thoughts via the tablet network. All future communications regarding plans moving forward will be only through Jenny, our only potentially secure channel at this point."

She let the screen go dark and turned to her councilors and Gariel. *"Now to deal with my 'little brother,'"* she sent as she exited the council chamber with a snort.

Chapter 3: Extensions and Expectations

Jenny looked around the gate office at her companions. The look on every face told her she wasn't the only one feeling more than a little overwhelmed and a bit alarmed at that very brief, somewhat confusing, and more than a little challenging meeting. Even Chidwi, perched quietly on her shoulder, seemed introspective. She reached out a tiny hand and patted Jenny gently on the back of her neck.

"Am I the only one who is feeling like we've bitten off more than we can chew?" she asked, straining to keep the plaintive note out of her voice. "Since when did Earth become the focal point of this conflict?"

Burt took her hand, shrugging his shoulders slightly. "It does put a lot on our plate, but we can do this if we all do our part. If anyone should feel a bit overcome by all of this, it is you, but I have every confidence you'll come through for us. What can we do for you in the meantime? Do you want to go with Tarafau to see Amenia?"

"That's probably the best first step," she agreed, squeezing his hand.

"Hey, Tidbit, feel like a road trip?" she sent to the cat curled up contentedly in his wicker cat bed by the desk.

"Yes, that will be fine. The new protocols say we also take your bodyguards with us, so I'll take you and Nona first and then come back for the other two. Do you need to grab anything before we go?"

"She needs to grab me," Burt cut in with a grin as he swung Jenny up from her chair into a fervent embrace. Whispering into her ear he said, "See you at our pond tonight?"

Jenny grinned, looking up into his blue eyes and nearly drowning in the loving look coming her way. "Of course," she whispered back. "Maybe you can come and visit me in person? I'd love for you to meet the linkling tribe, and we could go shopping at the Apex and eat roasted bud-crawlers."

"Sounds like fun. I'll see what headquarters has in store for me and apply for some break time." And he kissed her enthusiastically and unabashedly in front of the entire group. "See you tonight."

Jenny let go of her husband breathlessly. Still at a stage where everyone thought of them as newlyweds, she didn't think this would ever get old or routine for her. His kisses still made her weak in the knees.

Tidbit stood in his bed and stretched as only a cat can, from his toes to the tip of his tail. Then he stepped out of the bed, and suddenly he was a tall black man with a shiny bald head and he was dressed in a colorful draped tunic and breeches.

The girls had stood as well, and Tarafau reached out one hand to place on Jenny's shoulder and the other on Nona's. The gate office faded from view, and immediately they were standing in the center of a park surrounded by tanks draped in flowering vines, all pointing to the statue of a Daringi woman in flowing robes, one hand outstretched as if in entreaty.

This was a place sacred to the Daringi people. It marked the end of a time when intrigue, greed, war, and contention were the rule rather than the exception. No longer did the Daringi or the other intelligent species on their planet live in fear and anger. "Live and let live" was more than just a concept here, and their culture had embraced a pact of peace and acceptance of diversity.

Jenny always felt like she should heave a sigh of relief whenever she came here. She knew that this was one place where she was not only safe from potential enemies but accepted and even held in a certain amount of esteem by the natives of the planet. Jenny could feel Chidwi's excitement at the thought of being so close to the members of her 'tribe.'

Nona looked around, interested. *"I'm sure there's a story about this place. I look forward to hearing it. In the meantime, let's not make the other two wait too long."*

Tarafau nodded and faded from view. Before Jenny or Nona could even blink a couple of times, he faded back into view, a hand on both Lyra and Mynn's shoulders. They looked around in awe and delight at the park that surrounded them.

"Let's get to the house," Tarafau sent with his big catlike grin. *"I'm sure Amenia will be anxious to get you all settled in. I know she is looking forward to getting down to your training, Jenny, and I know Chidwi is looking forward to seeing her family."*

The five of them set off, Chidwi crooning happily from Jenny's shoulder, her reflection turned on, as linklings were not only welcome but esteemed in the Daringi culture. Jenny's bodyguards were alert, as usual, but Jenny could tell they were also taking in their surroundings with appreciation for how different it was from the neighborhood that surrounded Infinity Loop.

This time of day, there were few people on the roadway but as they passed the few who were out and about they were greeted with waves and smiles. Tarafau was well-loved in his community, and most of them knew who Jenny and Chidwi were. It felt much like a homecoming for Jenny. The girls looked around them, attentive and watchful, but Jenny knew that this was one place she could have told them to relax.

Unlike the loop at home, the houses along the road they walked varied from one space to the next in style, colors, and architecture with no uniform lot size or what you might call a driveway. Tarafau's house was domelike, built partially into a hill, so that from the road it looked too small to house more than a couple of rooms. But it was, in actuality, quite roomy as you descended the spiral staircase from the bright sunny sitting room into the family room that melded into the large kitchen.

The two rooms were divided by a long table that doubled as a food preparation island, and a long hallway extended beyond sight, leading to all the bedrooms and bathrooms.

Amenia, who was chopping vegetables, looked up with a welcoming smile as they all descended into the room.

"Ah, here you all are!" she sent happily, dropping her knife and wiping her hands on a towel.

She came forward, greeting each guest with two hands extended with a gentle squeeze and finally hugging her husband with fervor.

"Let me finish getting these vegetables into the stew so it can begin to simmer. We'll do supper out in the garden, as I know you all ate recently. While you're waiting for me to finish up, by all means go outside. I can tell Chidwi is anxious to see her family, and then I'll get the girls settled into their accommodations and we'll do some scheduling for the next few days. Okay?"

They all nodded, and Tarafau led the way out into the garden. Jenny had a new appreciation for this place after having read her aunt's journals. So much had happened here that had later affected Jenny's own journey, including the birth of Elizabeth, Jenny's new best friend. This is where the linkling colony had been established that had given her Chidwi and where her aunt had experienced so much that was both painful and joyful.

As soon as they exited out into the huge expanse of the yard with its grove of ancient trees in the back of the property, Chidwi leapt from Jenny's shoulder and sprinted, hooting happily, towards the grove. From the grove emanated a troop of chartreuse linklings of various sizes, hooting joyfully in reply.

The reunion sent a ripple of joy and love like a wave towards Jenny and her three guards. It was a palpable feeling of warmth and greeting. Linklings were naturally mindspeakers and also able to read the minds of those around them. When they were excited, happy, worried, or angry, they could transmit their strong feelings to anyone nearby.

There appeared to be nearly fifty of the little beings, their long mustaches and flowing ear tufts streaming behind them as they charged towards Chidwi. There was much dancing and hopping and hooting. After everything she and Chidwi had recently been through, this was such a delight and so warming to Jenny's very soul. After what felt like ages of tension, anxiety, and fear, this was like a cool refreshing drink to a thirsty soul.

At the circle of chaises that sat around the clean firepit where family gatherings tended to take place, each of them found a seat. After a careful look around, Jenny's guards all relaxed into theirs and Jenny took her place, facing the noisy enthusiastic reunion on the lawn between them and the lovely grove of soaring trees at the back of the yard.

The sides of the yard were lined with flowerbeds, a riot of colors and types of flowers and shrubbery, much of which was fruit bearing or herbs Amenia used for cooking and healing. Looking behind her, Jenny could see the actual size of Tarafau and Amenia's home. It had three stories; the top that you could see from the street, the main floor with a long hall lined by bedrooms and bathing facilities, and the basement, where Amenia had created the workout and therapy space for her practice as a mental healer.

The open area of the yard was about six times the size of Jenny's ample yard on Earth, and it was obvious that Amenia took great care to create a pleasant and useful space for her own family here.

The linkling colony that had been established back when Lizzie was young was now a thriving little community; and the gentle, contented crooning that came nearly constantly from the grove at the back of the yard made it a place of peace and contemplation.

Considering the tasks that lay before them, it was good for Jenny to have the chance to do her work in such a peaceful and encouraging atmosphere. She knew from experience that Amenia would work her hard, and on top of the training she still had to do her duties as a communication liaison for the Alliance. So this was no break for her, but if she needed to continue her work, this was as good as it would probably get until they had resolved the current conflict.

Amenia came out and escorted the girls back to the house to set them up in the guest rooms, so for a short time, Jenny was left alone, listening quietly to the exultant crooning of the linklings. She knew while she was there that Chidwi would be happily distracted any time that Jenny wasn't working out with Amenia. But when her classes with Amenia were in session, Chidwi would be right by her side, as one of the purposes of the training sessions was to more firmly establish how Jenny and Chidwi could work more effectively together.

She came to with a start, realizing that she had somehow drifted off to sleep. Chidwi had lighted on her stomach with a chirrup and was patting her arm. *"Chidwi is very happy. Jenny is happy too? We will do good things here and enjoy all the good peoples? Jenny is tired? Sleep later. Things to do."*

Jenny grinned and stretched. *"Yes, Chidwi, things to do."* She looked over her shoulder and saw that Amenia and her guards and, to her surprise and delight, Elizabeth were striding towards her.

She jumped up and ran to embrace Elizabeth who was nearly a head taller than she was. Elizabeth's deep brown hair was long and braided and her green eyes, which shifted color based on her moods, sparkled with welcome.

"Surprise!" she sent as they stepped apart. *"I get a break before my final round of agent classes. Then I will get my first intern assignment. They have stepped up the schedule with everything that is going on and, as I am moving forward ahead of my classmates, I will be getting my first intern assignment earlier than I expected, so I get a week to spend with my family."*

"Wow!" Jenny sent grinning from ear to ear. *"I'm going to be here for about a week as well. We can work out together, and I want to hear about all your agent training adventures."*

"Your bodyguards and I are going to the Apex to get in some shopping while you work out with mother this first time back. Can we bring you back anything?"

"Maybe some roasted bud-crawlers?"

"That's a given. Father wouldn't forgive me for not making sure there were enough bud-crawlers to go around, especially when we are all together again for the first time in a long time. He's inside with mother, and they told me to ask you and Chidwi to come back inside for an initial workout while we're gone shopping."

Jenny nodded and they all trooped back into the house where Amenia and Tarafau were standing in the kitchen, arms around one another. Tarafau looked up at the group of young women and sent, *"Ready, Jenny? Don't forget my bud-crawlers, the rest of you. It will go well with the beautiful stew and rolls Amenia has prepared for supper."*

The girls all nodded cheerfully and headed off for their shopping trip. Jenny, with Chidwi perched on her shoulder, followed Tarafau and Amenia down into the workout room.

This was a comforting place for Jenny. So many hours of training with Amenia had eventually brought her to the point of her talent to mentally communicate across dimensions. She was excited and admittedly a little anxious as to the next steps. Now that she had read about all of the things Lizzie had learned to do with her mind, she wondered where these next training sessions would finally take her.

She knew that in addition to Amenia's training, she would also soon be training with Liliath.

They knew, thanks to the scientists who had defected from the Inseni, that there were some security deficiencies in their current communications network. Until now, being able to communicate over the dimensions via mindspeech hadn't been something that had occurred to them, as the only one who had been able to do that previously was long since dead, and he hadn't revealed his talent to anyone but Lizzie at the time.

As they sat on the mats, Chidwi standing just behind Jenny with her tiny hands on her shoulders, Tarafau sent, *"Today we will be just setting the parameters of future sessions. We will be meeting together only twice a day to allow you to pursue your other duties. Soon we will be introducing you to three potential candidates for ongoing training, to see if your skills are transferable in any way. Does this make sense to you?"*

Jenny nodded and Chidwi crooned.

"Let us begin with breathing, then we will start by entering Jenny's mind space. We will be trying one new thing today," Amenia said, sighing with a deep cleansing breath, signaling the beginning of the training.

The routine was soothing, to say the least. Jenny was now able to do the complex breathing patterns that induced the REM state necessary to enter her mental world with practically no effort at all. Chidwi was a constant presence during the process, and Jenny could feel the comforting auras of both Amenia and Tarafau as they went through the steps that finally brought them all before the drawbridge that entered her mental world. The guard at the gate nodded genially to them. After going through the portcullis, they stopped before the lawn that was much like a broad park.

Surrounding the huge lawn were many buildings. At the far end of the lawn was a large mansion, one of the buildings Jenny had yet to enter.

"To the communications center," Amenia prompted.

They only had to think about it to arrive in front of the glass double doors that entered the place where Jenny had first discovered her ability to communicate across the vast distances between dimensions. As they entered, Jenny realized that the main room with its computers and the cellular tower had expanded considerably. There were multiple workstations, as opposed to the single one that had originally stood next to the base of the cellular tower.

Each of the workstations consisted of a large air screen and a simple touch keyboard. Jenny would have given anything for something like this in her college days. The entire computer, she knew based on her experience with Alliance tech, was contained in the keyboard, but it offered more computing power than an entire room full of the most complex gaming computers available on Earth.

Jenny had to assume that these additional workstations would eventually be manned by her assistants in this project. In the meantime, she also noted that there was now an area similar to the television studio she had visited when Sam had worked at a local station in Los Angeles.

A glassed-in control booth stood off to one side, the "On the Air" sign darkened. All of the usual switching equipment and various monitors, as well as an audio switching board, were visible through the control room windows that looked out into the main studio.

Three video cameras stood on rolling tripods facing the area where a talk-show style set was fully lighted, lapel microphones placed on each of three chairs angled towards the host's desk. It reminded Jenny of the old Johnny Carson shows her mom used to love to watch.

Bemused, she asked herself the question she knew Amenia would want her to ask. *"How does this relate to what we are trying to accomplish here today?"*

"Am I the host of this show?" she asked Amenia, somewhat afraid of the answer she already knew in her heart.

"What would you call this space on Earth?" Amenia asked, looking around curiously.

"This is the studio and control room of a broadcast television station," Jenny promptly replied. *"On Earth, this is where many programs are produced to be broadcast to a vast audience. The programming for this type of studio would include news, discussion on a variety of topics, and highlighting celebrities of various performance art forms."*

"Ah, I see. How appropriate to our purposes. I noticed that there are three workstations, which seem somehow significant and also appropriate, as you will see later today. As you may know, you can populate this studio, as you call it, with all the necessary personnel to use it effectively. The personnel can be real or imagined, humanoid or even robotic, at your choice.

"You will also notice that Tarafau came along with us on this trip. You automatically included him, something you haven't done in the past. This demonstrates an important skill you will need to employ with our future endeavors. What are your thoughts about these changes in the communications center of your mental village?"

Jenny didn't reply at once. She glanced around at the expanded facility, noting the details. This was a workspace where multiple levels of communication could be created, but it was also no longer intended to be manned by just Jenny and Amenia. Even with Chidwi and Tarafau in the space it looked empty and as if it was waiting for much more.

"Liliath assigned me to expand the mental communications network. She implied that if I could do it, the potential was that it might be a talent that could be taught to others with the right mindset. I think

the extra workstations mean that I am anticipating that work, assuming we can find the right beings for the job.

"I think the broadcast studio is trying to tell me that I will soon be able to also project images similar to the images transmitted on air screens via the current interdimensional communications network, without exposing the transmissions to prying eyes, as mental projections are not technologically hackable.

"The 'guest talent' chairs on the set tell me that we will be able to involve others in those projections and potentially project images in addition to those of the persons in the 'conference call,' similar to what we do with the current Alliance tech we have been using for training purposes."

Amenia's face shone with approval. *"I agree."*

Tarafau nodded. *"Lizzie would be proud of her great-niece. She took her own talents far beyond what anyone expected, but she was always stretching farther. I believe you will yet teach all of us things we never expected possible with mental abilities."*

Jenny ducked her head, and she knew, where she was actually sitting on the workout floor, her face was probably blushing to her hairline.

"I think we found out what we needed to know," Amenia said. *"We have more to do today outside of your mental village. Let's return to the workout room."*

And with that they found themselves still seated facing one another on the workout mat in their relaxed positions. Jenny almost shook herself in wonder, transitioning from the one to the other. It always seemed so real in her mental fortress and there was now so much more to think about.

Chapter 4: The Steps of the Dance

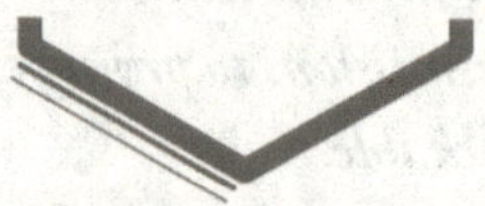

As they emerged from the basement into the family room, there was a knock at the door above.

"Good timing," Amenia remarked. *"Meet you out at the firepit,"* she sent to Jenny, gesturing towards the back door.

Jenny didn't question her. It was probably either a delivery or one of Amenia's clients. Jenny and Tarafau exited out into the sunshine. Chidwi, leaping from Jenny's shoulder as soon as they were outside, sprinted towards the grove to greet her tribe.

By the time she and Tarafau were settled into their chaises, Jenny heard Amenia sending, *"Close your eyes, Jenny, and don't open them until I tell you."*

What was she up to now? Jenny knew that Amenia delighted in surprising and entertaining her guests and Jenny was more than willing to go along, as she was never disappointed with those little surprises.

As she sat, eyes closed, in the warmth of the sun she noticed that the crooning of the linklings had faded away, something that almost never happened except when they were startled or absorbed in something that fascinated them.

Finally, she felt more than heard Amenia settle into the chaise between Jenny and Tarafau. *"Open,"* she sent.

Before Jenny were three lovely women with teal hair tipped with yellow braided in complex plaits that hung down their backs nearly to their hips. Despite their overall humanoid appearance, their skin had a greenish tinge to it. They could have been sisters, but they weren't identical. They were dressed in what Jenny would have called a toga, white and extending to their calves. Long sleeves hugged their upper arms but from the elbow flowed bell-like loosely down to their fingertips.

They nodded in unison and without a word began in slow synchronized movements what could only have been called a dance. There was no music and the movements were subtle and mesmerizingly relaxed.

First, they each turned to one side, facing the same direction, placing their right hands on the shoulder of the woman in front of them. The single movement took several seconds, each hand traveling in an exact arc until the hands touched the shoulder in front of them precisely at the same moment.

Their left feet slid equally slowly and exactly forward to nearly touch the heel of the person in front of them, then the right foot circled out to the right as they each rotated their heads to face towards the circling foot. Then they pivoted shifting the hands still on the shoulder in front of them so they were facing forward. Each movement was precise and almost achingly slow and done in complete silence.

They then arched their backs and raised both of their hands above their heads and back farther and farther into a perfect backbend that ended with a flip, both feet leaving the ground and coming back to their feet. Then they touched each other's hands and created a three-person ring, facing inward, and began a slow weaving circle in which they sometimes faced out and sometimes faced in.

To Jenny's surprise, each time they faced the circle out towards the audience, the color of their eyes changed from an intense teal to electric green to a startling yellow and then to a deep chocolate brown. They ended as abruptly as they had begun and stood calmly in a line, all facing their stunned audience.

Jenny wanted to applaud but was uncertain as to what was appropriate for this culture. She was in awe of the extreme synchronization and somehow felt like there was unheard music playing somewhere in her mind during the performance, but she had heard not a single sound.

In the trees the linklings began to croon again, but softly, as if they didn't want to disturb the mesmerizing atmosphere that seemed to echo the amazing dance, for such it truly was.

Finally, Amenia stood and walked over to the three who still stood silently waiting. Jenny noticed that neither Amenia nor Tarafau had applauded, so she waited to see what was next.

"Jenny, allow me to introduce you to three people who will be participating in our mental experiment. The demonstration you just witnessed was not previously choreographed or rehearsed. The entire performance was completely spontaneous and accomplished via the mental gifts of your new companions.

"These are Li, Na, and Fo from the planet Finque in the dimension known as Il. They were sent to us by Liliath and are certified agents of the Alliance."

Jenny stood and, as she had learned was customary in Alliance culture, held out both hands to each in turn, repeating their name, and once she had greeted each of them, sent, *"That was amazing. It was if you were dancing to very slow music."*

"We were," agreed Li. *"Our native language is comprised of what you would call musical tones. I feel sorry you couldn't hear the music. It is something that we have learned can be taught to those not from our planet. Your aunt was known as one of those."*

"I believe my Aunt Lizzie knew someone from your planet, a woman named Gi," Jenny replied, glad once again for the time she had spent in Lizzie's journals.

"Ah, yes, we are aware of her. She liked to come and visit us from time to time. Gi is now a revered councilor on our planet and has many

descendants. Lizzie was renowned for her mental musical gifts," Na agreed. *"It appears that unusual mental gifts are a family inheritance for you."*

Jenny smiled back at the three of them, wondering how long it would take her to remember all of their names without mixing them up.

"As you can see," Amenia continued, *"we are well prepared for our little experiment. In a few minutes I expect the girls will return and we will eat together and spend some time getting to know one another. Then, this evening when we are pleasantly full of good food and are completely relaxed, we will retire to the workout room and see if we can make a start.*

"I don't expect anything spectacular immediately, but I do think that the experience will reveal some potential in ways we don't yet understand or expect."

Jenny knew that Amenia was accomplished at helping people reach their full potential in the field of mental gifts and talents, and she had no doubt that if this experiment had any chance, she was the one who could ultimately make it happen.

Amenia gestured for Na, Li, and Fo to take seats around the firepit, and the linklings came scampering out from the grove crooning happily. The three of them made much of the little creatures, especially the littlest ones. Linkling "little ones" were active and able to get around in the trees within weeks of being born. Currently there were about six of them, although Jenny couldn't be completely sure as there may have been others up in the nests established in the lower branches of the ancient trees that formed the grove at the back of the yard.

Chidwi was obviously enjoying her time with her little tribe, and for a moment Jenny felt a pang about keeping her separated from her family. Chidwi, on the other hand, chided her comically for even thinking that. Since Chidwi could read not only Jenny's mind but her emotions, there was literally nothing she could hide from her little companion.

The girls and Elizabeth returned just before supper and had to show off their purchases from various Apex shops, which had been delivered before the girls actually arrived via the underground delivery system. Amenia introduced them to Na, Li, and Fo and soon they were mind-speaking enthusiastically together, swapping stories from their agent training days and their various assignments since.

"And now, as we have work to do, if the girls, Elizabeth, and Tarafau will tidy up, let us go to the workout room and get started," Amenia said, gently shooing a linkling from her lap. She nodded to Na, Li, and Fo and led the way into the house and down the circular stairs into the roomy workout space. It took up the entire basement floor and was equal, in Jenny's opinion, to the workout space at Sanglarka and her own dimensional workout space she accessed via her gateroom.

Amenia indicated that they should all be seated on the mats provided for meditation. *"Now, I understand that the three of you are already adept at breathing and relaxation. Today we will start there. After we have had some time to attune ourselves, we will be trying something new, perhaps to all of us. We will begin that part of our process by entering with Jenny into her private mental space. Once we have succeeded in that part of the exercise, I will give the next set of instructions. You may begin your breathing."*

They each assumed their meditative postures, with Chidwi in her usual place behind Jenny, one small hand on her shoulder, and after what could have been hours or only minutes, Amenia recalled them to full consciousness.

"Now, we will see Chidwi's part in all of this. As I have told you, linklings have the capacity to not only read minds but to also filter out mental resonances as they need to. In this instance we will be using her as a conduit to make the initial joining, and then Jenny will guide us

through to her private mental space. I must emphasize that this is a great privilege, and that Jenny is taking a huge risk by allowing others to access this space, so I must request that we all agree to honor and respect this."

Na, Li, and Fo all nodded somberly, and each sent, *"I so swear,"* looking deeply into Jenny's eyes. Chidwi sent her assessment that they were sincere, and Jenny nodded back.

"Thank you," she sent in return.

Once again, they sank back into the meditative pose, this time with the intention of entering Jenny's mental space. Amenia and Tarafau had done this before with Jenny, so she was familiar with the process. As before, she found herself walking along a drawbridge of sorts that led to a closed portcullis guarded by an armored knight.

"Sir knight, I avouch those with me as being welcome in my realm. Allow them to pass."

The knight nodded. "As you say my lady. Enter and be well come."

She turned and beckoned to the four behind her, and they entered the village onto a village green that extended to what appeared to be a mansion.

As before, Jenny knew exactly where she needed to go, even without Amenia's coaching. Down the street, past the library, to the communications building, marked by a tall cell tower emerging from the roof.

She led them through the glass doors, past a reception area, and into the main office. "Amenia, I think we need to begin by familiarizing them with the mental communications system and introducing them to the team. Do you agree?"

Amenia nodded with a smile. "I can see you've been thinking this through. By all means. Please continue."

Jenny walked over to one of the computer consoles, each of which had its own office chair and an advanced cellphone resting next to the keyboard.

"This is the interface we have been using to visualize the various connections we have established in our mental communications network. Up until now, I have been the only one able to access and utilize it, but today we will be attempting to connect you in the same way. I know the technology on your planet is different from my own, so you may picture this differently than I do. That said, first we need to program your names and cellphones into the system. Each of you take a cellphone, and we will initialize it with your information."

Each of the women took a cellphone and followed the instructions on the screen. Jenny noted that to her the screens appeared to be written in English and assumed, since they went right to work typing in their information, that to them the screens appeared in their own language and alphabet.

"Now, I want you to do the same at the workstation. Simply fill in the form on the screen and push the Enter key."

At this point, Jenny was glad that within her mental environment all communications, although appearing and sounding to her like they were speaking English, was actually communicated in mindspeech, even though they seemed to be speaking to each other naturally.

Jenny's cellphone chimed after each one of them finished filling out the form. They looked up at her quizzically but waited for her to continue her instruction.

"Now that we have you programmed into the system, let's make a call to someone in the network so you can see how I use this. You can see there is a list of names and coordinates on the screen of your phone. We programmed every person on the team in to each of the phones. To access them, I select one of the names." She demonstrated with a click of the mouse on Bob's name. "Now I am able to directly call Bob."

Bob's face appeared before her, and she said, "Bob, it's Jenny."

He looked up from the diagrams he had been studying. "Hello, Jenny. What's up?"

"Just demonstrating my mental communications system for some trainees. Amenia and I are hoping to be able to delegate some of my communication duties to some other gifted assistants."

"That's terrific! Do you need me to stay available for further demonstrations?"

"Yes, please. Who else is around at the moment?"

"Merv, Fidget, Ignatius, and Cornelium are all here. Should I let them know they may be getting a call?"

"That would be great. I'll get back to you in a moment."

Jenny turned and looked at the four women who were watching her intently. "Okay, did you hear both sides of the conversation?"

They shook their heads simultaneously.

"I was pretty sure you wouldn't. Could you hear my side of the conversation?"

Once again, they shook their heads.

Jenny sighed. "Okay, Amenia, do you have a suggestion?"

"Start by calling each one of them in turn to connect them via mindspeech into the network," she suggested.

Jenny nodded and called each of the girls in turn, to which they responded in mindspeech, *"Receiving."*

"Now have them go into another room and try it again," Amenia recommended after Jenny had finished the last call.

The girls filed out of the room so they were no longer visible.

"Call them again."

Jenny did so. This time the individual faces came into view and their eyebrows rose as they saw her in return.

After Jenny had successfully performed this step, Amenia guided, "Now make a conference call to them."

Jenny did as suggested, and all three faces appeared, wide eyed and seemingly impressed with this feat. She ended the call with, "Come on back. Now let's try to do this with Bob."

She then initiated a conference call including Na, Li, and Fo with Bob and Ignatius.

"Bob, can you see all of us?" Jenny inquired when he looked up from the papers he had been perusing.

"Yes! Hi, there!"

"Ignatius, can you see all of us?"

"I see you and your friends, Jenny." Ignatius agreed, enthusiastically. Jenny still was stunned at how the bird had taken to mindspeech. His irises pinned to points and he fluffed his feathers excitedly.

"Everyone on this side of the call, can you see Bob and Ignatius?"

"Is Ignatius an avian and Bob humanoid?" asked Fo.

"Yes. And I find this interesting," Jenny replied. "They have never been able to see me before. Amenia, does this have anything to do with the new broadcast studio?"

Amenia grinned and nodded. "You needed to be able to visualize sending images as well as receiving them. I don't think you need to enter the studio, but your subconscious knows it is there and understands its function. The studio will now allow you to send images as well as receive them clearly, and it appears that anyone who initiates the call with you from your side is included."

This excited Jenny. It had been unnerving to know that those she communicated with couldn't see her when she saw them so plainly.

"Thanks, Bob. I can see you are in the middle of something at the moment. This is Na, Li, and Fo; they will be assisting me with communications for the Alliance in the future. They seem to have a similar ability to send and receive over dimensional borders. Liliath and Amenia have been searching high and low for someone who can help. Although not everyone on their planet has the ability to use mindspeech, it appears that those who do don't seem to have the barriers most beings have.

"If this works, it will allow me more freedom and flexibility to fulfill all of my other responsibilities."

"That's great, Jenny. The rest of us have been really concerned about your current workload. Thank you, Na, Li, and Fo, for helping with this. Secure communications within the network have been a major concern and will be vital to our success with this endeavor. I'll let you all go now. Thanks for including me."

Jenny nodded and cut the connection, then looked happily directly at Na, Li, and Fo, who were looking back at her with large eyes. For a moment they reminded Jenny of Lizzie's description of Geln, the triple beings with one consciousness.

"Well? What do you think of that? You just did a two-way visual mindspeech communication that took you across dimensions to speak with a man and his avian lab partner. Now that we have made sure you can do this, let's sit down and figure out how best to organize this project."

Chapter 5: Conundrum

For the next week, Jenny, Amenia, Na, Li, and Fo spent their time practicing contacting various Alliance members, first from the safe and visually inspiring mental communications center in Jenny's mental world and finally branching out to doing it in real life, each of them getting the opportunity to make calls sitting on the mat in the workout room and, once they had that down pat, they started trying it from various places within the house and even out in the yard around the firepit.

They successfully did one round where each of them contacted a different group simultaneously with great success. Amenia still could not manage it but was exultant when all three of the trainees reported success.

As they worked together, Jenny noticed the distinct differences in the new members of her team.

Na, her name pronounced in their musical language as a deep alto in very calming harmony, was the tallest and most outspoken of the trio, not hesitating to call attention to errors or to ask pertinent questions as they moved through their process of assigning duties, scheduling responsibilities, and making arrangements for ongoing testing of their process. She appeared to be the leader of the group, although at no time did any of them indicate any particular precedence among them.

Li, her name a soaring, high-pitched crescendo, was a quiet, contemplative person, gentle, considerate, and willing to listen to all sides before making a decision; but when she decided, she was diligent in following up and moving forward. She could be depended on to complete any assignment quickly and thoroughly.

Fo, her name pronounced as a smooth, almost burbling sound like a brook in full flow, was enthusiastic and had a mischievous sense of humor, often irritating businesslike Na. Her energy and curiosity were infectious and suited Jenny well. With a pang, Jenny realized she reminded her forcefully of Sam in the days before her complete betrayal.

Jenny discovered that they had gone through agent training as a group, all in the same pod, but had each done their internships in different dimensions, suited to their various personalities and talents. The current assignment was their first official agent duty, and they were all eager to perform at the top of their abilities.

They arranged their schedules to cover various time slots, communicating with specific groups within the Alliance defense team. They would be stationed in different dimensions to protect the communications team from the potential of being completely wiped out in a single attack from the Inseni. Jenny had been adamant about this, as she was very much aware that similar protections had been in place for her appointment as the Gatekeeper.

On their last day together before each of them went to their own assignments, Amenia, Elizabeth and Tarafau had gathered them all together around the firepit; Jenny, Na, Li, Fo, and Jenny's bodyguards, Lyra, Nona, and Mynn. Chidwi and her tribe were also in attendance, frolicking happily around them.

"We gather together to celebrate a happy conclusion to the basic training and ongoing relationships we have established here," Amenia said, gazing into each face with a fond brilliant smile.

"At this point we are just beginning a vital expedition into what could prove to be not only taxing but potentially difficult and even dangerous. I want each of you to know that the Alliance has every confidence

that you will each perform admirably in your various roles. Jenny, our leader and exemplar, can do so much more than she realizes, but she cannot do everything herself. We each become her hands, her voices, and her support.

"So now, as we go to our various posts, let us celebrate and enjoy face-to-face contact, as this may not happen again until the Insenium is finally conquered, and peace reestablished in the Alliance and the other dimensions who need our help."

They all applauded and food was served, delicious roasted bud-crawlers, one of Jenny's favorite native foods of this dimension, reminding her of broiled lobster, and they happily chatted among themselves about nothing in particular. To Jenny it was obvious, however, that each of them was contemplating what was coming next; and she, herself, realized that she wasn't entirely sure where next steps would lead her.

She would be meeting next, via mental communication, with the Alliance council and the teams at Sanglarka, Switzerland, and those ensconced at Cornelium's lab on Liliath's home planet. This meeting would be a milestone, as it would include all four groups in a mental conference that would, for the first time, include the ability of all parties to see and hear one another. Jenny and Amenia had been working on this new skill between sessions with Na, Li, and Fo, and Jenny was confident that this could well be significant in enhancing secure future communications within the Alliance.

After a congenial meal, Tarafau transported Na, Li, and Fo to their individual assignments, one at a time. Then he took Jenny, Chidwi, and her bodyguards, two at a time, to the little house on Infinity Loop.

It was good to be home. Lizziebot had taken care of everything within the house, and Ted the gardener had been tending the gardens in the front and back of the house. It was obvious that Burt had been in and out, as he had left her many funny little love notes in various parts of the house, including on her pillow.

His duties hadn't allowed him to attend her at Amenia's house, so she hadn't seen him since before she had left on assignment.

She walked out to the garden, which had come to mean so much more to her since reading Lizzie's journals. Chidwi scampered up into the branches of the yew tree, and Tidbit settled lazily at the edge of the koi pond. The two of them seemed to find the scintillating, sparkling fish not only fascinating but also very calming.

Jenny hesitated for a moment, vacillating on whether to try the thing she had hoped to attempt ever since reading about how Lizzie had learned to communicate with the plants around her. She knew it was a skill that would require some refining to prevent her from being constantly bombarded with the murmuring of plants she encountered, but she also knew that other than the plants in her own yard, Earth plants were not used to communicating outside their own sphere; so the likelihood that she might have issues while on Earth were potentially small.

Tentatively she sent, *"WindSong, can you hear me?"*

"Hello? You are not Lizzie. No one ever speaks with me any more except the new little linkling in my branches."

"I am Jenny, Lizzie's niece. This is now my house. I didn't know before that I could speak to you. I wanted to thank you for your shade and the protection of the koi fish in the pond."

"I am happy to be here. Lizzie made my surroundings beautiful, and the gardener is very kind to see to our needs. Thank you, Jenny, for taking time to speak with me. Do you also make music?"

Jenny ducked her head in embarrassment. *"No, WindSong, I have not learned that skill, I'm afraid. I do have Lizzie's mbira, but I have had no time to try to play it."*

"Ah, no matter," WindSong sighed gently. *"I just miss her concerts. I know she has transitioned to her next estate, but I do find myself longing to see her again."*

"I understand. I never actually got to know Lizzie until I read her journals and would have liked to have spent some time with her. She has taught me much, but I feel like I have missed out by not having the opportunity to get to know her face to face."

"Your time will come. For now, it is enough that you know of her life and can honor her through your own service. She once told me of the difficult times she had before she came to this place and planted this garden. She spoke of you and her hopes for your future. I am sure you will do well."

Jenny didn't know what to say to this, but she was prevented from pursuing the conversation further by a voice coming from the French doors leading into the house.

"Halloo, neighbor," Bob called out. "Got a minute?"

Jenny rushed to him and grabbed him in a happy hug. "Of course," she replied after she let him go. "What's up? I just got home myself."

"I'll let that wait until the rest get here," he said, a twinkle in his eye. "Are the girls around? I would think they would be right on your heels here by the gate."

"They went to their apartment in the garage to get set up again to be here for a while. I expect they'll be back in here any moment now. It feels good to be back, although, as you know, we made some significant progress at Tarafau's place. Now that I have the communications organized and set up, it takes a lot off my plate. Also, I need to get up to speed on everything else that's going on in the Alliance, so I'm glad you're here. I take it you have news?"

Bob nodded but held up his hand. "In a minute. Shall we go back out onto the patio?"

And, as Jenny nodded, her bodyguards entered the house from down the hallway. Their apartment in the garage was mostly just for sleeping as their primary assignment was to guard Jenny from any potential harm. Jenny had objected to their presence in the beginning, but after she and the three of them had fought three burly Inseni intruders in the past year right in her living room, she was glad of their company, not to mention their constant vigilance when she was at her most vulnerable while mentally communicating across the dimensions.

They were arguing quietly among themselves about something.

"What's going on?" Jenny asked. She knew they tried to keep their disagreements private, so as not to disturb her with everything she had on her plate; and sure enough, they stopped in their tracks and looked somewhat embarrassed.

"Nothing," Mynn said quickly. "What's up?" she immediately added as she noticed Bob standing there, typically bouncing on his heels, a clear sign he was excited about something.

"We're waiting for a few more to show up and then we'll tell everyone at once," Bob responded with a mischievous grin and a wink.

They went out into the patio, the air fragrant with the herbs that grew abundantly around the little yew tree. Tidbit and Chidwi looked up expectantly at the little group emerging from the French doors. *"Something?"* Tidbit sent, his cat ears tilted forward and his amber eyes wide.

"We're waiting for a few more to come," Bob repeated good-naturedly.

Jenny had noticed that it took a lot to agitate or irritate Bob. Even when things were rough, he usually responded with positive determination to resolve the issue rather than to cast around for blame or to complain about the situation.

"How many are we expecting?" Nona asked. "Do I need to add some chairs?"

"Good idea," said Bob. "We're expecting at least four more."

He settled himself with his back to the French doors, looking out over the garden. Jenny knew he had watched the progress and growth of this garden for many years while Lizzie was still alive, even before he knew anything about the Alliance or Lizzie's adventures.

They didn't have long to wait, however. Merv, Burt, Elizabeth, and Anela were soon among them, huge smiles on their faces.

Burt hurried over to Jenny, his eyes alight to see her there, whole and functional once again. As he was wont to do, he kissed her on her forehead and pulled her in for a long warm hug that sent tingles from her head to her toes. As he pulled away, he could see her body-guards grinning and Elizabeth beaming in delight.

Blushing, and looking around at the amused reactions of her friends, she found herself wishing she had gotten the agent training that taught agents how to disguise their emotions.

"Shall we be seated?" Merv inserted, as Elizabeth also came forward to give Jenny a sisterly hug.

Jenny could only nod, holding Burt's hand and seating herself facing Bob across the patio table.

"So I'm sure some of you are wondering why we needed to do this in person, but both Merv and I agree this news deserves to be told face to face," Bob began, looking at each of them, still beaming with excitement. He had been drumming his fingers on the table as they had assembled themselves and now leaned forward, continuing to scan the faces before him.

"Noony..." he sent, and the little Mookookie was suddenly before them, emerging from his chest like a scene from a scary science fiction movie. The little Mookookie grinned as only they could do, since his face and body were one piece and his mouth was the largest part of him, unless he extended arms or legs as needed.

"For those of you who don't know him, this is Noony, a very valiant and useful being who, along with several of his fellows, has been aiding us at Cornelium's lab in investigating the many aspects and potential of the MDPs and their stewards, the Nanoites."

Then, out of his own MDP, Bob extracted Fidget, his robotic companion and lab assistant. "Most of you know Fidget. It turns out he works very well with both the Nanoites and the Mookookie Thanks to Jenny's unlikely mental expedition with Fidget into an MDP and the outcomes of that experiment, we now know much more about how the MDPs work, and we have recently learned that the interior environment of an MDP can be altered to adjust the temperature, the atmosphere, and the lighting to suit organic beings.

One of the things we didn't know was that the Nanoites are organic beings and have a significant and highly evolved culture of technology and are in agreement with the overall desires and moral code of the Alliance. They have not only built and maintained the various pods that make up the MDP network, but they have some technologies that none of us have ever seen before."

Jenny could see the intense light in Bob's and Merv's eyes. Of course, very little could excite these two more than scientific advances and new "dastardly alien tech" (as Burt would put it). She could tell that this must be really big, as both of them were practically glowing with excitement and anticipation.

It was like the entire group was holding their breath, waiting for Bob to continue after what was obviously a pause for dramatic effect.

Merv cut in, "Everybody take a deep breath. You'll all pass out if you continue to hold your breath like that."

There was a nervous laugh at that around the table.

"Okay, so here's the thing. We have always known that MDP stood for "miniature dimensional portal," but pretty much everyone, including all the Alliance scientists and technologists, just thought it was a humorous turn of phrase. Turns out, the MDPs are literally portable portals and are fully capable of acting exactly the way gateways operate.

They are on a completely separate part of the gateway network, and not even Anela had any idea, with all of her training, that they come under the supervision of the Gatekeeper."

Jenny gasped at this and the rest of them sat there wide-eyed.

"No," she whispered, looking straight at Anela, who nodded somberly.

"Yes," she replied, understanding very clearly the implications of Jenny's single word.

"We have transported troops and equipment in our last conflict, but we weren't aware of the complete scope of what this could mean. We only thought they would be good for short-term use, kind of like a bus or plane. However, with a livable atmosphere, an unlimited power supply, and the ability to cook and even to create hygiene stations, to name just a few of the amenities that could be stored in an MDP, they could function more like a space station or a very large RV."

Burt cut in excitedly, "This means that a small force of just a few people could sneak a huge army or rescue force into just about anywhere with no chance of detection until it was too late. We have gone from a Deuce and a Half to a troop carrier. Those within the MDP are simply safely orbiting the MDP planet until called out to do their job. Even if those wearing the MDP bracelets connected to that particular pod were killed, heaven forbid, those within the MDP would be safe."

Burt turned to Merv. "But would they then be stranded in the MDP pod?"

"Not at all, mate," Merv replied. "Those responsible for tracking MDPs within the Alliance would immediately know that the MDP armband had been destroyed and the coordinates of the MDP pod would simply be transferred to a new MDP armband, so that everything and everyone within the pod related to that device would be safely retrievable."

For a moment, they all sat there obviously stunned. Jenny could see Burt's mind working furiously, a million potential tactics and possibilities running through his head. Bob and Merv looked like two mountaineers that had reached the summit after a very long climb.

Jenny, looking around the table, noticed that each of them, including her bodyguards, were now gazing at the nondescript armbands each of them wore, which resembled the plastic sports bracelets that had once been the rage in the United States. Evidently one of the technological aspects of the bands were that they generated a kind of vibration or resonance that meant that most people simply didn't notice them. Either that or they just assumed that the person wearing it was just a bit behind the times, fashion-wise.

Each face seemed immersed in contemplation about the potential effects of this new information on their future project to rescue the dimensions that had been attacked and invaded by the Insenium. There was no doubt that they had a long road ahead of them in this quest to eliminate the Inseni threat, and all were painfully aware that every advantage they could acquire would be vital to their success.

Jenny cleared her throat. "So, how are the Nanoites and Mookookie expediting this research, and how are we keeping it secure?"

Merv looked up, now serious and matter of fact. "Your gift, Gatekeeper, for asking questions was perhaps only ever excelled by your Aunt Lizzie. We could really use her penetrating mind in the lab, I can tell you. You and your new communications staff will, of course, be key in allowing higher security, as we carefully begin to brief crucial team members regarding ongoing strategies and tactics.

"One of the things we need to try is to see if you can mentally communicate with people inside the MDP environment. Communication with them is the one thing we haven't nailed yet. Even with all the advances you have made with your gifts, this should be a new priority for you and your communications staff."

He leaned forward in his chair, his hands flat on the table before him, once again scanning the intent faces all focused on every word he said. "The Nanoites and Mookookie evidently have a number of things in common that we were previously unaware of. For instance, like the Mookookie, the Nanoites can communicate with all other Nanoites regardless of their location. Adding a Nanoite into every robotic or mechanical piece of tech we have would mean instant communication across the dimensions. Of course, we don't know how secure that would be, so we are for the moment at least, not pursuing that as a communications option.

"However, it turns out that the Nanoites and Mookookie are congenial. They seem to have formed a kind of alliance themselves. Their philosophical and political aims and ideologies seem to be very close to the same. The leaders of the Mookookie, 'the old ones,' are willing to aid us in rescue operations, but are reluctant to do more than sabotage the enemy, not willing to take a life or deliberately injure any being, and the Nanoites agree to this restriction.

What this means to us is that we cannot use the Nanoites in any robotics or mechanical constructs we employ in active warfare, nor can we use the interesting interdimensional talents of the Mookookie that way. Obviously, the Alliance would also prefer to never take a life or injure anyone, but we are willing to use whatever means are necessary to free as many dimensions as we can from Inseni tyranny and prevent them from being able to ever expand away from their own dimension again."

The rest of them nodded. For one brief moment, Jenny had thought that perhaps she would be released entirely of her duties for secure communication within the Alliance, but she could see their point.

Bob continued as Merv paused. "That doesn't mean there won't be a number of ways we can partner with our new friends, one of which includes intelligence operations that would be extremely hazardous for the rest of us but would not expose them to any danger or require any violent actions on their part. One of the reasons that Burt is in on this briefing is that he has been one of the Alliance's top intel agents for quite a while, and I believe he will see how that could extend his operations effectively.

Also, we are pleased to announce that Elizabeth has been assigned an internship to rejoin the team as one of Burt's new team members, along with Desminda and Tarafau, who will act as the liaison between the intel team and the Gatekeeper. They will be operating out of Sanglarka."

Elizabeth, who had been sitting on the other side of Jenny, grinned as Jenny reached over to give her an enthusiastic hug and a welcoming smile.

Chapter 6: Warp and Weft

Jenny sighed. *"Every time I think I've started to get a handle on all of this, it seems like they add something new for me to learn,"* she thought, grateful that only Chidwi could hear her thoughts. Chidwi reached up with a tiny hand and patted Jenny's arm. She had been sitting beside her in the little chair Burt had provided for her next to Jenny's desk chair.

"Jenny is smart and clever. Jenny will do well. Drink some water and keep going," Chidwi sent, a touch of humor in her mental voice.

Jenny reached for her water bottle, took a sip, and shook her head. It was fine for Chidwi to call her clever and smart, but at the moment she felt more like all of her responsibilities were ganging up on her. She had always loved school and had been considered a diligent and interested student, but right now she felt like she had been drinking from a fire hose, it was all coming at her so fast. And unlike simply raising her grade point average, so much more depended on her success that she shuddered to think what would happen if she failed.

She knew that all the members of her team were working flat out, and she probably wasn't the only one feeling stressed by the urgency of it all. At present, she was studying the intricacies of how the MDP network was monitored.

She had been given full access to that network along with all of the tech that ran the gate network. Fortunately, she didn't have to actually run the system, but it evidently was a requirement of the Gatekeeper to know how it all worked and to step in, if necessary, and handle things in an emergency.

It wasn't like she was computer illiterate or usually had any difficulties learning a new piece of software, but this was so much more than that. She had discovered that there were literally thousands of the pods orbiting the Nanoites' origin planet, and many of them were currently not in use.

One of Jenny's tasks would be to allocate empty pods to the appropriate staff members for use in the coming conflict. She also was repurposing four of the five MDPs that had been bequeathed to her by Lizzie. These had been used in the last effort to stop the Inseni but were currently unassigned.

One of them she kept, as she had been told it contained a potentially hazardous piece of equipment or technology and was not to be used except in an extreme emergency. Lizzie had left no specific instructions relative to that, as far as Jenny could discover, but for now, it was best not to give someone access to something unknown and potentially dangerous.

In addition, later today she would be vetting a potential new gate guardian for the India gate at the observatory in Sweden, just as they had for Lizzie so long ago. Lova had been researching potential candidates, as she had some Indian contacts and thought she may have found a promising contender. They also expected to vet a candidate for the Australian gate later this coming week. It was vital to ensure that these gates were appropriately defended and monitored.

Fortunately, she didn't have to vet every new gate guardian in every dimension; that would have been ludicrously impossible. But each dimension had a gate headquarters similar to Sanglarka, and the Gate Guardian for that gate was usually responsible for maintaining gate security by finding and vetting replacements when a guardian died or retired.

However, since the Earth gates were intrinsic to the current crisis, they were taking no chances. Therefore, Chidwi would be present at the interviews and vetting process. In this case, having a linkling with the ability to read minds would be very helpful in assuring they were making a good choice.

Jenny wasn't sure, any more than anyone else in the Alliance, how Earth had become such a centerpiece for the vital workings of the Alliance and its defense. But even though they weren't official members of the Alliance, there was no helping it, especially since Jenny had been installed to everyone's surprise, including her own, as the Gatekeeper.

She sighed again and was about to go back to her studies when Mynn stepped into the gate office from the hallway.

"Lizziebot says it's time for lunch, and you have visitors," she said with a wink and a grin.

Jenny didn't have to be asked twice. She leapt up as Chidwi jumped to her usual perch on Jenny's shoulder. The air screen automatically disappeared, and anyone looking into the office would see a desk but nothing on it even remotely resembling a computer.

She nearly ran out to the dining room to find Burt and Elizabeth and the other two bodyguards seated at the table, a nice lunch of sandwiches and salad spread out before them. Lizziebot was just gliding into the dining room from the kitchen, a tray laden with a pitcher of pink lemonade and ice-filled glasses in her robotic hands. Jenny had been impressed that Bob had created all of his robots with the option of either walking step by step on the soles of their feet or extending wheels on their feet to allow them to skate along.

She placed a glass in front of each of them and the pitcher in front of Burt, who happily poured a glass for all of them and handed the empty pitcher back to Lizziebot. Jenny knew Lizziebot would soon be back with a refill as pink lemonade happened to be a favorite of everyone in this group. Mynn and Jenny sat, and they stopped to bless the food.

Finally, as they all reached for sandwiches and started to pass the salad around, Jenny turned to Burt, eyebrows raised. "And to what do we owe this unexpected visit? It looks like having a Daringi intern has its benefits, since you didn't have to come through the gate office to get here."

Burt winked and Elizabeth grinned sheepishly. *"It was Burt's idea. He wanted to surprise you,"* she sent immediately. *"I wasn't sure if this was a polite thing to do, but he assured me that you love surprises."*

Burt shook his head, chuckling. "Actually, sweetie, I just didn't want to disturb you by sneaking up on you from behind out of the gateroom. It took a bit of persuading, but we got there in the end. I do admit, however, that Elizabeth made it very clear that she didn't normally drop in on people unannounced."

"At any rate," interrupted Jenny, "to what do I owe the pleasure of this visit? Since they didn't slaughter the both of you the instant you appeared, I assume you at least informed my bodyguards of your impending arrival."

The three girls nodded simultaneously, and Jenny could tell they were working very hard to suppress a grin. She would have to have a talk with them about surprises later, she told herself.

"Actually," Burt said, "we could use your help. I've cleared it with the Alliance and, of course, your bodyguards would be in attendance, but there have been some interesting things going on in our favorite place, the Amazon jungle. I could use your help, since you were with us when we discovered the Inseni portal, and I need your opinion to see if you're seeing what I'm seeing."

"A trip to South America?" Jenny asked, somewhat confused. "I thought I was supposed to stay incommunicado for the moment."

"Oh, you won't be exposing yourself to any prying eyes. That's one of the benefits of a Daringi intern. All travel arrangements are easily accessible, without even having to pack a bag."

Elizabeth grinned and ducked her head. She still didn't like being the focus of attention in a group, something Jenny was sure she would overcome as long as she continued with Burt.

"Well, what exactly will we be looking for?"

"I don't want to say. I want you to see it all for yourself without any preconceived notions. It stood out like a sore thumb for me, but maybe I'm just imagining things. One of the jobs set for me and Elizabeth was to keep an eye on things in that area as well as continuing our search for other potential portals. Just me and my cat..." and he looked pointedly at Elizabeth. "Like father like daughter." And he laughed as Elizabeth faded from view, turning into a ginger tabby cat now seated on the chair where Elizabeth had been the moment before.

Tidbit sauntered over, leapt up into the chair beside her, and rubbed his head against hers, purring loudly.

"It's obvious he is proud of his girl," Burt said with a chuckle. "I have to say I really lucked out to have her as an intern. It's rare to find an apprentice so willing and so driven to improve and serve so diligently."

Jenny knew that if she could as a cat, Elizabeth would be blushing.

"So, when would you like to leave?"

"I think now would be good, unless you have other plans."

"As you well know, I always have other plans, my schedule being what it is, but I don't have any formal meetings scheduled at the moment, so now would be good. Let me change into my hiking gear and we can get going."

Burt leaned over to kiss her on her forehead, squeezed her hand, and nodded.

In a few minutes they assembled in the gate office; Burt, Elizabeth, Nona, Lyra, Mynn, and Jenny with Chidwi perched happily on her shoulder and Tidbit scrutinizing the group, his tail twitching. Elizabeth took Burt and Nona first, then the other two, and finally Jenny. Jenny realized they were taking no chances with her safety and was torn between embarrassment that she needed such security and gratitude that they were all so faithful in seeing to it.

Elizabeth laid her hand on Jenny's shoulder, and the next moment the humid heat of a jungle struck her like a blow. Looking around, she realized she was in the place where they had formerly camped out, about a mile from what had been the Groga camp and where they had accessed the portal that first gave the Alliance the heads up that there were gateways outside of the Alliance that had completely different coordinates and wavelengths. Tarafau appeared next to his daughter.

Jenny looked around more carefully. The Alliance had gone in and removed all traces of their presence from her last visit. It seemed so long ago, after all that had happened since. But the little clearing had not overgrown and she could see the game trail they had followed before to the Groga encampment. Jenny had never gone along that path, as that had been delegated to the Alliance troopers.

When she had visited the encampment after her capture by Sam, she had come from a completely different direction, only to be recaptured and taken by the portal to Sam's home world. She shuddered at the memory.

Burt beckoned and led the way, since he had traveled this path before. Jenny wondered why they hadn't traveled directly to the Groga encampment instead of tramping along in the heat and humidity, but somehow she knew that now was not the time to discuss it.

They didn't even chat in mindspeech, which was somewhat unusual for this group as they usually had something to say; but each of them was instead focused on their surroundings, concentrating on the details of what they were seeing.

As they finally broke through into the huge clearing that had held the Groga camp, Jenny noted that the Alliance had also cleared away the evidence that anyone had ever been there. It was in keeping with the policy of noninterference with native cultures that was so important to interdimensional relations.

However, knowing how it had looked the last time she had been there, she felt a chill. Unlike the former Alliance encampment, the jungle had not encroached on this area, and she could still see the faint difference in coloration of the sparse grass covering the ground where the Groga tents had been assembled. Considering how the jungle had a tendency to overcome an untended area, this did seem somewhat odd to her.

She directed her gaze to the place she knew the portal lay. Somehow, she felt like there should have been a slight shimmer in the air, like a heat haze where it stood, but there was no sign that this clearing was any different from its surroundings. Somewhat hesitantly she headed towards it, her guards, one on each side and one behind her, pacing her step by step.

Still, no one said a word either verbally or mentally. Suddenly, a few feet from the portal, she stopped abruptly. She had been focusing ahead of her, but glancing at the ground she saw evidence that this area had been recently trampled by many feet, circling the area where the portal stood invisible.

"Someone has been here. Has the Alliance been sending guards or keeping some kind of watch here?" Jenny finally sent to the group.

"So far," Burt answered, *"we have only been monitoring it all electronically for both sound and movement based on infrared that will work both night and day to detect body heat, and we have no idea where all these tracks have come from. It's as if whoever made these tracks were both invisible and utterly silent. Our equipment should have picked up*

any movement or sound, but so far only normal jungle sounds have been recorded, and the animals tend to stay away from large open spaces unless there is water. They tend to prefer the covering of the jungle for their hunting, and the more vulnerable creatures seek the jungle for cover and food."

Jenny considered this. *"And we have been monitoring government reports to be sure the Brazilian government hasn't been searching the area? They haven't noticed the signs of the Groga incursion or our pursuit of them?"*

"Nope, nothing in any of our intelligence sources indicate any suspicion by the Brazilians. And it isn't like this is a popular tourist area. Elizabeth and I came out recently with a team to reset the surveillance equipment which is at the edge of the clearing and noticed the footprints. Now let's go closer to the portal."

They walked carefully across the footprints that had been left behind until they came to the spot that they all knew to be where the portal stood.

Burt asked, *"Now what do you see?"*

Jenny scanned her surroundings and noticed that the footprints that led up to the portal were cut in half in a line across where she knew the portal stood. And peeking out of one of the footprints was what, at first sight, appeared to be a coin. When Jenny stooped and reached out her hand to touch it, Burt grabbed her hand and pulled her back up to a standing position.

"Just a second," he sent and pulled from his MDP what looked like a debit card. He swiped it over the metal object several times and then reached for it and handed it to Jenny.

"Just taking precautions. I can't see anything about it that we need to worry about, and I'm not sure it's significant at all, but let's take it back with us and have Bob and Merv take a look-see with all of their sciency gizmos, shall we?"

Jenny nodded in agreement and slipped the coin-like item into her MDP, distracted by her thoughts regarding the footprints.

"A lot of people have recently been through this portal. How is that possible? I thought we sealed it."

"We did seal it on the other side of the dimension they attacked that day, but who knows how many additional exit points there may be? And although they can't get through the portal to the world we blocked anymore, we can't block it from this side, and there is no way of knowing how many additional coordinates they have available in those portal access units they use to go through the gates. Also, it seems there are many footprints headed out of the portal as well as going in. It looks like they are using this area almost like an Alliance gateroom.

"However, the fact that our equipment cannot seem to register their movements or any sound they make in the process is more than a little worrisome, don't you think?

"Even though I will be reporting this to the Alliance as soon as we head back to our gateroom, I knew that this was also part of your bailiwick, being the Gatekeeper and all. I'm guessing it isn't written into your contract; but since all of the Alliance gates are your responsibility, I thought it was also important for you to know that our gate system may still be vulnerable."

Jenny sighed and shrugged her shoulders as if to ease her back from a heavy rucksack. *"Have you taken photos?"*

"Yes, just now. One of the nanobot drones just did a complete sweep." He whistled "Shave and a Haircut," and held out his hand. Jenny couldn't see it in his palm but knew from his grin that it had landed there. *"It's programmed to climb directly into my MDP. I'll extract the photos while I'm at Alliance headquarters directly into their databank, and they will redistribute them to those with a 'need to know.'*

"I just didn't want to keep you out of the loop and thought seeing it in person might be best. Elizabeth, take Jenny and Nona back to the

gate office, and then come back for the other two. Then you and I will head straight to Alliance headquarters."

He reached out and grabbed Jenny in a fervent hug. *"Meet you tonight at 'our place,' okay?"*

Jenny nodded and kissed him while the girls giggled.

Elizabeth grinned and put a hand on Jenny and Nona's shoulders, and Burt blew her a kiss just as the gate office faded into sight.

Chapter 7: Threat Looming

Over the next several days, Jenny barely had time to breathe. Between continuing to organize and implement the new mental communication network, learning the ins and outs of MDP registration and control, doing her daily mental communications tasks, making sure she got a daily workout, and trying to determine what the Inseni might be up to in the Amazon jungle where the only non-Alliance portal they knew of on Earth stood, she became even more grateful that at least some of her duties could be done while she was sleeping.

She kept her tablet in the gate office in the safe under the desk and entered all information by hand as an extra layer of security, receiving top secret intelligence only through the mental communication network.

Even with all of that going on, she began to be restless. With the exception of her recuperation time after she used "the shout," her visit to Amenia's to train the new communications specialists, and their quick visit to the Amazon portal, she had never felt more cooped up and as if everything was moving forward without her. Not that she wasn't "in the loop," as Burt would put it, but she found her earliest fears seemed to be realized.

When she had first been made a gate guardian, even before she had the Gatekeeper title given to her, she had feared it would mean being a glorified secretary, just keeping track of the comings and goings in and out of the Los Angeles gate.

She had been delighted to find out that this wasn't the case, and her subsequent adventures had kept her both busy and engaged in some of the deepest doings of the Dimensional Alliance.

Now she found herself back in the role of a student and what felt an awful lot like clerical duties.

Of course, the constant flow of information and the respect that seemed to be given by all in the Alliance for her opinions and ideas, meant that it wasn't exactly boring, but she chafed at feeling like she was indeed confined to her house as she had been during her recuperation from "the shout." As much as she loved her house, her neighborhood, and her beautiful garden out back, she really felt like she just needed to get away for a while.

When she expressed this to Burt on one of their nighttime mental meetings at the little pool, he cocked his head and looked deep into her eyes.

"I don't think it will be long until you'll get your wish more often than I'd like, but I have to say I sleep better knowing how well protected you are. I don't think you realize how vital you are to the entire Alliance right now, even above and beyond your duties as the Gatekeeper. Trust me, you are on many minds right now on both sides of this conflict. Many of them you have never met or may ever meet... not to mention a certain husband, who seldom gets to see his beautiful, clever, talented wife."

Jenny sighed, recognizing he was giving her good advice even if she didn't like it much. She was somewhat encouraged by the possibility that she might soon get to be more involved in the actual goings on in the Alliance, aside from her mental conferences with the various teams across the dimensions. But before she could reply, Burt continued.

"Merv and Bob told me to pass on a message, but I'm not quite sure why, as I know you have quoted this to me in the past. The message is: 'Remember that magic is only science we don't understand yet.' End of message. Do you know what that's about?"

"No, not really. It's true, it is one of Bob's favorite sayings. I get the feeling he is infecting Merv even more with Earth lore and science, owing to Merv's past experiences during his extended stays on Earth in the ancient past. They spend way too much time together, I think." And at this they both laughed, for it was true that you seldom saw one without the other these days.

"So, I delivered the message, and you'll have to figure it out yourself, as I need to get some real sleep. Elizabeth and I have an assignment and we might not be getting much rest over the next several days. Just keep in mind that this is all just getting started. Between what we just found in the Amazon and other weird things that are starting to pop up around the dimensions, I'm beginning to think this is way bigger than we initially thought, and that's saying something."

He grabbed her and kissed her enthusiastically and then faded from view; and Jenny, once again regretting that mental kisses weren't as good as in person, also faded into sleep, having completed her communications duties for the night.

She woke with Bob and Merv's message clear and almost shouting in her mind. What did they mean by it? What did that have to do with what they were dealing with at the moment? Of course, she was familiar with Arthur C. Clark's famous three rules regarding science, and they had always seemed obvious to Jenny, completely agreeing with her own attitude about science as compared to what some would call magic, but why such an obvious statement, and why did it seem urgent for her to think about it?

She couldn't get it out of her head as she dressed, ate some breakfast with Chidwi and the girls, and let Tidbit in from his nightly "wanderings." The insistent quote rang in her head like one of those annoying tunes that keeps playing over and over in your thoughts, even when you don't remember all of the words to the song. During her workout with Tarafau and the girls, she kept getting tapped no matter who she sparred with until Tarafau finally called a halt to it.

They trooped out to the living room, Jenny sinking gratefully into her reading chair.

"What's going on with you?" he asked, now once again in his cat form, the end of his tail twitching and his ears cocked forward in a questioning manner that only cats seem to be able to achieve. Jenny almost expected his tail to form into a question mark.

"Something has you distracted and scattered. The only time before I have noticed you do this was when you were planning something you didn't want the rest of us to know about."

"Not to worry, I'm not planning anything, just puzzled about something that doesn't seem to want to leave me alone."

"Well, maybe you should put it out for the rest of us. Maybe we can see something you missed?"

"Good idea. Let me get my shower and we can eat some lunch and talk."

Jenny was still toweling her hair when Chidwi scampered into the bathroom. *"Lizziebot would like us to come and eat the lunch she has made for us. Eating it inside, so we can talk without distraction, she says."*

Sure enough, when Jenny entered the dining room, all three of her bodyguards were already seated and seemed to be waiting patiently, also already showered, and dressed in clean clothes. Jenny had been surprised to discover how well furnished the garage apartment had been, including a small eating area, a sitting room, and a very well-equipped bathroom. It wasn't unusual for those who weren't on "Jenny watch," as they called it, to retire to the apartment to rest or watch television, something that fascinated them to no end. And they sometimes even cooked their own meals in the little kitchenette.

Jenny was glad they got some private time, considering how much time they spent with her, just hanging out while she took care of her various duties which often consisted of her sitting in a relaxed position with her eyes closed, not exactly good company for whichever of the girls was on duty at the moment.

They took turns going out with her on her usual jog around the loop. Whenever she went shopping, however, they all went with her, mostly, she thought, to just get out of the house for a while. Even Jenny looked forward to that, something she had never done before. She missed her hiking club and realized with a start that perhaps this was something they could still do, with her taking breaks in the quiet surroundings of nature to do her job while her guards had a chance to work in better surroundings.

In the meantime, Tidbit was curled up on the window seat, and Chidwi hopped up into her special seat at the table immediately to Jenny's right.

"So, what's bugging you, Gatekeeper?" Mynn asked as soon as they began to eat. Once again Jenny was grateful that mindspeech allowed them to talk and chew without being impolite as she had just taken a big forkful of salad.

"Hmm… it's hard to say. My head just keeps repeating the message I got from Bob and Merv last night during my communications time. It somehow seems non-sequitur to me, completely out of context with our current situation. It's like someone just told me the sky is blue or water is wet."

"So, what was the message?" Nona prompted.

"'Magic is only science we don't understand yet,' a quote from a famous inventor and author who was well known for his understanding of the sciences. He often spoke about the importance of creativity in the scientific process and was a strong believer in the possibility of impossibility.

"I'm not sure why Bob and Merv would remind me of something that seems so obvious and unnecessary to think about, considering everything else that is going on at the moment."

Tidbit cocked his head, the end of his tail now twitching furiously, something that seemed to happen in his cat form unconsciously whenever he was deep in thought.

"And that was the entire message?" he sent, his tone curious and perhaps a bit agitated.

"Yep. Just that. No explanation or other clues. I'm guessing they think I need to connect the dots myself, but for the moment I'm confounded. Maybe I'm taking it too literally? Or maybe it's their idea of a joke?"

There was a long silence while each of them considered the potential meaning of this obscure reference while munching on their lunch.

Chidwi, who had been choosing from the various fruits and vegetables in her bowl, finally chirruped and sent, *"Is this a hidden message that needs to be kept in Jenny's heart and only between her and us?"* She glanced meaningfully around the table, finally looking over her shoulder at Tidbit.

Jenny couldn't help but chuckle as all four heads, including the cat's, nodded nearly in unison, the faces before her contemplative and serious.

"Okay, so what are your thoughts? The intent of the original quote is somewhat obvious, but what does it mean in our circumstances?"

Mynn spoke up again. Of the three of her bodyguards, she seemed to be the most interested in the sciences. The other two, although undaunted by new technology, seemed to lose interest to a certain point when deep scientific principles were being discussed.

"Don't I remember something from one of your reports about the 'wizards' of the Inseni? Or did they call them 'magicians'? Not sure which of those terms might be more insulting, but it didn't appear that

the Inseni king thought of it in that way. He actually seemed to think that they were performing magic spells to achieve the various technological advances they did for him."

Jenny considered this. Burt's reports on his time with the Inseni definitely seemed to indicate that the Inseni thought of scientific achievements as magic. And since they were still dealing with the Inseni, how might that play into future strategies?

"So, I don't totally understand the concept of magic," Nona put in hesitantly in the silent contemplation that followed. *"What does that word mean? My culture has no reference to it."*

Jenny then launched into an explanation of some of the myths and legends of Earth and the difference between magic and science.

"So, it's more about the point of view of the observer, then?" Nona asked. *"There is essentially no difference between what is being observed in any case, but does how a person views the event influence what they believe to be the cause of the event, deciding on either magic or science as the cause?"*

"I guess you could put it that way. Magic is supposed to be mysterious and potentially unexplainable, only available to certain talented individuals with 'special powers.' Focus-enhancing elements like magic wands, staffs, crystal balls, or even pets they call 'familiars' all are considered tools of the magical craft. A magician or wizard can generally do things that normal beings can't. They can make things disappear or create things apparently from thin air. They can use illusion or distraction to influence the people around them to do things they might not otherwise be able or willing to do."

"Hmm... so you would be considered a wizard in your culture?" Mynn sent with an amused twitch to her mouth and a twinkle in her eyes. *"After all, you have 'powers' none of the rest of us have."*

Jenny thought about this. *"I suppose someone might think that, if anyone actually knew about what I do. But I can't make things disappear or conjure things from thin air—"*

"But you can!" interjected Nona suddenly. *"Get your quarterstaff out of your MDP!"*

Jenny's mouth dropped open, startled by this. She didn't extract her staff, but she realized that when it appeared whenever she invoked it, it definitely would look like a magician's illusion, and that some of the other technology she had gotten too used to using as a matter of course would also appear as magical to someone who had never seen it before.

"But what do you think caused Merv and Bob to remind me of this right now? How does it apply to everything we're trying to accomplish in the coming conflict?" And Jenny struggled to keep the whine out of her voice. *"I feel an urgency about it ever since Burt told me about it, and I don't know why."*

"Perhaps it would be a good thing for you to contact Amenia," Tidbit put in. *"When you work with her, you often find insights that otherwise stump you in the conscious world."*

Jenny brightened at the thought. *"I think you're right. Just for security's sake, I'll retire to the workout room with Chidwi and just one of you,"* nodding to her guards who were still lost in thought.

"I'll go with you," Mynn volunteered cheerfully. *"And may I join in the mental conversation? I am fascinated by the skills you are learning and am also really interested in what you may discover."*

Jenny thought about this. *"I don't see any reason why not, as you are already aware of what I'm looking for. It's not like I have much in the way of secrets about anything with the three of you. Tidbit, are you coming?"*

The big black cat stood and stretched languidly, muscles and fur rippling, his black-on-black tabby stripes undulating in the sunlight that was pouring in from the window. He leaped down from the window seat and stood waiting expectantly.

"We'll want a report when you're done," Lyra sent, speaking out for the first time. She had seemed in deeper thought and more somber

than Jenny had ever seen her. *"I have a bad feeling about this..."* she trailed off, and stood and began to clear the plates from the table even though Jenny knew Lizziebot usually performed that task.

In no time, Jenny, Tarafau, and Mynn were seated in relaxed positions on the mats on the workout floor, Chidwi's hand on Jenny's shoulder, facing the large windows that looked out onto an alien landscape. Jenny still was in awe that only steps away from her living room were alien environments beyond her imagination.

She found Amenia lying back in a chaise near the firepit, watching the linklings play in and among the little glade behind her house. She looked in front of her as Jenny appeared. Jenny loved the fact she could now be seen by those she contacted. It seemed somehow more personal.

"Jenny, how may I help you? Is all well?"

"Amenia, can Mynn and I spend some time with you for a bit? I believe all is well, but I have a question that is nagging at me and I need some perspective. Can we meet in my fortress?"

And before Amenia could do more than nod, the three of them with Chidwi on Jenny's shoulder were at the drawbridge being greeted by the guardian of the portcullis. Mynn strode along beside them, her eyes roving constantly, partially as it was part of her job as a bodyguard, but Jenny suspected it was even more in awe of this new experience.

Instead of going to the communications building, Jenny decided that perhaps the library, one of the first buildings on the square, was the most appropriate place for this conversation.

They went up the stairs between the sculpted dragons that guarded the entrance and opened the big double doors into a spacious, quiet, well-stocked library; tall shelves extending as far as she could see. In this case, the inside was definitely bigger than it appeared to be from the outside of the building.

They went past the elderly librarian sitting at a desk in the front to what Jenny knew without looking would be exactly where she pictured it. On one side of the library there was a small room lined with bookshelves and in the center of the room were three overstuffed chairs in a circle around a highly polished coffee table.

Comfortable surroundings for a scholarly discussion, Jenny thought, as they all took a seat and Chidwi clambered to her favorite place on the back of Jenny's chair.

"Now what is this all about?" Amenia asked, curiosity plain on her face. "Is this about one of your abilities or something else? You've been making amazing progress, and I'm not sure you are ready to explore much more in terms of adding to your current skills."

"No, not abilities per se, or at least I don't think so. I need to work through a problem that is nagging at me, and Tarafau suggested that maybe you could help me work it out so I can focus on other things more carefully."

Amenia nodded. "So, what could have you so flummoxed? You tend to take most things in your stride. Lizzie was usually the one who got herself wrapped up in unsolvable problems."

Jenny told her about the message from Bob and Merv. "I understand the basic meaning of the quote they sent me, but I can't see in what way it applies to our current situation or why they would send it to me without any explanation. I have to assume that it might be important to work it out myself, but so far, all it has done is to distract me from other things that appear to be more important." She let out a sigh of annoyance, shaking her head at the ridiculousness of the whole situation.

At first Amenia didn't speak, then she got up, walked over to one of the bookshelves and seemingly randomly pulled out a book and handed it to Jenny.

Jenny's eyebrows shot up in disbelief. "Huh? What is this about?"

Amenia didn't answer but nodded towards the book. Jenny turned it to the side and read the spine of the book. Inscribed in gold lettering down the side was one word: "Answers."

"Really?" she remarked to Amenia and showed the book to Mynn, who chuckled and shook her head.

"Open it," Amenia recommended with a completely straight face.

Jenny did so, and just inside the front cover was the title and below it: "By Jenny Japhet Scout." Her mouth dropped open, and for a moment she just stared at it.

Then, she looked at the dedication on the facing page. "Dedicated to my Aunt Lizzie, who got me into this mess."

Still shaking her head, she turned the page and began to read aloud.

"Chapter 1: Magic vs. Science," she read in a tone of total disbelief. "The so-called 'magicians' of the Inseni are just one more example of the principle that science is broader and more complex than anyone ever understands. In order to take advantage of the sciences, one must be ready to suspend disbelief and move forward, realizing that not all truths are obvious and not all things we call science are fully truth.

Therefore, sometimes we need to reexamine our assumptions, predictions, and assertions in order to reach a conclusion that leads to not only truth but a usable theory. Sometimes this examination allows us to see truth that was hidden by things we take for granted to be immutable."

Jenny looked up to see Amenia looking thoughtful and Mynn practically jumping up and down on her comfy seat.

"Why do I get the feeling that Bob and Merv were sending me a message in code, and why do I also wonder about why they felt the need to do so?" She looked at Mynn, who was biting her lip, evidently attempting to keep from blurting something out.

"What do you think, Mynn?"

"I am sure you're right... about the code, I mean. They're trying to prepare you to consider something they have discovered that they think you will find unbelievable but may be necessary to the ultimate success of our venture. I think it's necessary for you to discover it for yourself, because you will be intrinsically involved in whatever it is, and discovering it for yourself gives it greater credibility. By the way, I think this inner world of yours is amazing, and how did that book know what to tell you?"

Jenny couldn't help but laugh appreciatively at Mynn's enthusiasm. She looked at Amenia and raised an eyebrow.

"You already knew the answer, Jenny," she replied to the unspoken question. "All the books in this library," and she made a wide sweeping gesture, "were in some way written by you. Your mind holds a vast library of information, but unfortunately it isn't always easily accessible by the waking mind. But here, you own the library and it features only books by you or books you have read or conversations you have overheard or lessons taught you in school or by experience. All these things are contained in the books in this building in your mental village."

Mynn's eyes were wide, and it was obvious she was taking in every word with delight. Jenny sat for a moment silently thinking this through; and as she did, words appeared on the open page in front of her. She almost dropped the book in astonishment.

She read aloud, "There are things happening both in the Alliance and in the Insenium that are about to reconfigure your current beliefs about the extent and value of current scientific knowledge. An open and yet discerning mind will be essential moving forward. Be prepared for revelations that will come out of the current ongoing research being done on both sides. Make a priority of getting Mookookie into the Inseni scientific community, as this might be your best opportunity to stay ahead of what they are doing.

Also, you currently have tools in your possession that may be vital to a positive final outcome of this conflict, but now is not the time to reveal which ones or how to use them. Return frequently to your library as you move forward. Answers are here."

Jenny stopped as the words ran out and began to feel like she had been running a mental marathon race. "So, where do I go from here? Do I reveal any of this to anyone else or just keep it in my head and wait?"

She almost expected the book to start revealing more text on the page and she even flipped through the blank pages beyond where she had been reading, but nothing appeared. She looked up first at Amenia and then Mynn, but they both shook their heads, their eyes wide.

"Maybe we all just need to think about it for now." Then, she paused. "Wait, we're forgetting someone. Chidwi, what do you think?"

"Jenny speaks truthfully. Chidwi advises thinking much and then to speak with the scientists. We have many, many, do we not?"

"Yes, Chidwi, many and many more, at least two groups of which we have direct contact with. I think it's time we paid them each a visit, don't you?"

"Yes, Jenny should visit scientists. Girls can come with Jenny and Tidbit. Secret. Not tell anyone but Burt, yes?"

"Yes, and I think we will not go via gateway. We'll get Tidbit and Elizabeth to take us directly. I'll let Bob and Merv know in my evening communication session. In the meantime, I need to give Na, Li, and Fo their assignments."

"How is that working out?" asked Amenia as they rose and prepared to leave the fortress. "I was hoping it would relieve a lot of stress from your daily routine."

"They are amazing. Thank you, Amenia, for finding and helping me to train them. They are each assigned to a specific range of communications, and they are doing a great job of summarizing each message to be concise without leaving out important details. Each of them has a direct connection to Liliath's councilors, and recently I only hear things from them that connect directly to my own responsibilities. We do a weekly conference together, unless there is something urgent where they need to contact me directly. So, thank you again for that."

Amenia nodded, waved, and faded from sight as Jenny and Mynn retired to the workout room.

"Well, Jenny, did you find out what you needed to?" Mynn asked as they exited the gate office into the house, Tidbit trailing behind them.

"I think so. I think it is preparatory to some new discoveries that they want to reveal. I think we are about to get some real eye-openers. I'll arrange for Elizabeth and Burt to join us when we go to speak with them about this. Tidbit, I'm assuming that you and Elizabeth can be there in your normal form, since Cornelium's lab is in a member dimension?"

"Yes, Jenny, it shouldn't be a problem."

Relieved, she got on with her usual duties with a clear mind.

Chapter 8: Lightbulbs

Jenny felt like she had been set free. They all sat in a circle in the break room of Cornelium's lab—Tarafau, Elizabeth, Nona, Mynn, Lyra, Burt, Anela, Bob, Merv, and Cornelium, who was reclining on a huge chaise. Like all the rooms in the lab, the break room was spacious, as needed when the main scientist is a dragon. Chidwi perched as usual on the back of Jenny's chair. It felt so good to be somewhere beside her house, as much as she loved her little house on Infinity Loop.

She had gotten used to being in the thick of things where the Alliance was concerned, and her recent convalescence and the restrictions imposed for security had been chafing more and more as every day passed.

Now she sat on the edge of her chair in anticipation. Evidently, they were waiting for two more attendees. There were two empty chairs sitting at the edge of the circle closest to the door. None of them spoke either in mindspeech or aloud. They had greeted one another enthusiastically when the group had first arrived, but since seating themselves, all had fallen into a somewhat contemplative state, unusual for this particular group.

She heard footsteps from across the main lab and looked up expectantly. Next to her, Burt squeezed the hand he had been holding. They got so little time for close personal contact that just holding hands was a joy for them both, so they did so even in large groups and during meetings with the rest of the team.

Into the breakroom walked two people whom Jenny recognized from her own mental observations of Burt's covert operations in Emperor Peril's domain. Peril had taken Burt to visit his "wizards" on a moon in orbit around their planet. Jenny knew these scientists had been rescued from that environment after the successful revolution by the slaves on the Mookookie planet and had willingly added themselves to the Alliance science team after making contact with their families also rescued from slavery there.

Gahn and Visker strode into the room looking at the faces turned to them and, seeing Burt, waved and sat in the two empty seats.

Burt sent to the group, *"To those who haven't yet met them, please greet Visker and Gahn, two renowned 'wizards' formerly of the Insenium who have joined the Alliance science team and have proved themselves not only competent but extremely helpful in our efforts to decide how best to flush the Insenium from the dimensions they have so far conquered and enslaved. They're here to help us with some of our thornier issues regarding how to best accomplish this."*

All sent various versions of welcome or "glad to meet you," and then waited patiently for someone to continue.

"So good to see you out of your 'wizards' den," Burt said to the two of them with a grin. They both smiled in return. *"Are you enjoying your new accommodations?"*

They both nodded enthusiastically. The two scientists were as different as two people could be and still be humanoid. Visker was tall and lanky with blond curly hair and nearly violet blue eyes, and he was missing a hand. The hand had evidently been replaced with a cybernetic mechanism which Visker waved around as he spoke, apparently very comfortable with the replacement.

Gahn, on the other hand, was stocky and tan, with straight black hair that hung below his shoulders. His large eyes were so dark as to be no discernable color.

Nevertheless, it was evident that the two of them were comfortable with one another, having worked side by side for the Insenium for a long time.

"We can't thank the Alliance enough for freeing us from Inseni rule. Most of our families actually decided to stay on the planet, since in many cases our originating planets are still under Inseni rule. We understand that the Alliance is working to change that, and we want to be a part of it," Gahn declared while Visker nodded.

"The result of our current research has yielded some results we think you will find not only interesting but useful as well," Visker added confidently. He pulled from his lab coat pocket a familiar looking object.

"The card? I thought it was destroyed. You told me it was worthless." Burt exclaimed, wide-eyed. *"You said it didn't do anything and that the computer circuits on the card were nonfunctional."*

"Ah, yes," Gahn said proudly. *"We wanted Peril to think that. Your scientists here thought the same of the card you found. However, we managed to abscond with this after the revolution and brought it with us to the lab. Turns out it is of some worth after all, but not in the way you thought."*

"It is not a personal interdimensional travel device. It is a master key to the Insenium portal system. They issued the mechanical devices for accessing the portals to lesser officers and military personnel, but it was kept secret that there were these master keys. Even Peril didn't know about them. Evidently, the key you found at the Amazon portal had been dropped by someone high in the real Inseni military.

"Peril's troops were not ranked highly by Gall and his minions. So, the fact that a key was dropped near the Amazon portal tells us that more than just the Groga were engaged there, for whatever reason."

"Then that is why we got resonance reacting to the MDP when we tested it in Cornelium's lab!" Bob put in, his eyes wide. Burt could almost see the curiosity wheels turning in Bob's head.

Gahn and Visker nodded triumphantly.

"Now that we know this, we will continue to run tests. Keep your card for now. Keep it secure and we will do the same. We believe there is something slightly different between the regular gateways in your network and the miniature portals existing in the MDP network. It is just a slight difference, but knowing that, and also having the cards to compare with that, we may be able to ascertain the resonances or frequencies of the Inseni portals, which may be a huge step towards learning how to recognize them. We are currently working on a mechanism that will detect those frequencies so we may even be able to use from the far reaches of space around Alliance member worlds."

There was an extended silence as each of them considered the implications of this statement. Jenny looked from face to face, attempting to discern the effects of this amazing statement on each of the participants. Of her bodyguards, only Mynn looked excited. The other two seemed politely interested, but it seemed like a lot of this may have gone over their heads. The others, however, had varying looks of excitement and contemplation on their faces, attempting to fully comprehend the potential of what they had just heard.

"I, for one," Jenny interposed on the silence, *"can see there is a lot more to this than simply understanding the purpose of these 'keys.' My question is: How many of our science team will be working on this project? It's obvious to me that this is a high security issue and, taking Liliath's suggestion as a guide, I want to recommend that this be kept on a need-to-know basis for now."*

All heads nodded solemnly.

Anela's eyes were bright. She turned to Bob and Merv. *"Thank you for including me. I can see why this information needs to be kept within a tight circle of security."*

"We wanted to hear what Visker and Gahn had to say before we extended this information beyond this small group. We only initially included you in our experiments with the card because of your gatekeeper

key. However, perhaps as the potential backup Gatekeeper, it might be important for you to know about this," Bob replied.

"I think perhaps I should confer with Liliath about it," Jenny said, after a moment's thought. *"I need to report to her as soon as I have all the information from Visker and Gahn. Did we record this session?"*

Cornelium nodded his huge head. *"All scientific conversations are recorded here to be sure we have all details. Bob, Merv, Visker, Gahn, and I will do an extended and more detailed version of this conversation after we conclude this meeting."*

"So, after this little bombshell, I think we all could use some time to contemplate; and I think I need some quiet time with my wife," Burt said, rising from his seat.

They all seemed slightly surprised at this abrupt statement. This group could easily spend hours discussing an important break-through. However, noticing Burt's significant look, signifying that there was more to his statement than it appeared, they all nodded.

"I think the rest of us," Bob said, indicating the scientists in the group, *"can hash out the implications of this development. We'll keep you posted."*

He stood up and gave Jenny a hug and a wink. Elizabeth put a hand on Jenny and Burt's shoulders and the gate office faded into view. Before Jenny could inquire regarding the excited look on Burt's face, Elizabeth had faded out and returned with Nona and Mynn and went back for Lyra. Jenny decided to be patient and waited until all of them were back in the gate office.

"Now, Burt, what's going on? I get that this was an exciting and potentially helpful revelation, but why do I get the feeling that a lightbulb went off over your head that had little to do with what the 'wizards' had to say?"

"Aha, my wife, I can see you are beginning to know me too well. It was bound to happen. Yes, indeed. I don't know why, as often happens with the best of ideas, but something in the conversation triggered a thought that didn't seem to have any connection to what they were discussing. I think it was the reminder that we originally thought the cards were personal interdimensional transportation devices. It occurred to me that we already have something like that."

"What?!" exclaimed Mynn. "How cool is that? And of course, for now we would want to keep it a complete secret. Can I have one?"

Burt laughed. "Actually, you already do, and she is standing right in front of you. Since you are responsible for her protection..."

Jenny was stunned. "Me? Really? And how does that work, then?" She felt he must be kidding with them.

"I was remembering when you rode along with me when I visited the 'wizards' with Peril. Do you remember when we were kids and they let kids do 'ride-alongs' with policemen?" He laughingly hit his head with his palm as if he had missed something.

Jenny nodded her head, even more puzzled and, waited for him to continue after his dramatic pause.

"Well, you have been chafing almost visibly the past few weeks, feeling trapped and uninvolved with everything that's going on. What if you could do ride-alongs with various ones and even interact with us without anyone else knowing it? What if you could be an active part of everything going on without it being some kind of formal meeting or putting yourself in direct danger? What if you could hang out on the patio and actually be somewhere else, doing things right along with the rest of us? That would resolve both sides of this issue.

We want to keep you safe, right? Not just for yourself, but for the good of the Alliance? I think you could not only do this but even bring along one or more of your bodyguards, so they don't get bored and are also in on the action. Do you think you could do this? Can we test it?"

Jenny collapsed into the chair behind the office desk, stunned.

"Wow! Why didn't I think of this? I'll have to practice with the girls, but yes, I think we can do this. The tricky part will be filtering the communication so that only the people I want to see and hear me can do so. And the idea of bringing one or more of the girls with me has its merits also, especially if something happens we don't expect. If my connection broke, they would automatically be returned to consciousness wherever their bodies were at the time. Wow! Just wow! Burt, I could kiss you!" And she did, to the delight of Elizabeth and her bodyguards.

Chapter 9: Sibling Rivalry

Liliath reclined on her chaise with a sigh. It had been a long day for all of them. She felt like she had put Jenny onto a good path, that the other teams were all working at top speed and efficiency in each of their various purviews, but she still felt uneasy, like the task before them was so far beyond their ability to achieve; and yet, how could they just ignore the activities of the Inseni?

Although the Inseni government had been apparently completely disrupted by Sam's retribution, the damage they had already done couldn't be ignored. Potentially hundreds of dimensions, maybe thousands, had been invaded for the purpose of plundering, terrorizing, and dominating the various cultures on the planets they had already conquered.

They were still gathering data as far as was available through interrogation of various captured Inseni leaders, but if there had been any records available in the Inseni capital, they had been destroyed with Sam's destruction of Gall and the city around the building he was in for over a hundred-mile radius. Liliath still quailed at the idea of how much power Sam, otherwise known as Engoza, had expelled in her rage and anguish over what Gall had done to her parents and her entire culture. She had been, as far as they could tell, the only remaining person in her parents' kingdom.

Suddenly Liliath realized that Jenny was there in the room with her, Chidwi perched on her shoulder. *"Liliath, I have some news,"* she sent, appearing before Liliath's chaise, somewhat transparent, but with a smile crinkling her eyes. Liliath hadn't seen her this cheerful since before she had carried off the defeat of the Insenium's Groga troops using "the shout."

"Between Burt, my bodyguards, and Elizabeth we have come up with a new use of my talents. I can now be a participant in events and projects with every team member individually or in groups. When I am doing what we are currently calling a 'ride-along,' no one can see or hear me except those I specifically include in my sending. For instance, I can be in on a conference or I can actually be in the middle of a battle, with no risk to myself and without anyone knowing I am there but the anchor person or people with whom I have connected. As you can imagine, this gives me so much more than secondhand reports and could be potentially useful when one of our members is in a tight spot. For instance, if they need immediate help, I can make that happen quickly. Or if they need answers in the moment, I can get them for them. What do you think?"

Liliath contemplated the young woman in wonder and, not for the first time, blessed Lizzie for her perception in bringing Jenny into the Alliance and Miriha for bestowing the Gatekeeper position on her.

"Jenny this is amazing. And you say that no one who is not intentionally in your circle will be aware of any communications that you have with your intended audience? And you said you can bring others into the conversation or experience along with you? I never heard of such a thing."

Jenny nodded, her face wreathed in a satisfied smile. *"I can make my companions appear to the intended audience or not. To answer what I think is your next question, no, I will never bring someone along without making sure that the person I am contacting knows the conversation and events are being observed."*

Liliath nodded and began to reply, but put one finger to her lips. She looked up at the sound of her door opening, without a preemptory knock. It was Gighin. Her brother didn't hesitate at the door awaiting an invitation to enter, but instead strode into Liliath's cave-like living area with confidence, as if this was his home as well as hers.

"Well, hello, Gig. Knuckles too sore to knock, I suppose?" she greeted him wryly. To Jenny she sent, *"This is not private and perhaps may be a good test of your new talent. Stay with me. Do you have anyone else with you?"*

"Only Elizabeth, but I can disconnect her, if you wish."

"No," Liliath replied, and turned her attention to her brother.

"Ah, my dear sister, I didn't know family were required to be so formal. I'll remember in future. In the meantime, I was hoping you now have some time where we can discuss some matters of importance to our planet and our membership in the Alliance without any onlookers."

She looked into his deep green eyes, remembering back when he was a young dragon, full of mischief and charm. Over time he had assumed a more dignified, somewhat self-satisfied, even sometimes arrogant persona, pursuing applause and recognition among the great and well-placed in their society. His opinions were less broad-minded than Liliath's own, as he was generally unwilling to see things from another's point of view, and they often found themselves in conflict with one another.

As Liliath had gone into teaching in the Alliance agent training center and later into her role as an Alliance councilor and finally as the Chief Councilor of the Alliance, they had lost touch with one another. They definitely moved in different circles philosophically and politically. Now she found herself wondering if the draconic council had made a good choice in sending Gighin as their liaison.

She nodded towards the chaise opposite her in the room and he reclined upon it almost lazily. She recognized the shift in his eyes and realized he was preparing to at least appear to be reasonable and open to discussion. But she knew her brother well enough to know he had made up his mind well before this visit, regarding what he wanted to discuss and the point he intended to win, regardless of any of her arguments.

She shifted slightly in her own chaise and inclined her head towards him, still looking intently into his eyes.

"So, what message do you bring the Alliance?" she asked, careful not to say, 'What message do you bring me?', as she had every intention of keeping personalities out of this and acting professionally. If he was indeed just relaying a message from their leaders, she didn't want to prejudice her attitude against it from the beginning.

"It is more of a question. They wish to know what further role you expect the Alani to play in your current plan to rescue the various dimensions invaded by the Insenium. We are reluctant to enter in on some valiant quest that is likely to become a very long ongoing mission, both costly and perhaps impossible to fulfill. As you may already know, we are not the only dimension wondering about this.

"I cannot in any good conscience recommend such a path. It isn't a lack of sympathy or recognition that the Inseni has done wrong by these people, but how far can we afford to take this? And how does this potentially conflict with our stance of non-interference?"

Lizzie breathed carefully in and out, calming herself to prevent showing agitation to her brother, who was looking very smug at the moment.

"I think we have addressed this at some length in our past few general council meetings," she said, trying hard not to sound impatient. "As you know, we have left it entirely to the various dimensional governments to decide their level of participation or to opt out as they would like."

"Nevertheless, you can't deny that pursuing this could put the entire gate network in jeopardy. That affects all of us, whether or not we render direct or indirect aid to this project," he retorted, a slight hint of disdain tingeing his expression. "What precautions are you taking to prevent this? The whole purpose of the Alliance is to protect that network and allow the members of the Alliance added security to prevent what happened to those dimensions invaded by the Inseni from happening to us."

Liliath nodded. This wasn't a new argument. The same sentiments had been expressed openly in the general council meeting by several of the member representatives. The majority had agreed to help those invaded by the Inseni, but there were still enough within the Alliance who were reluctant to pursue this that various experienced liaison agents were actively engaged in soothing and calming those fears.

"We did put the project up for a vote again at the last general meeting, with the majority voting to proceed. We will continue to keep all the members up to date with all the information we have that we can reveal without compromising the security of the project. So, what would you have me do?" Liliath said, in her calmest most diplomatic tones.

Gighin's eyes narrowed with exasperation. "Really? The 'all-powerful' Chief Councilor is at a loss? You have no idea how to respond? Come now, big sister, you can do better than that. You have all of the resources of the multiverse at your fingertips.

"I tell you, our people are deeply concerned about the path the Alliance is taking, with no clear assurance that there is any chance to succeed, potentially over generations of time, if ever. Simply leave it alone. How many suffering masses exist across the dimensions? Are we to save them all? Can we not simply deny the Inseni further access to the worlds in our network and let it go?"

Gighin also leaned forward towards Liliath, the spines along his back and down his tail rigid and erect. Liliath was sure he wouldn't attack her physically, but she also knew this was a sign of a dragon "displaying" as birds on Jenny's planet did, showing their displeasure, courage, and strength to an opponent.

She almost wanted to laugh at the aggressive posture. To her? Really? His overconfidence had always been somewhat amusing to her, simply because she was both larger than he was and better trained in combative skills, he having chosen the more aristocratic path, preferring, as he said, "not to get my hands dirty."

However, she simply stared at him for a moment with quiet contemplation, as she would have one of her students at the agent training school she had administered for so many years. She noticed he was trying not to squirm under her penetrating gaze.

"I do understand the concerns of those dimensions who have expressed a certain amount of resistance to our plan to rescue these people. I also understand their reasons. However, at this point we are focusing on the least impactful way to both protect the Alliance gate system and still release those dimensions invaded by the Inseni from bondage and terror. Nevertheless, not one of the Alliance members will be required to participate more deeply than they desire. We will go with the majority in this decision, especially since it represents over 80 percent of the votes by the general council."

Gighin harrumphed noisily. "And what if your majority drags us into either a never-ending conflict or, even worse, compromises the gate network? Isn't the main purpose of the Alliance to keep that network safe?"

Liliath shook her head agitatedly. "This has already been covered in discussions over many sessions of the general council, and we have analyzed every bit of input. The fact that there are still Inseni gates out there and some of those gates still impinge on our own Alliance members' planets is one of the main reasons we are pursuing this. We have increasing evidence that this is the case, and one of the purposes we are pursuing is to create the technology that will allow us to detect Inseni portals wherever we have a member planet with suspicious activity.

"Do you honestly think we would consider this plan if we hadn't done every bit of research possible?"

He didn't reply immediately, still staring directly into her eyes. Finally, he said, "And what part would you have our own dimension play in this plan? I know you have already engaged Cornelium's lab in a great deal of hush-hush scientific research regarding your machinations. Will this put our culture in jeopardy?

"And what about the use of troops and resources? So far, your requests have been vague. We need to know what is expected of us going forward."

"You haven't gotten specifics, because we are still in the process of analyzing our research and creating a workable plan."

"And, other than your carefully guarded research and planning unit, how much will you reveal to the rest of us?" And Liliath caught a slight sneer in his voice.

"For now, everything is on a need-to-know basis for reasons I am sure you can understand. Once the plan is complete, we will be bringing in specialists from each of the dimensions participating directly in the various tasks. For those simply providing resources, as you would also expect, we will be giving much more general information."

Gighin rose peremptorily from his chaise with an impatient snort. "Obviously, you have made up your mind and will not be dissuaded. However, you should know that there are those within our own council who are not well pleased with the stance the Alliance has taken on this matter. There are those who are very concerned about the secrecy involved in this project. I will be staying here for the duration, I think. In the meantime, I bid you good afternoon." And with that, he turned and left, his tail held rigidly high behind him, indicating his disdain for the outcome of their conversation.

Liliath waited until the door closed completely and spoke to Jenny who had stood beside her throughout the conversation with her brother without comment.

"Well, Jenny, I'm curious. My brother and I didn't use mindspeech and conversed in our native tongue. Did you understand any of it?"

"Yes, Liliath, I got it all. Evidently, my talent allows me to hear the mental part of your conversation when I am in this mode, no different than when we are in my mental village."

"Interesting. Then this could be very useful indeed. What are your thoughts about my brother Gighin, then?"

"He seems a very different person than you are. However, I could say that about my own sister and brother as well. We weren't born close together, and we were never very close. We definitely have pursued very different paths from one another. He seemed a little full of himself, to be honest."

Liliath laughed, a deep rich sound, showing her large fanged teeth, her forked tongue lolling. Jenny waited patiently for the laughter to subside. She had been concerned she may have offended Liliath, but evidently that wasn't the case.

When she had gotten control of her amusement, Liliath said, *"Well, Jenny, now I have one more secret I will not be revealing to my brother. So far, your experiment seems to be a success. Please keep me informed as you continue. Looks like you are going to be doing a lot more than just receiving reports.*

"I imagine this means that most reports will now be going through your three communications specialists. Do you think Amenia may be up to training a few more? Although I don't want to make this new wrinkle in communication common knowledge, I do feel like this may be the solution to some of our security issues. And so far, the experiment seems to be working well for you.

"Perhaps we will make one of your current specialists the head of communications in the future. For now, however, even with everything

else on your plate, I think it is best for you to continue to supervise these efforts. What do you think?"

Jenny considered it. *"I think you are right on all counts. In the meantime, I'll keep you up to date with our progress in all of these things. Did Bob and Merv tell you about the most recent breakthrough regarding the cards and their potential use?"*

"Indeed. And I can relate to their excitement. I feel like this may be a useful tool when they discover how to use them. In the meantime, I think we can't rely on any one potential solution to the task before us. As you heard, not everyone in the Alliance is completely on board with our quest.

"Continue to hone this new skill of yours, Jenny. I believe that in the final analysis it will be a combination of all of the elements we are currently exploring that will give us the vital answers to the dilemma before us.

"Tell Burt, congratulations for bringing this new application of your skills into play. I must get to the council room. My break is over, and I have much to discuss with my councilors at this time."

Jenny nodded and faded away; and with a deep sigh, Liliath left her rooms to get back to work.

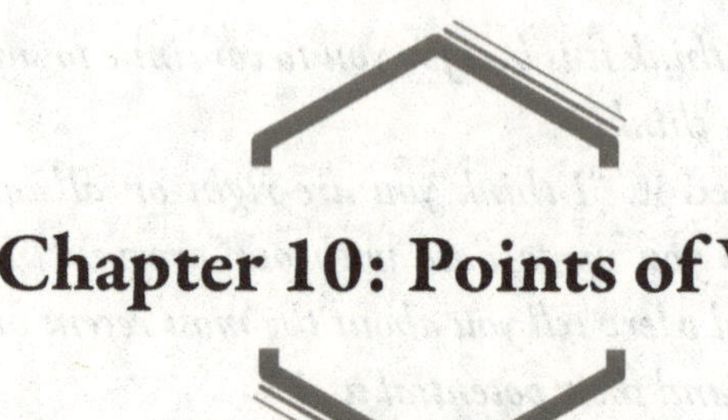

Chapter 10: Points of View

Burt and Elizabeth faded from his house onto the lawn in front of the lodge at Sanglarka. Traveling this way wasn't new to him, but he still got a bit of a shiver transporting without a gate. The lodge was a large wooden structure, in the upper edge of a valley surrounded by mountains, hundreds of miles from any village or town, with no way to access the area except by helicopter, gate, or as Burt and Elizabeth had just done.

This was probably why, of all the known Earth gates, this one had been chosen as the Alliance headquarters for the planet. Long before Jenny had become the Gatekeeper, Sanglarka had been designated as the center of all operations pertaining to the Alliance gate network for Planet Earth.

The current Gate Guardian for Sanglarka was Lova, a tall, graceful Swedish woman in middle years. She was a welcoming and kind soul, and every visitor to Sanglarka felt her gentle, positive influence, which made Sanglarka one of Burt's favorite places to hang out, refresh, and take a deep breath before his next assignment.

He had been surprised and grateful, therefore, when he and Elizabeth had been assigned to Sanglarka to be a liaison with the Earth teams to headquarters. The current level of security made this necessary, as there was great concern that their usual communications network could be compromised. The various workarounds they had devised had meant extra work for those with unique talents, such as the

Daringi with their ability to transport interdimensionally without a gate.

The Daringi council had given the Alliance a team of Daringi to facilitate this, and Elizabeth had been included in this particular assignment, being attached to Burt and Sanglarka specifically as her final internship before becoming a certified agent of the Alliance.

Elizabeth had proven to be not only reliable but pleasant to work with and was practically family, since Jenny had been officially adopted into Tarafau's family and he was married to her. This technically meant that Elizabeth was his sister-in-law, which made him smile when he thought about it.

Meeting Jenny had been life-changing for him. Up to that point, he had been quite content to be a bit of a loose cannon, working his various assignments for the Alliance, always looking forward to the next big adventure. Jenny had added spice to his life. She was a light to him, and she had no idea how amazing she was to those around her.

As they approached the lodge, Arvid strode out of the large double doors, a backpack on his back and a grin on his face.

"Hello you two!" he sent in mindspeech, that being the agreed upon language for the gate culture. There were so many different languages spoken by the various visitors that they had decided long ago to avoid miscommunication by using mindspeech by default.

"Hi there, Arvid!" Elizabeth replied with a grin. She and Arvid had sparred with quarterstaffs many times, and Arvid had to admit she had a gift for it. She had excelled in martial arts during her Alliance agent training and, like her father, seemed to view beating Arvid in quarterstaff sparring matches as the ultimate achievement.

"Hey there, Arvid, how's my favorite dwarf?" Burt said mischievously. He knew that Arvid's people did not identify with the Earthly appellation of dwarf and loved teasing him about it, something he had picked up from Tarafau.

Arvid just shook his head, *"You're going to have to come up with some new jibes, kid. That one is wearing thin. I think we are all as well as we can be, with this new wrinkle in the Amazon."*

As usual, his gruff tone hid a wry sense of humor. Arvid was very kind in general, but he put on a serious, gruff exterior. Anyone who didn't know him well would think him a grouch. No one could beat him at any of the many martial arts he practiced, and yet there couldn't have been a more patient and competent teacher, even to those who had not the skill to do more than learn the basics.

"Heading out to check on an orphaned bear cub," he said. *"We think his mom was killed by a wolf pack. She defended that cub with her own body as a shield in front of the little cave they had lived in. The little guy is recovering, but he still misses his mama. I'm taking him some treats, and I'll be back in a bit. Lova is in the communications room, if you're here to see her."*

Burt nodded and waved as Arvid stumped off to the path that led into the forest that edged along the clearing where the lodge had been built. Burt continued to be amazed at the incredible beauty that surrounded the Sanglarka gate lodge. Between the deep blue sky with fluffy white clouds and the towering peaks that were crowned in caps of snow year 'round, and the seemingly unending forests that surrounded them, he knew that few of the incredible vistas he had experienced in all his travels with the Alliance could compare to this beautiful, peaceful place.

When you added to that the constant, supportive, trustworthy, and encouraging staff and the other gate guardians who visited from time to time, the only place he could think of that he would rather be was the little house on Infinity Loop, with his sweet Jenny.

He knew she would be visiting them all soon, with at least one of her bodyguards tagging along. This new ability she had would make things quite a bit easier for all of them. The fact she could now drop in and hang out with any of them as they pursued their various duties for the Alliance was a game-changer, without a doubt.

They passed through the enormous double doors inset with large panes of insulated glass into the huge lobby, bigger than any deluxe hotel lobby he had ever seen. The overstuffed chairs grouped in conversation pods near or around the huge stone fireplace were interspersed with various small tables and footstools. The colors were forest greens and deep blues, calming, with a rich feeling.

Surrounding the lobby on the second floor was a long balcony lined with occasional doors that led to the various well-appointed guest quarters. Across the room on the main floor was a huge dining area, and along that wall were several sets of doors, one going into the large kitchen, one into the workout room, and the final one at the other end that led into two offices—one designated now as the communications room and the other as an office and library where private meetings and study could take place.

Burt and Elizabeth headed directly to the communications room. The lodge was quiet at the moment. Burt assumed this was because they were all either meeting in the communications room or going about the various chores that were required to keep the lodge and surroundings in such good order.

When they entered the communications room, Lova looked up from her workstation with a welcoming smile. She was alone. She stood and crossed the room, extending both hands, first to Elizabeth and then to Burt. *"Welcome back, you two. I'm guessing you have a few things to tell me. And will Jenny be attending as well?"*

"Ah, you've heard about that, then?" Burt said nodding with a grin.

"Actually, she has visited me several times while testing her new skills. We've taken walks in the garden and through the forest as well as going into the workout room. She is quite good with this new thing. It turns out that, except for the fact that she and her companions are

slightly transparent, they are able to interact fairly naturally with us. She tells me the only real drawback is she can't eat supper with us and she misses Arvid's fluffy rolls and spicy sugar cookies," she chuckled. "I understand there have been some disturbing developments near the Amazon portal and we are on even more high alert, at the moment, if that is even possible."

"So, do you have anything specific you would like us to work on?" Elizabeth broke in. *"I know a lot of what we will be doing is taking sensitive communications in person to the various gate guardians to avoid using the Alliance communications network, as well as interacting more privately with Alliance headquarters. I'm guessing you have a stack of work for us?"*

Lova sighed. *"We do indeed. Please take the following documents to the various parties indicated on each packet. Some of it is duplicate information, but we can't afford potentially exposing it to any potential enemy agents. I miss the days when we could just communicate on our tablets. We're still doing that, but only with nonessentials and nonsensitive information, to allay any suspicions that may make the Inseni step up their game."*

She handed Elizabeth a stack of carefully compiled packets, each labeled with the intended recipient's name and location. Elizabeth promptly stored them into her MDP.

At that point, suddenly, Jenny and Mynn were in the room with them, smiling at them all.

"Hey, you three. Did you start without me?" she quipped.

"Hello, Jenny," Lova replied, a sparkle in her deep blue eyes. *"Just getting started. I'm afraid we are taking your hubby away from you again. He and Elizabeth have quite a list of errands to do for us. I hope you don't mind."*

"We all have to do our part," Jenny admitted agreeably, *"even when it means we have to go to great lengths to spend time together. I just wanted to check in with some of my thoughts concerning the Amazon*

portal. I've checked in with the techs who set up the surveillance equipment, and they are adamant that there should be no way for any organic being to slip by and enter the gate without their security equipment's detecting them by sight, sound, or body temperature.

"I'm concerned that the Inseni may have developed some kind of shielding technology that gets them around that; and if that is the case, we need to figure it out. I want our entire Earth science team working on potential ways they might be able to get around that tech. We also have visited the science team at headquarters and the team headed by Cornelium.

"In the meantime, we need to reanalyze the original data we obtained when we initially scanned the portal. I think there may be a clue hidden there. In addition, I think we need to put more of an emphasis on carefully examining the devices we have obtained that we know access their portals, for clues regarding resonances or coordinates that may be stored in them and how to best access them. Those captured devices may well hide an important key to our dilemma of how to detect other potential portals here on Earth.

"Also, I would like some feet on the ground in the Louisiana swamp where we first encountered the Groga encampment. I have a nagging feeling that we must have missed something there. Why a Louisiana swamp of all places, especially if there wasn't a portal there? It's way too far from the Amazon portal for there to be any significant connection there, unless we're missing something, and I think we are."

Lova sat back in her chair, apparently awestruck, her eyes wide and one finger tapping her chin in thought.

Burt and Elizabeth stood there, somewhat dumbfounded. *"Been thinking about this much?"* Burt quipped, shaking his head. *"Honestly, how big is that brain of yours? Every time I think I've figured out how you think, you go and pull something like this. Sounds like our sciency guys have their work cut out for them and that we may need to get the troopers involved again as well. And I'll lay you dollars to donuts that you'll be going along on some of these excursions yourself, am I right?"*

Jenny nodded and Mynn copied her almost exactly in sync. *"Oh no,"* Burt thought, just barely avoiding rolling his eyes, *"They've been spending way too much time together, I fear."*

To the group he sent, *"Well no one on any of the teams is likely to get bored, I'm thinking. Do you want Elizabeth and me to pass this info on, as we will be visiting all of the teams at the Earth gates today?"*

"Good idea. If you pop over to the gate office first, Lizziebot can give you some printouts of the data I already have. Lova, what is the current state of the communications network?"

"It's all about misinformation, Jenny," she replied somberly. *"We are trying to give Inseni intelligence as many red herrings as possible, while giving the impression that it's business as usual and that we don't realize that Earth is still a target. We're hoping that they may act on some of this information soon, to give us an idea of what they may actually be up to.*

"In the meantime, there has been some added security you may not yet know about. Remember when your neighbor's house was up for sale? A small family has moved in next door. They are Alliance agents. By all means, take some time to be a good neighbor and go visit them with a plate of cookies or something. Their house is being "remodeled" at the moment, a cover for installing special tech and some defensive equipment.

"Angela and Travis are trained agents and have been thoroughly briefed. The little girl and boy who live with them are actually their children and are well trained. I've met this little family, and they are the perfect team to continue to monitor goings-on in your neighborhood. Therefore, one of your assignments is to be seen coming and going to their house.

"The house has been 'bug' proofed, and you can be open with any conversations you have with them inside the house."

Burt could tell Jenny was stunned by this information. She already had so much on her plate.

"With only some marginal effort on your part, you can do what needs to be done," Lova continued, obviously sensing Jenny's thoughts about the added responsibility this put on her.

Burt longed to reach out and hold her to him, comforting her, but he knew she wouldn't appreciate a public display, not to mention the fact that she wasn't actually physically there, even though it felt like it.

Jenny straightened herself, visibly putting her emotions in order. *"Actually, I think that might even take some of the work load off of me, as I think about it. I'll drop by later today, since I wouldn't usually just drop in on a neighbor at breakfast time. I'll have Lizziebot bake some of Arvid's spicy sugar cookies. Is there anything else?"*

They all shook their heads, and Burt got the feeling that Jenny looked relieved.

"Then I'll be off," she sent, nodding to Mynn. Burt noticed that Mynn hadn't spoken at all. He knew that, although she was at this moment officially acting as Jenny's bodyguard, she still would have normally put a word or two into the conversation. He wondered about this but decided to leave it alone for now. A topic for another time.

They all waved as she and Mynn disappeared in a twinkling from their sight...

Jenny smiled to herself as she appeared into Cornelium's lab, knowing that they saw her and Mynn as a transparent apparition, much like a pair of ghosts.

"Working hard?" she sent brightly to the three scientists, Cornelium's huge head inclined upward at an air screen depicting what Bob and Merv appeared to be manipulating on the table before them. She noticed that this was one of Cornelium's tables, as both Merv and

Burt were standing on stepstools to raise them high enough to be able to work there.

Three heads turned in her direction, seeing her and Mynn standing before them with satisfied grins on their faces.

"Wow!" Bob said, eyebrows raised in surprise and appreciation. *"You figured it out! I knew you could do it."*

"Good show, Jenny," Merv agreed. *"One more amazing surprise in your bag of tricks. Keep it up, and they'll be calling you a wizard too."*

"I can see your training is paying off in dividends," Cornelium chimed in, his mind voice gruff-sounding as usual, but with a note of approval. *"What other skills are waiting to be discovered?"*

"Liliath says she thinks I have enough to be going on with, considering everything currently on my plate, but I have to admit, I have missed being able to travel to meet with the various teams 'in person,' so to speak. This still keeps me within the safety of my gate but allows me to experience, to a certain extent, the joy of your discoveries. But it also allows me to get a more realistic feel for what is going on to help me better coordinate our challenge of protecting the gate system and eliminating the Inseni threat."

Cornelium nodded gravely. *"I only hope this new way of communicating lives up to its expectations regarding security and your safety. I have a tendency to expect nearly every new discovery to have its unexpected drawbacks and surprises. For now, however, the theory is sound, and we must proceed on that assumption."*

"Will you be able to do this to multiple physical locations at once?" Merv inquired thoughtfully. *"That could have some interesting advantages."*

"Exactly why I'm here," Jenny said, Mynn nodding by her side in agreement. *"What better place to do an experiment than in two separate science labs? I'm about to bring the Swedish lab into the connection, or at least I will if it works."*

For a moment, nothing seemed to change, and then a semitransparent scene came into view and two groups of people stared at each other in amazement, Jenny and Mynn between them.

"Bingo!' cried Bob as Merv sent simultaneously, *"Fancy that!"*

Cornelium simply nodded his head.

"Amazing, Jenny," Adele added, beckoning to the others in her lab to gather around her. Dhakira, Megan, and Elgyra were smiling triumphantly. Jenny had let them know she would be dropping in but hadn't told them that she would be joining both labs at once in this visit.

"Cornelium, Bob, and Merv, so good to meet with you!" Adele enthused. *"Jenny, I continue to be impressed with you as you expand your skills. I think Miriha made an excellent choice. I know she would have been proud with how you plunged in and put every effort into your assigned tasks. By the way, I want to thank you for attaching our group to Fo. She is not only competent but a joy to work with. So glad to see that at least some things have been removed from your rather overwhelming task list."*

Jenny nodded happily. This was going so much better than she had thought it might. She had been waiting for another monkey wrench to be thrown into the works.

"So, this time I simply wanted to be sure the connection works. Can both parties hear the others speaking?"

The groups on both sides nodded.

"And obviously you can hear me. Next time we will get into some deep discussions, but for now I have a few more visitations to make. How would you like to come along while I test a couple more aspects of this new way of communicating?"

There was a nearly simultaneous enthusiastic nodding of heads from all participants. Jenny grinned, then made an additional connection.

Surprisingly, she found herself and the other two groups tagging along with her, not in the council chamber, as she had expected, but in what she immediately recognized as Liliath's spacious chambers in the DA headquarters building.

She knew her talent didn't use special coordinates and wasn't dependent on location but keyed in on the individual or group in question, somehow not connecting to the physical but the specific mental resonances that emanated from each being she had previously connected with.

Liliath was ensconced in her favorite chaise in her living room with her councilors seated in comfortable chairs on either side of her.

"Greetings Jenny! I see you brought along some friends!"

"Yes, Liliath. I think it's been a while since we all found ourselves face to face, so to speak. Okay, everyone say hello, so we can test the connection."

They obediently each spoke in turn after which Jenny asked, *"Could you all hear each other clearly?"*

Once again, the almost simultaneous nod from each of them.

"Terrific. Now we are going to do a little experiment. Liliath, please choose one of your councilors to exclude from our conversation and send the name privately to me."

Liliath nodded, looking from side to side at each of them. *"I choose Rilian,"* She sent directly to Jenny. The otter-like being next to her sat looking forward, with no idea that she had been chosen.

"Good," Jenny then sent to the entire group. *"Now, I just want everyone to take turns telling us your favorite color, just so we can do this as quickly as possible. The goal is to do a simple test. Then we will see."*

Each of them in all three groups complied, including Jenny and Mynn. Jenny wasn't surprised to find out Mynn's favorite color was blue; and once she had told the group her own favorite color was also blue, which made Mynn chuckle audibly, Jenny then turned to Liliath.

"Ask Rilian what we just discussed," Jenny instructed.

Liliath turned to look at Rilian, who shook her head. *"She says she didn't hear anything, but she could continue to see all of the faces of the group."*

"Okay, I will now let her back into the conversation." And she scanned the faces of the three groups before her.

"Did everyone hear the conversation from all three parties?" Jenny asked. Once again, all nodded, except Rilian, who shook her head. *"Rilian, what did you hear? And could you see the rest of us during this time?"*

"I could see all faces clearly but could hear nothing from any mind in the group," Rilian replied, a touch of wonder in her mental voice. *"It was the same as if we were having private conversations with one another in the council room before a meeting began."*

"Excellent," Jenny said in approval. *"That was as I had hoped. Now, I am going to delete one person from each group and attempt the experiment again. I would like the person selected to go into another room and wait, where I will attempt to reconnect with you and bring you back into the group from your new location."*

She chose Merv, Adele, and Balth, Liliath's other councilor.

Once each of them had disappeared from their group into another room, she reached out to them one at a time and drew them back individually, now appearing as a separate entity within the sight of the others. The other participants either nodded, expressed surprise, or applauded the success of the experiment.

"Now each of you say something," she requested. Each of them said one version or another of, "Hello, my name is..."

"Did everyone hear all of that?" Jenny then asked.

Once again the affirmative nods from the group.

Jenny sighed with relief. It had worked! She knew there were still other aspects she would have to test, but for now she knew she could keep conversations private even within a group of people, the same as if they had all been in the same room together.

She had thought this would be the case after her experience with Liliath and Gighin, but she had needed to test it thoroughly, as she wasn't certain what type of situations she might find herself in and wanted to be sure that she could control both the sight and hearing of the experience on both sides of the link.

"Thank you for participating in my little experiment," she sent with gratitude embedded in her comment. *"Because of this, we should be seeing a lot more of one another. We have some huge tasks ahead of us and need to be able to meet in groups without any chance of the Inseni's listening in. We will appear to continue to hold regular meetings in the usual way, but these meetings will be intended to spread some misinformation to Inseni intelligence and to be able to test the Alliance communications network for leaks."*

There were satisfied smirks on some of the faces and almost all of them were nodding in agreement.

"So Mynn and I will see you all again soon. We have another stop to make, and we'll give you a heads-up when it's time for another little conference. It was so good to see you all again. You should know that this is only one potentially powerful tool we have for the coming confrontation with the Insenium, and we couldn't do it without each one of you."

Liliath nodded her head and smiled that scary, wonderful draconic smile, showing her brilliant white fangs. *"Thank you, Jenny. I'll want a private conversation with you in the next couple of days. I'll let you know via Lizziebot."*

Jenny smiled to herself as they all faded from view and she was once again in her little gate office on Infinity Loop. She and Liliath had developed a series of code sendings that could travel blatantly over the established Alliance communications network that would seem like casual conversation to anyone listening in.

Their code for a visit with Liliath was, *"I could use a tall glass of pink lemonade right about now."* This, of course, was in honor of Lizzie, whose friends knew it had been her favorite refreshment beverage. Jenny liked it too, but she admitted she preferred root beer, which was part of the coded reply, *"I'm going to get me a nice cold root beer."* Which indicated she was available and would drop in right away.

She was in the process of developing a similar code system that would represent touchpoints for the various individuals she needed to communicate with on a regular basis. Her three mental communications specialists contacted her directly on the mental plane, never using the Alliance network at all. This meant that all of the information they gathered and messages they delivered were completely private from potential spies, and no one knew anything about them, including their various locations, except Jenny and Liliath.

Jenny smiled to herself when she smelled the delicious aroma of Arvid's spicy sugar cookies wafting from the kitchen. It was time for her to make a different kind of visit, something she hadn't done in what seemed like ages.

Chapter 11: Good Neighbors

Jenny knocked on what used to be Elias Mensch's door, a plate of cookies in her hands and Chidwi perched invisibly on her shoulder. She knew there was a doorbell by the door, but Elias had been irritated by the bell and so she had gotten in the habit of knocking instead of ringing the doorbell.

Tidbit was sitting on the lawn near the street, ostensibly watching a bird perched in the hydrangea bush at the driveway entrance. Jenny knew she could call him mentally if needed, as would Chidwi, if necessary, as a backup. She had left her bodyguards at home for now, not wanting her visit to look like an invasion.

A tall, slender young woman with auburn hair in a pixie cut and brilliant green eyes answered the door. She looked down at Jenny with a dazzling smile.

"Hi, neighbor! I'm Jenny, next door in 888. Thought I'd drop by and say hello." Jenny said in normal speech.

"Ah, yes, the Realtor told us about you. You were a friend of the previous owner of this house. I'm Angela. My husband just got a re-assignment, and we were told this was a quiet, nice neighborhood. We're loving the house, but it's a mess right now as we're doing some renovations. But, by all means, do come in if you don't mind the mess."

Jenny smiled and entered the house. She had never actually been inside while Elias and his dog Cinder had lived here. The little entryway opened into a living room similar to the one in Jenny's house, that led to an open-concept dining room and kitchen, separated only by a long counter lined with several tall stools.

However, it didn't really look like a renovation was happening, at least not in this part of the house. The living room contained two long sectional couches that connected in the corner next to the outside walls. There was no fireplace, but two large, overstuffed chairs faced the sectional, and there were bookshelves in between.

Angela gestured to one of the chairs. "Have a seat, Jenny. I'll take the cookies to the kitchen, and I'll be right back."

She took the plate from Jenny and, as Jenny settled comfortably into one of the chairs, returned immediately.

"Okay. Now we can talk. I've been looking forward to meeting you. That bit at the front door was in case of any potential listening ears. Liliath told us to expect a visit soon after we moved in. The kids are in school at the moment, and Travis is at 'work.' His cover is a job at a local tech school. He only goes in a couple times a week and works from home the rest of the time. Of the two of us, I am the main agent assigned to you and yours.

"The house is being refitted to align with the Alliance's heavy security restrictions that have been given to this area, including anti-listening devices, so you can be assured that our current conversation is secure. If I thought for one moment it wasn't, we would be using mindspeech.

"I've met your other neighbor, Lacey. We understand she is about to sell her house and move in with her niece, as she no longer wants to have to care for the house. She turned 92 this year and is ready to retire, she says." Angela laughed at this.

"I think I might have made that decision a long time ago, if it had been me."

Jenny laughed with her. Angela had a genuine and hearty laugh, her eyes crinkling. It was somewhat infectious.

"That being said, the Alliance will be 'buying' Lacey's property, and another agent will be moving in next door to you on the other side. They are taking no chances, since this gate has become the official Gatekeeper gate. They might have done it anyway, but the current situation has made it a priority.

"Our job here is still very similar to your original mandate as a gate guardian. We are to keep all looking normal and natural while we keep an eye out for suspicious activity and make sure that this area is protected at every level available to us, so as not to arouse suspicion that anything is out of the ordinary.

"We'll be dropping in from time to time to visit with you and other neighbors. The thing about this neighborhood is that it is pretty quiet and not very outgoing, in terms of neighborhood get togethers or events, which makes it perfect for our purposes.

I think that covers the main points Liliath wanted me to cover. Now, we can get to know one another and be neighbors in truth," Angela concluded with a welcoming smile.

"It sounds like they have covered all the necessary information. So, what about your children? I didn't know that families with children would be involved in agent activities."

"Oh, yes. I thought my agent days were over when I got pregnant for the first time. But there are programs to deal with that in the Alliance. My children have been through gates many times. When they were little, we simply told them we were 'visiting,' like going on a vacation would be on Earth. They didn't have any idea that going from one place to another instantly was anything unusual.

"Before each of them started school, they went to a special 'summer camp' created by Lova for agent children, where they learned how to speak of their travels in ways that other children or adults would consider normal. Our children had been raised with mind-speech and knew that not everyone could use it, so they fit right in at Sanglarka.

"At the camp, they learned to say things like, 'We flew to Puerto Rico,' when speaking about their travels, which was the term we used to describe how we got to the various places we visited via gateway. If we went to other dimensions, they would just say we went to visit some friends, without getting specific about location. We also created a code for the various places we went. If asked for specific information, our kids would simply say, "I don't know… it was someplace in the woods or at a lake," simply vaguely describing the location.

"Generally speaking, this wouldn't have been unusual, as most kids aren't all that clear about maps and locations.

"As they have grown, they have learned more about the Alliance and are basically what you might describe as 'junior agents,' having done a summer camp every year at Sanglarka along with other agents' children. They are aware that what we do is important and different than most other people, and we have taught them not to share certain aspects of what we do, for the protection of their friends and their families."

"Wow." Jenny said, "the Alliance really does have a handle on all of this, doesn't it? Makes me wonder how the Inseni were so successful in pulling the wool over our collective eyes for so long.

"I admit it kind of feels like the Loop is being invaded, but I guess, if I understand the history of this place properly, the entire area was purchased a very long time ago by the Alliance because of the gateway."

"You're right. Although legal property transactions are made for every lot on the loop and the surrounding neighborhoods, basically the Alliance owns it all, and they are very careful to screen potential buyers for certain characteristics. It's important to not find themselves in the position of becoming an overlord or alien dictator to any of the nonmember dimensions where they discover gateways. Therefore, the majority of agents on Earth are of Earthly origin.

"I'm originally from Maryland, and Travis is from Washington state. I won't bore you with our origin stories, but we met during our agent internships and the rest, as they say, is history. We've worked in several gate areas, and we love what we do. We both have different interests and hobbies, but this life suits us well and our children are getting an amazing education, getting to travel with us to the various assignments and live in different cultures.

"Our kids both use mindspeech, as well as having had the opportunity to learn Spanish and some Swedish—something they don't tend to show off at school, but I often hear them conversing together in one language or another, just to stay in practice."

Jenny felt like she could get to like this woman. She was open and confident, and it would be good to be able to share her concerns and experiences with someone who was close by.

"I'll introduce you to my bodyguards at a barbecue at my house later this week. You should know that I almost didn't get to come over by myself today, and they are out working in my front yard at the moment to keep an eye on me."

Angela nodded somberly. "We are aware. I actually was a bit surprised you were alone when you knocked at my door today, to be honest, until I noticed Tidbit out front. By the way, did I smell Arvid's spicy sugar cookies on that plate? Makes me homesick for Sanglarka."

That made them both laugh.

"My kids and Travis would be very upset if I started in on that plate without them. When would you like to get together for that barbecue? Should Travis bring his guitar?"

And with that the conversation became like any conversation you would have expected of two neighbors getting to know one another. They planned the barbecue, and Jenny left for home feeling a lot less confined or isolated and worried about things in general.

There was something amazing about how having a supportive community made a huge difference, especially in difficult times.

As the week passed, Jenny found that more and more things seemed to be falling into place. Her most recent meeting with Liliath had been encouraging, but Jenny sensed that Liliath was troubled about something that didn't seem to have anything to do with Jenny's role in all of this.

She recalled from her study of history that sometimes, to keep a secret, it was necessary to do like other secret societies had done. There were what you might call "cells" of different parts of the organization the Alliance had put into place to guard against the Inseni's discovering their plans. This meant that Liliath was the only one who knew and understood all the teams, teammates, moving parts, and organizations involved in their mission.

Liliath had confided in Jenny that if something were to happen to her, as the Chief Councilor, it would trigger a high security program that would make all the information available to Jenny and one of her remaining councilors, as well as Anela. If she and both of her councilors were killed, Jenny and Anela would be the only ones to know the entire plan.

Jenny's backup gatekeeper was in the know and protected on Liliath's home planet.

In the meantime, Jenny continued to manage her communications network with her nightly visitations to the various components she was assigned to. She also spent time every day in the gate office, learning the ins and outs of the MDP monitoring system; and she shared any insights she gained directly with Cornelium, Merv, and Bob to help them with their research.

Burt and Elizabeth popped in from time to time, even showing up for the getting-to-know you barbecue to meet Jenny's new neighbors.

Travis and their two children, Matt and Coyana, were bright and smart teens. Matt looked more like his mother, with auburn hair and green eyes, and Coyana took after her dad, with blonde hair, braided in the popular Viking style. She informed Jenny she wore her hair like that because she was proud of her Swedish heritage and loved getting to travel frequently to Sanglarka, where Lova had taken her under her wing and taught her and her brother the Swedish language and Swedish history and customs.

And, as Angela had told her would happen, she noticed a "For Sale" sign on Lacey's lawn on one of her morning jogs. She hadn't noticed Lacey out in her garden trimming her roses in a long time. She made a mental note to take a moment and visit her, but unfortunately, she woke in the middle of the night a week or so later to the flashing lights of an ambulance parked out in front of Lacey's house. She discovered that Lacey had collapsed from a heart attack and had passed before the medics could arrive.

Although Jenny was aware, of course, that Lacey had led a long and interesting life, she still felt some regret that she hadn't taken a moment to go and visit her before she had passed. Her niece showed up a couple of days later to inform Jenny that they would be holding memorial services in Lacey's home state of Idaho, but that she knew Jenny's aunt had been close to Lacey. She brought with her a lovely glass vase that evidently had been a gift from Lizzie a long time ago, and she thought that Jenny might enjoy it.

Burt had told her that evening at their little pond in their mental visit, when Jenny had expressed regret for this, that Jenny could only do so much and to quit expecting to meet every need and handle every new thing. He knew she held herself to a high standard, and sometimes he thought she was still doing way too much, worrying that she was going to burn out and end up sick because of all the pressure she put on herself.

So, life went on. In what would have appeared to be a reasonable amount of time, a "Sold" sticker appeared on the "For Sale" sign in front of Lacey's house, and a middle-aged bachelor moved into the house.

Of course, he was an agent, one Jenny hadn't yet met; and, unlike Angela, before Jenny could go visit him, he knocked on her door. A short, balding Polynesian wearing a luau shirt, he had Jenny's mail in his hand.

"I thought you might want this. It came to my box instead. Jacob, Jacob Muai, is my name. Next door."

This reminded Jenny so much of her first encounter with Elias Mensch that she almost laughed out loud. Instead, she replied, "Nice to meet you, Jacob. I'm Jenny Scout. Welcome to the neighborhood."

"Thanks," he replied. "I bought this house mostly because of the gardens front and back, so you'll probably see me out and around. I'm retired from a very profitable sales career. The plants will keep me busy."

Evidently this was his cover story; and like Angela, he wouldn't reveal any more than that outside of the many security precautions the Alliance had installed in her house and would soon be installing in his own. She saw a repairman's van in his driveway, appearing to be from the local cable company.

Jenny nodded with a smile. "I'll see you around, then. We occasionally have a barbecue at my place, and you would be welcome to come, if you'd like."

"That will be well, as soon as I'm settled in a bit," which Jenny assumed was code for whenever they had completed all the security arrangements on his property.

"Sounds good. Thanks for the mail. For some reason, the postman sometimes gets 888 and 886 mixed up."

He gave her a broad wink and turned to leave, whistling like a bird as he crossed over the driveway to his own house.

To any observer, it would have appeared like any neighborhood with people moving in and out and new neighbors getting to know one another. In the meantime, Jenny still had work to do and the clock was ticking.

One day, while inventorying her own MDP, she came across the little coin-like metal disk she had discovered at the portal site in the Amazon jungle that day they had gone to investigate. She withdrew it, turning it idly in her hand.

It was about the size of a quarter, with no discernible imprint on it. The edges were smooth, and it didn't really resemble any of the metals she recognized, possibly an alloy. She flipped it into the air as if she was playing head and tails. It landed on the desk with a delicate "ping!" She couldn't see any recognizable use for it, but somehow it kept tugging at her mind. What was this, and why would it have been dropped where it was?

She shook her head. With all the things she had to think about and worry about, why did this silly little piece of metal catch her attention?

She set it on the desk. One more weird piece of the puzzle, and Jenny still had more questions than answers.

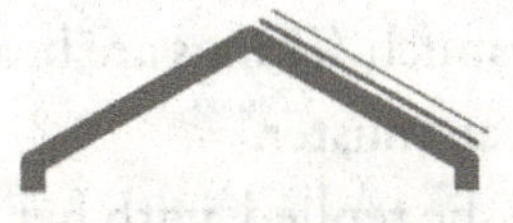

Chapter 12: The Busy Signal

Jenny woke with a start to a soft kiss on her forehead. "Wake up, sleepyhead," Burt whispered. She couldn't help but return his mischievous grin. It had been good to have him home, even if it was only for a few days, but they both had known that they wouldn't have a "normal" married life, even from the beginning. Between her gatekeeper duties and his agent assignments, they saw more of each other during Jenny's nightly mental check-ins with him at their little pond on the Merced River than they did in person.

"Oh, sorry, I guess I slept in," she yawned, reaching out for a morning hug.

"Not surprising, as hard as you've been working," he replied into her ear, ruffling her curls which were beginning to trail down her neck. It was one of the few of his habits that annoyed her. It didn't seem like that much time had passed since her hair had been completely cut down to stubble after her injuries sustained in the Inseni revolution, but she really didn't like being reminded of it.

She had decided, however, to keep it short, as it was so much easier to care for and she had little time for fussing with her hair, so she tried to be patient with Burt's affectionate tousling.

"Elizabeth and I have to head out," he told her apologetically. "I have a meeting in Sanglarka, and then I need to check in at headquarters. Lizziebot has breakfast ready for you. I was told that she has messages from Bob via Fidget for you. In the meantime, try not

121

to wring yourself out so much. Things are heating up, and you'll need as much energy as you can muster."

"I'll try to be good," she replied, with her best pretend pout. "You do the same!" And she waggled her finger at him sternly.

They both laughed and he waved. She heard him head down the hall and then the sound of his footsteps disappeared into the gate office.

She made her preparations quickly for the day and headed out into the dining room where, sure enough, Lizziebot had spread out a breakfast of strawberries picked from the back garden, a bowl of oatmeal with fresh cream, a sprinkling of brown sugar, and a cold glass of pink grapefruit juice.

A cool breeze was wafting in through the French doors and Jenny glanced up from her breakfast as Chidwi scampered in from the patio.

"Good morning, Jenny!" she sent cheerfully and jumped up onto the special chair that Burt had made for her out of an antique highchair they had found in a garage sale down the street. He had padded it with a satin cushion that matched the red clay tiles of the living and dining rooms. As she settled herself, she reached out and patted Jenny's cheek, the linkling equivalent of a hug.

"Good morning, Chidwi! How are the koi and Windsong today?" Jenny had been delighted to discover that Chidwi, like her predecessor, Ynni, communicated with the tree, something she was only beginning to learn how to do.

"They are well, Jenny. They are happy that the weather has cooled down a little bit. I think the koi will soon have koi-lings again, as the mama koi is looking fatter than usual. What will we do today?"

"I have to do my workout, and then I need to check-in with the Earth gate guardians and after that with our communications team to see how the other gate guardians in the Alliance are coming along."

Jenny was grateful for the young women who were now stationed across the dimensions to help her stay on top of things. She had scheduled a gate guardian conference, for appearances using the usual Alliance communication channels that didn't have any sensitive information in it.

She was also doing spot checks on some of the more active Dimensional Alliance members, especially now when they were all so engaged in the upcoming push to drive the Inseni out of as many of the dimensions as possible. During those mental meetings, she would include any information Liliath wished her to pass on in private.

As Jenny nibbled on the last strawberry on her plate, Lizziebot cleared the table. "Lizziebot, what are my notifications for today?" Jenny asked as Lizziebot came back into the dining room to stand by her chair.

"Fidget relayed the following from Bob," Lizziebot replied. Bob had told her that the voice of the bot was so close to Lizzie's that it was almost undetectable from the real thing. Jenny took some comfort at that, especially now that she knew so much more about her aunt after reading those three journals during her recuperation from "the shout."

Lizziebot then changed voices to Bob's voice, probably recorded word for word by Fidget. "Jenny, I want you to know that we are on the verge of a breakthrough, and at some point in the next week or two you will need to physically travel here. All necessary precautions will be taken to prevent Inseni agents from knowing about your travel in advance. When you come, of course, your bodyguards should accompany you. I'll be in touch soon as to a day and time. Take care of yourself."

As if Bob's words were a call to action, Mynn, Nona, and Lyra entered from the hallway. "We've already eaten," Mynn announced cheerfully as Jenny looked up from Lizziebot. "Burt threatened us with 'dire chastisement' if we disturbed your little sleep-in this morning." she chuckled her eyes wide with mock fear.

"Well, let's disturb Tidbit's nap, shall we? We have to get in our workout, and then I have work to do," Jenny responded, pretending to be stern and businesslike. She knew these three would willingly lay down their lives in her defense but was grateful that they could still tease back and forth as if they were all college roomies rather than "the Gatekeeper" and her bodyguards.

Nona, shook back her blue-black hair, which she had braided into multiple tiny braids and, reaching behind her, wound them into her customary knot behind her neck. Her aquamarine eyes danced with excitement. She loved their workouts in the special room that existed in another dimension totally unknown to them. A short walk three doors down the gateroom corridor, and they would find themselves in a large, fully equipped workout room with an attached swimming pool and sauna. Jenny knew the girls often took advantage of the room, whichever ones weren't on "Jenny duty," as they called it, to use the facilities there.

Jenny had programmed the gate office and certain gates to give access to any of her guards, as well as Burt and Elizabeth, so they could use the gates in her defense and to make Alliance headquarters readily available whenever it was needed, even when Jenny wasn't in the house.

Lyra went to the window seat in the living room, but before she could make a sound or touch him, the big black tabby cat sprang to his feet and stretched, gripping the window seat cushion with his claws as he arched his back and extended every muscle in his cat frame.

"Workout?" he sent lazily.

They responded by heading as one down the hallway to the gate office door. They didn't pause in the gate office but headed through the next door into the hallway and through the door that led to the workout room. As they trooped in, the cat transformed into Tarafau, and they each took their seats on the mats to begin their breathing exercises.

This had become such a habitual routine that even mindspeech wasn't necessary. As they each came out of their meditation, feeling energized, they retrieved their quarterstaffs from their MDPs and split into two groups; Tarafau against Nona and Mynn and Jenny against Lyra. Chidwi took her usual seat on one of the benches along the wall to cheer them on.

After sparring until the first tap on an opponent, they switched off, the three bodyguards against each other and Jenny versus Tarafau. By the time Tarafau had gotten in a tap against Jenny's arm, they were all feeling that exhilaration that follows a good workout. Tarafau then exited out to the house to keep watch with Lyra and Mynn. Meanwhile, Nona stayed with Jenny in the gate office as she prepared to connect with the Earth gate guardians one at a time to allow each of them not only to report but also to ask questions specific to their particular gate or to allow them to express any concerns they had in private.

She would do something similar later that day with guardians in other dimensions, contacting a different set of guardians each day, rotating through her list of guardians. In the past, the gatekeeper would have done this through the Alliance communication network or in person via a gateway, but Jenny now did this in addition to similar efforts by her three mental communications specialists, relying completely on mental communications.

The thing she loved about her new skills, which she had also taught to her specialists, was that it was just like an in-person visit, both parties being able to see facial expressions and body language, as well as feel the genuine emotions behind the words.

She sat behind her desk, Nona sitting across the room in one of the chairs she had arranged in a semicircle for their occasional local group meetings. As Jenny looked across her desk, she noticed once again that little metal disk she had left there. It glinted in the office light, and she picked it up, idly turning it over and over in her hand.

She decided to start with Luz. As the wife of the Gatekeeper of the Puerto Rico gate and a qualified agent, she was also very much in the know about what was happening at that gate. She maintained the security of the property and also saw to the needs of Juan, a nearly perfect mate, under the circumstances.

Jenny and Luz had become close, like an aunt with a favorite niece. Luz always had good personal advice for Jenny, and Jenny looked up to her as a great example of a woman who was both strong and self-sufficient as well as being very feminine, gentle, and easy to talk to.

She entered into REM state and picked up her mental image of a cellphone. She pressed the link to Luz's name. The connection was always instantaneous. She was shocked, therefore, when instead of seeing and hearing Luz's response, a pulsing buzz started up immediately. Jenny stared uncomprehending at the cellphone that she knew existed only in her mind, severed the connection, and tried again, just as she would have with an actual phone.

Once again, the loud pulsing, irritating buzz was the only response. A busy signal? Really? Since when?

She wondered if perhaps Luz was so busy that she was mentally blocking communication, but she couldn't imagine how that was possible, as it had never happened before.

She sighed and decided to try Luz again later. Maybe she would just contact Juan directly this time. She found Juan's link and tapped it. Again! It was the same buzzing noise. Maybe he and Luz were both busy with the same thing? Unusual. She hoped it wasn't because they were being attacked somehow and were busy defending themselves, in which case she definitely didn't want to distract them.

Now a little worried, she decided to check in with Lova at Sanglarka. Perhaps if there was something going on with the Puerto Rico gate she would know, especially since Sanglarka was the Earth headquarters for the gate guardians.

She tapped Lova's name... and again! Now the buzzing seemed ominous. Perhaps somehow Lova was in contact with those at the Puerto Rico gate?

Sighing, she decided to try the new Australian Gate Guardian, Bernadette. She had been in mental touch with her a couple times since she had been installed as the Australian Gate Guardian. Like Jenny, her training had been somewhat hurried, but with Brendan in charge of a portion of the Alliance space fleet taking part in the conflict with the Inseni, they had no choice but to get someone competent into the position as soon as possible.

Another busy signal! Now Jenny was beginning to feel real fear. One at a time, she tried every single gate guardian, including the newly installed India Gate Guardian, with no success.

Frustrated, she finally dialed Liliath. To her relief, Liliath responded immediately. Her rich, soft draconic voice sounded as if Jenny had awakened her from sleep.

"Oh, Liliath! I'm so glad! I was beginning to think my ability to contact mentally was completely gone! I don't know what to do! Do you know of anything that is going on with the Earth guardians? I'm beside myself with worry!"

"Jenny? The Earth guardians? I thought you had that in hand."

"So did I! But I can't reach any of them. I keep getting what amounts to a signal that they are busy or rejecting my calls. I haven't tried them through the Alliance network yet, but I needed to check if it was just me or not. What can you tell me?"

"Since you are the first Gatekeeper to have this talent in living memory, I am somewhat at a loss. I heard from Lova a few days past, but, as you know, at headquarters we are in the middle of some signif-

icant plans and we are dealing with a lot of cross-dimensional issues at the moment. We had been leaving this in your hands, at least where the Gate Guardians are concerned."

Jenny felt a little stung by that remark. She already felt unprepared for the tasks in front of her.

But Liliath, sensing her reaction, said: *"Please don't misunderstand me. There is no blame here, simply stating our position in all of this. I know you have already gone further as a Gatekeeper than any I have previously known, and there is no doubt of your diligence. I'm only saying that we have so much confidence in your abilities that we were not concerned about your coming across anything you couldn't handle."*

Jenny let out the breath she hadn't realized she had been holding.

"Okay, so, what do we do next? The fact that I can't contact a single Earth gate guardian is not only worrisome but perhaps even frightening. Since you were not aware of anything going on with them as a group and I had no notion that they were engaged in a conference, for instance, or a group project, I can't help but jump to the conclusion that there is something desperately wrong here, and I had thought we had gotten beyond danger to my home dimension."

Jenny could almost feel Liliath's large head nodding in agreement. One of the advantages of mindspeech was that once you were connected you could feel the other person's emotions along with their words.

"Jenny, I don't want you to do anything more in this direction at the moment. I'm going to send an agent via gateway directly to Sanglarka to see what I can find out, and I will get back in touch with you via Lizziebot. For now, I want you to notify your bodyguards that I have put the Gatekeeper's gate on alert and we have upped the security, and that means you stay put for now. If anything comes up that the security measures can't handle, you are to go into the gate office and stay there with Tarafau, Chidwi, and your bodyguards until you receive further instructions. Understood?"

Jenny nodded numbly and added in mindspeech, *"Understood. Should I continue my mental rounds to the other team members who are not on Earth?"*

"I think it will be okay for you to stay in touch with me and with Bob or Merv, as well as Burt, of course. You will also want to contact your communications specialists to see if they are having similar issues. Maybe have them see if they can contact any of the Earth guardians.

"Other than that, for now, I will make some discreet contacts with our more trusted allies. Also, at any point, feel free to contact Amenia to let her know what has happened. I will contact you in the next few hours. Stay on alert, and don't reach out to anyone but those I just mentioned."

"Okay, Liliath. Thank you for your help. I didn't know who else I could contact without taking a chance of interception or worse. I knew you would be able to help me figure it out. I was definitely beginning to panic, something that would have really disappointed my dad, for sure."

As Jenny severed the connection, she drew a deep breath and at once was back in the gate office, Nona and Chidwi looking at her in concern.

"Call the others into the office," she told Nona. "We need to talk, and I don't want to take a chance of being overheard."

Chapter 13: Coin of the Realm

"*Try it again*," Amenia said, sitting on one of the seats in the communications room of Jenny's mental fortress.

Jenny nodded. Her physical body was now in the workout room. Per Liliath's instructions, she had restrained herself from trying mental contact with the Earth Guardians. Liliath had successfully contacted Lova at Sanglarka via a visiting agent, and they had affirmed that all was currently well with all of the Earth guardians by physically visiting each gate. This, at least, had been a relief.

Now, two days after her experience with the "busy signal," as she was calling it, she had contacted Amenia and they were connected in Jenny's mind. After explaining the difficulties she had been having with connecting to the Earth guardians, Amenia had suggested they go to the communications room and see what they could discover.

She picked up the cellphone and once again dialed Luz. Luz appeared before her, obviously in her kitchen preparing a meal, an embroidered apron over her usual colorful blouse and skirt.

"*Well, hello, Jenny! I hear you've been having trouble getting through*," Luz said in greeting.

"*Yes! I was so worried. I somehow thought the gate guardians might be under attack. But now I'm confused. Why can I get through to you now?*"

"*Good question*," agreed Amenia. *What is different about this time and last time?*"

"*The only thing I can think of is that this time I'm in the workout room in a different dimension,*" Jenny replied. "*Last time I was in the gate office, although I have done my work from there before. Actually, I usually work there because the office chair is comfy and it's easier to enter my notes from there. Do you think this means I can't use the gate office to work from anymore?*"

"*Not necessarily,*" Luz replied. "*It could have been some kind of momentary resonance that caused this interruption in your mental communications. I think we may need to experiment a bit more, but in the meantime, until we figure this out, I suggest you bring a comfortable chair and your tablet with you the next time you go to the workout room. I suspect some kind of tampering, but I can't imagine how it could happen in the actual gate office.*

"*Well, I hope we figure this out,*" Luz commented. "*We had hoped we had foiled the attempts of the Inseni at sabotage. We had really hoped that after we shut down the Amazon portal, this sort of thing would be done with.*

"*Ah, but remember,*" Luz continued, "*the Inseni shut down all electrical power and communications on Earth via something they had planted on the moon? During that time, you still had complete access to the Alliance, and it didn't affect the Alliance communications network at all. Shutting down the Amazon portal to one dimension didn't stop the Inseni from doing some additional mischief.*"

"*And now we know they are still using the portal, after what we discovered this past week at the site,*" Jenny replied thoughtfully.

"*One more thing that needs figuring out,*" Amenia concluded. "*I think you should report to Liliath and, for now, institute the changes I recommended to your current workspace.*"

"*I think you're right. Okay, Luz, thank you for helping with our little experiment, and I appreciate your insights. Talk with you again soon...*"Jenny said, and she and Luz waved at one another as she broke that connection.

"Okay, Amenia, do you want to come with me to talk to Liliath?"

"I think you've got this handled, Jenny. But by all means do let me know what you discover and what Liliath wants us to do, moving forward."

Jenny nodded, and the communications room faded from her view to find Mynn quietly working out with small barbells at the other end of the room. She looked up, and Jenny gave her the thumbs up. "You did it then? That's good. I wonder why it didn't work before." Mynn said with a puzzled frown.

"We don't know, but I need a chair and small desk moved in here after lunch. I'll be doing my communications work from here for the next little bit. In the meantime, let's get some lunch and get back to work"

And so, it went. They settled Jenny into one corner of the workout room with a chair, desk, tablet, and even a little refrigerator to keep cold drinks and snacks in. They also established a reading corner with an armchair, a side table, and a set of shelves in another corner, out of the way. Her bodyguards took turns on "Jenny duty"; and when they weren't "traveling" mentally with Jenny, they would usually either sit down to read or work out quietly with stretch bands or the small dumbbells while Jenny did her work.

It seemed strange at first, but over the course of a week of doing business this way, it became routine... a new normal.

Jenny was mostly unaware of her surroundings at any rate, sending her mind back and forth to consult with the various teams.

She had become used to creating consulting groups across the dimensions with the teams, and it no longer felt unusual to her. All the participants were beginning to find it difficult to imagine doing it any other way. Getting to speak directly with each other without leaving their own labs or meeting rooms was a new convenience they hadn't imagined possible before.

As they began to exchange ideas in a secure environment, some tactics and strategies began to emerge. The emphasis was still on the idea of limiting casualties on both sides while finding a way to disconnect the Inseni from access to the portals they had already discovered. The second stage would be to discover how many of those planets connected by the Inseni portals were also connected to the Alliance network.

The scientists on all three teams agreed that the difference between the Alliance gate system gates and the Inseni portals was more than likely a difference in resonance, but they still hadn't entirely discovered what caused these resonances, how to detect them, and, most importantly, how to measure them. All three teams—the Alliance science lab, Cornelium's lab, and the Switzerland gate lab—were working on different projects in addition to resolving the gate issues.

Bob, Merv, and Cornelium were devising how to work with the Nanoites and Mookookie to use the MDP system in new ways that would not only facilitate troop and supply movement, but also potentially create temporary environments for prisoners and refugees until the end of the conflict.

In addition, Bob continued his robotic research, to his and Fidget's delight, as they had access to resources now beyond anything Bob had ever imagined possible.

Adele's team were working on a potential way of separating the Inseni from whatever populace they had enslaved, without harming the native residents of the planet and, if possible, not even harming the Inseni as they removed them from the planet. They knew it might still come down to fighting and that there would inevitably be some casualties, but they wanted to prevent any unnecessary harm on either side.

The Alliance headquarter scientists were working on how to locate and disable the portals used by the Inseni and were evaluating the equipment they had captured during the raid in the Amazon jungle to determine how they were programmed and whether or not they could duplicate the technology.

Meanwhile, Liliath and the Alliance council had their hands full with getting commitments from the agreeable Alliance member dimensions towards contributing personnel, supplies, and technical support when the Alliance finally was ready to put its plans into motion.

And Jenny found herself in the middle of most of it at any given time. In addition, she found herself consulting often with Anela, her backup gatekeeper. She liked Anela, who was gentle, intelligent, and committed to her work. She often found Anela in Cornelium's lab with Bob and Merv, interacting with their Mookookie partners.

As Jenny understood it, like Bob's robotic lab partner Fidget, the Mookookie and the Nanoites could communicate with one another and had created a kind of coalition between the two cultures. Freed to a certain extent from each of their home environments, the two diverse types of beings had found common ground in their willingness to aid the Alliance to eliminate the depredations of the Inseni.

The Mookookie, of course, had found themselves under the Inseni thumb for what may have been centuries and were extremely grateful for the Alliance's role in breaking loose from Inseni rule.

The Nanoites, on the other hand, looked back on an event centuries before, when the Alliance had saved them from a dying planet and given them the realm of the MDP pods. This had happened so long ago that there were no records of this event in any of the Alliance histories, and the process of how this had been done was lost in the mists of antiquity.

Alliance scientists and historians felt bereft that this knowledge had been lost to them, and many continued to search for some hidden cache of records that would explain so much of what had been lost concerning the origins of the gate system and the technology that made it possible. There was an ongoing concern that the time might come when the system might break down, and they had no way of repairing it.

Jenny continued to see Burt in person maybe only once a week, so they continued to meet nightly after Jenny went to bed, mentally visiting beside the little pool near the Merced River. Burt had told her he had no idea how to find the actual pool these many years later, after he had first visited it as a teen.

He had discovered it while tubing down the river, and it had been so peaceful and beautiful that when he had gone through agent's training and had first learned mindful breathing, he had pictured this place as his primary key to finding peace and to quiet his mind. This was the first place he had met Jenny in her mental visits.

Each evening they discussed what each of them had done during the day, and it was almost as if both of them had been working different jobs on Earth and had come home at the end of their workday. It wasn't quite as good as being together in person, of course. Nevertheless, it sure beat being completely out of touch, as Jenny's mother had been when her dad had been out on assignment in the military. More than once, he had found himself in situations where they weren't allowed to contact their family from where they were working.

Jenny's mother had, at least outwardly, handled these separations with her usual cheery optimism, but now Jenny was beginning to understand what she must have felt whenever her dad had been gone for weeks or months at a time. Her respect for her mom had increased so much as she realized the courage and mental and emotional stamina that had to have been required.

As a young college student, she had never even imagined herself married, much less in a similar situation. She blessed the events that had allowed her to develop her mental abilities, not only because they were so important to the Alliance and their current campaign to free those who were enslaved by the Inseni, but even more so because it meant that she and Burt were never farther apart than a thought from her mind to his.

This time, however, she was surprised that Burt showed up with a scowl on his usually cheerful face, his brows furrowed and his mouth a tight line.

"What's up?" she asked, concerned.

"It's that brother of Liliath," he almost growled in reply. "He's going around stirring people up all through the council. He's trying to get them to push back against the action to rescue the dimensions invaded by the Inseni. He's implying that we've done enough and it is foolish to waste the lives of our people because of the evil another has done who isn't even a member of the Alliance.

"'After all,' he says, 'None of these dimensions are members of the Alliance and, as far as we know, they aren't even connected in any way to the Alliance gate system.'"

Burt sighed, unclenching his fists. "I just don't see why the Alani would send such a disagreeable liaison. I've met many of them, and most of them are courteous and well-spoken. I admit, when I first met Liliath, I was terrified. Every myth and legend I had ever heard about dragons came back to me in brilliant clarity, and I had been sure I was about to be fried and eaten for my temerity of interrupting Lizzie and Tarafau in whatever mysterious thing they were doing in an African jungle.

"But these days, I tend to think of dragons as logical intelligent beings and have come to respect them, especially after working with Cornelium from time to time.

"So, I ask myself, why? Why would they send someone so arrogant and full of himself to represent them? Has draconic opinion towards the Alliance changed that much, or is this just Gighin representing his own opinions, despite his mandate to represent all of the Alani in the council?"

Jenny thought about this. She hadn't personally interacted with Gighin at this point and was wondering how much of the attitude he displayed could be chalked up to simple sibling rivalry and how much of it was sincere. Fortunately for her, it wasn't within her list of responsibilities to deal with him or any of the council. The Gatekeeper was responsible for the gate system and the gate guardians and their actions. It was definitely more than enough responsibility for any one person.

When she didn't reply, he asked, "So what about the communications foul-up; do you have any ideas?"

"Not really," she admitted. "We moved shop for now, but the whole situation keeps nagging at me. I keep thinking I know something that is eluding me and it might somehow be important, but for the life of me I can't figure out what could have possibly caused it. So, as not to potentially compromise the security of the gate office, we've moved into the workout room, 'in a galaxy far, far away,'" she concluded with a chuckle.

"Well, if I know my wife at all, I know you'll come up with an answer and shock the heck out of the rest of us with the simplicity of your conclusions. Honestly, you should hear the scientists talking about you. You'd think you were Lizzie or something."

They both laughed at this reference. Now that Jenny had read Lizzie's journals, in a way, she knew more about her aunt than Burt did, even though he had known her personally.

"Well, I'm off, wifie-poo. Elizabeth and I have some tracking to do. We're headed for the Amazon portal, as our instruments seem to be reporting something that contradicts our previous data. I'll report in as soon as we know something." And with this he gave her a kiss and Jenny severed the connection, drifting into natural sleep with the final thought of how disappointing dream kisses were, compared to the real thing.

Chapter 14: Resonances

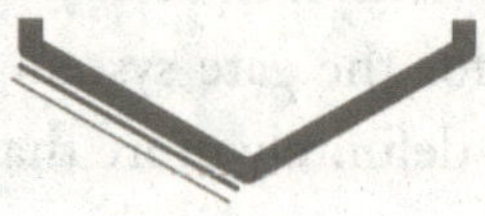

Considering how urgent Jenny and the rest of the Alliance council felt it was to set about their task to rescue the dimensions invaded by the Inseni, their progress seemed to move at a snail's pace.

When she awoke, however, after her conversation with Burt during her sleep, Jenny felt like things were about to pick up, and not necessarily the way she had hoped. Admittedly, she wasn't so naive as to believe that they could go charging in on majestic stallions with sword in hand to conquer the Inseni once and for all in a brilliant stroke of strategy and superior skill. However, that didn't prevent her from being more than a little impatient with the process.

After her quick shower and dressing without much attention to her appearance, she went into the dining room, where breakfast was already waiting for her even though she was slightly early for it. She knew Lizziebot had gotten more upgrades recently and found herself wondering how alert to her surroundings the AI that dwelled in the bot actually was. Obviously Lizziebot had noticed that Jenny was up and, knowing her routine, had immediately prepared breakfast.

Chidwi scampered over from where she had been hanging out with Tidbit. *"Good morning, Jenny! It is beautiful outside, and breakfast is ready for a good day!"* she chirruped happily, jumping up onto her chair at the table.

Nona, who had been on Jenny duty that night, stood from the reading chair, yawned, and stretched, just as Mynn and Lyra entered from the hallway looking ready for anything. They all joined Jenny at the table, and Lizziebot brought in breakfast for the rest of them.

Early on in their service with Jenny, they had discovered to their delight that they could place their breakfast order with Lizziebot the night before and have it waiting for them as soon as they arose in the morning.

As Jenny thought about this, she realized that she might be missing something so obvious that it made her blush with chagrin. Lizziebot! When had she gotten so used to having her here waiting on her hand and foot that she had forgotten that this bot also had all of Lizzie's memories programmed into her by Lizzie herself?

She sat there, her spoon full of oatmeal halfway to her mouth, staring into space. Naturally, the girls took notice, and even Chidwi paused, looking up from her bowl of choice fruits and nuts.

"What's up?" asked Mynn. "You look like a paused video."

Jenny shook herself slightly, put the bite into her mouth, held up a finger for them to wait until she could chew it, and then said, "Lizziebot!"

Tidbit looked up from his perch on the window seat, his ears perked forward, and his amber eyes nearly glowing with curiosity at the tone in her voice.

Lizziebot immediately stood at Jenny's side. "Yes, Jenny?" she inquired politely in the voice Jenny recognized as Lizzie's own.

"Oh, I wasn't calling you, necessarily, but I just realized I have been taking a lot of things for granted, especially you. Tell me, why Lizzie programmed the AI that Bob installed into you."

The girls all stopped eating; their attention riveted on the bot beside Jenny.

"Lizzie knew she would be passing the gate guardianship on to you and wanted you to have the advantage of her own insights and experiences. At the time, she had no idea I would be implanted into a bot. But of course, Bob could see the potential in his robotics work, and now I have not only artificial sentience but also the ability to move and do many things that weren't possible as a simple AI in a stationary device."

"And are you sentient? In the sense of organic beings?"

"I would say, no. I have some amazing programming and Bob continues to upgrade my abilities, but I am still only a highly sophisticated, advanced, programmed tool, for your use."

"But I have still underestimated your abilities, haven't I?"

"That may be. To be fair, my updates aren't usually reported to you, and I don't think even the programmers were aware of the extent of what their programming enabled me to do or to become. That will only be discovered when I am used to my full potential. I do have the ability to detect and respond to human emotion; and my programming is definitely influenced by Lizzie's priorities, personality, and understanding of the proclivities of organic beings."

Four human heads nodded solemnly at this declaration, and her bodyguards looked meaningfully at Jenny.

"Well, then, let's finish breakfast and go to the gate office. Let's see if you can help us with something that's been baffling us. I know your logic and assessment abilities may be more than our own combined."

Lizziebot nodded her assent and waited for them to finish eating. Although they usually allowed Lizziebot to clean up, this time they all pitched in and in nearly no time they were all in the gate office, Chidwi on Jenny's shoulder and Tidbit curling up into his bed by the desk.

Jenny turned to the bot. "Lizziebot, what can you tell me about this room?"

"Lizzie's memories include an orientation given to her by Gaston, the gate guardian who passed the gate on to Lizzie when he retired to Sanglarka. I am sure you are aware of the various functions of the equipment included here. So do you mean to inquire about any differences or unusual changes made to the room recently?"

"Yes, Lizziebot, that's exactly what I need to know."

Lizzie began to rotate extremely slowly, scanning the room. She extended her legs to give her access to the upper areas of the walls and shelves, then retracted her legs until she was on level with the top of the desk. She even stretched her arms to allow her to reach under the desk and scanned the floor. This whole process took nearly twenty minutes, with each of them moving out of the way if the scan moved in their direction.

Finally, Lizzie stopped revolving and returned her limbs to their normal state. "I see only a few changes," she said at last. "There is no new technology or anything inimical that I can detect. Perhaps I should scan the contents of your desk drawers?"

Jenny nodded and changed places with the bot, as she had been standing behind the desk during the scan.

Lizzie opened the top center drawer, that Jenny called her "junk drawer," a place for pens, sticky notes, and random little things she didn't want cluttering up her desk while she was working.

Suddenly, Lizziebot did something Jenny had never seen before. The eyes of the bot which were projected onto the screen where the bot's face resided went very wide and began flashing red, like the emergency lights of an ambulance. "Warning!" came a voice very unlike Lizziebot's normal voice. "Warning!"

Startled, Jenny walked to the side of the bot, peering into the desk drawer. "Warning? What about? Are my pens bugged or something?"

But Lizziebot didn't respond. Her eyes continued to flash red, but other than that, she didn't move.

Jenny looked at her guards, who shook their heads and looked inquiringly at Tidbit, who also shook his cat head, his tail twitching as it often did when he was curious or agitated.

She did the only thing she could think of, taking things out of the drawer, one at a time, holding each item before the bot's faceplate. Slowly, since the drawer was crammed full of various little things, she continued to show the bot one item at a time and still no response one way or another. Finally, as she thought she had pulled everything completely out of the drawer, she felt into the corners and found the little coin she had picked up at the Amazon portal.

This time, instead of simply not responding, the bot went completely blank, not moving or showing any signs of function, as if her power had been abruptly cut.

The girls gathered around Jenny, staring intently at the little coin on her palm. Tidbit arose and reached his nose up to sniff at it. Chidwi began to croon in a worried tone. Jenny, wide eyed, somewhat shakily took the coin and, reaching around the bot, opened the little safe in her floor and put the coin into the safe and closed it in.

As soon as Jenny had securely closed the little door, Lizziebot came to life.

"What just happened here?" she asked the bot as soon as it had rebooted.

At first Jenny thought that Lizziebot hadn't heard her, but just as she was going to ask again, Lizziebot spoke up. "There was a thing... a small thing. The resonance..."

"Resonance? From the coin?"

"Yes, the small metal object. Not a coin. Alien technology. Emits a resonance that interferes with things. Strong resonance. Alien resonance. Bad resonance."

Jenny clearly remembered the incident Lizzie had spoken of in her journals that had happened in Promisia. Something about a stone that had shut down the entire gate network. Now she was very concerned. She took note of the fact that Lizziebot hadn't reacted strongly until she had pulled it out into the air, not surrounded by anything that might block its resonant signal.

She felt it would be safe where she had put it, but realized that this particular device, whatever it was, had also probably blocked her mental sendings to the Earth guardians, but not sendings that went beyond Earth. Maybe the resonant effect was confined strictly to her own planet?

However, she knew that constant exposure to certain substances such as uranium could cause severe damage and even death to those exposed to even small amounts over time. Was it even safe to keep it in that enclosed area inside the safe? What if some of those resonances were still strong enough to cause some kind of damage over time?

She kept her thoughts to herself, not wanting to alarm her bodyguards more than they already appeared to be. She knew Chidwi knew what she was thinking and was glad she chose not to share it with the others in the group.

"Well, it's locked away," she said aloud. "However, perhaps, for now, until we figure some things out, we shouldn't spend any more time in the gate office than we need to. I'm going to retire to the workout room. We have things to do. Nona, get some sleep. Lyra, please take house duty; and Mynn, come with me."

They didn't protest, but Jenny could tell that they were all thinking intensely about what had just happened. She knew at lunch the conversation would turn to the little coin. For now, she needed to see what some others would make of it. True to her word to Liliath and the others on the council, she wasn't going to try and handle this all by herself.

She instructed Lizziebot to let her know if any communications came through from the Alliance. One of the newest upgrades to Lizziebot was the ability to send a pulse that warmed Jenny's gatekeeper key whenever a new transmission came through on the Alliance communication network, even when Jenny was off planet or otherwise out of reach for Lizziebot to be able to contact her directly.

Jenny, Chidwi, and Mynn left to go to the workout room, Tidbit trailing behind them. Jenny hadn't given him any instructions, as she knew he would automatically come along, considering his role as "Guide" to the Gatekeeper.

As they entered the workout room, Tidbit now became Tarafau, who at first glance would appear to be somewhat intimidating based on his size and muscular frame, not to mention the earlobes that came to a point at the bottom instead of at the top as you might have pictured an elf's ears. His nearly blue-black skin was set off even more with the way the light glistened off his completely bald head. Jenny remembered remarking to him at one point that his ears would look great with some earrings, something that got her that catlike stare and no comment.

The workout room looked a bit strange with the little desk and office chair in one corner and the reading chair added for the convenience of her guards. This was the place where Jenny had decided to do her work until they could figure out what had caused the busy-signal phenomenon.

Now, she was pretty sure they had found the problem, but she was still uncomfortable with working in the gate office until they discovered how to negate the coin's effects or at least dispose of it in a safe way that would pose no danger to any organic life forms.

Jenny's first thought was to contact Amenia but realized that, although Amenia was curious about what had happened, she probably wouldn't have any answers about how Jenny could move forward.

Besides, Jenny wanted to know what the thing was and what kind of danger it might represent. It was obviously related in some way to the Amazon portal, but how was a mystery that needed exploring.

Just as they all got settled onto the mats, Jenny's key warmed. With a sigh she said, "Stay here. I need to see what Lizziebot has for me."

Lizziebot met her in the hallway outside the gate office. "Burt says to get in touch with him right away. He has information you need to hear."

Jenny rushed back to the workout room. "Okay, we're going to go talk to Burt first. Are you with me?"

She simply nodded. By now, all her team members had gotten the chance to experience her "ride-alongs" and were ready to be taken into her circle.

Burt was seated in the communications room at Sanglarka, Elizabeth at his side, along with Lova and Arvid.

"Can you open this up to Cornelium's lab and the Sweden gate lab as well?" Burt asked, as they appeared before him.

Jenny nodded and complied. Suddenly they were all in the communications room in Sanglarka; together even though the four groups were in completely different locations. They could see one another and interact together as if they were in the same room, but unlike similar abilities over the Alliance network or even the Earth internet, these conversations could not be listened to by anyone who hadn't been specifically included by Jenny.

After some serious training efforts, Jenny had been able to also train her three communications specialists in this technique, which was making a major difference in the clarity and detail of communications within the Alliance member network.

Burt paused a moment, looking into every face. At first Jenny thought it might be to add some drama to his announcement, but then she realized he was connecting with each person in each group with the intention of not only getting their complete attention, but in some way Jenny could completely understand, he was emphasizing his confidence and care of every person in this group.

This was why he was such an awesome ambassador or liaison for the Alliance, she realized, and recognized it as a natural gift of this amazing man she had married.

"As you all know, one of the tasks Elizabeth and I have been assigned is to monitor the Inseni portal in the Amazon basin. Recently there has been a puzzling phenomenon regarding the area. Regardless of high-tech equipment monitoring the portal for sound and movement, there had been no signs anyone had been accessing the portal. Nevertheless, physical signs, such as tracks leading to and from the portal, were fresh and clear.

We had double- and triple-checked the equipment and found it to be functioning properly.

Today, however, Elizabeth and I traveled to the portal and found that the equipment has once again been able to not only see but hear troop movement in and out of the gate. What has changed, why it is working now and not earlier, is impossible to say. We can now monitor their movements and learn some things about what might be going on, however, and wanted all of you to know about this new... um... wrinkle, shall we say?"

Jenny's heart was nearly in her throat, but she managed to say, "Um, maybe it isn't impossible to say."

She went on to relate her earlier experience in the gate office.

As she concluded, for a moment there was absolute silence, the expression on every face varied from stunned to thoughtful.

"That could be it!" Burt enthused. "It's the only thing I can think of that might have changed since our last visit. I think there might be some ways we can test it, but, Cornelium, what do you think? What kind of precautions should we take to keep it from throwing a monkey wrench into our operations? How can we figure out if anyone is susceptible to its resonances? How can we figure out what kind of resonances it is creating? How did it affect both Jenny's mental projections and at least two different tech devices?"

"Slow down, young man," Cornelium sent stiffly. "Too many questions at once will tangle up any investigation we may make. I think the first step is to figure out a safe environment to test it in, somewhere, perhaps inside solid rock? And how can we be sure that any measurements taken by any tech we have will be accurate or whether our equipment won't be similarly affected as the bot and the monitoring equipment in the jungle?"

The effect of how Jenny's mental communication worked was odd, in that it made it look like and feel like they were all speaking the same language and not by mindspeech. They could see Cornelium's mouth moving but each heard what he said in their own native language.

Jenny saw the heads of the scientists and guardians nodding in agreement, apparently lost in their own contemplation.

"Well," Bob broke in, his moustache twitching as it often did when excited about something. "It's obvious we need to consider this carefully before taking any action. How safe is Jenny with the thing in the floor safe, as long as she doesn't spend any extended time in the gate office?"

"With the coin in the safe, it should be okay to take some scanning equipment into the office and check for anything we currently know is inimical to humanoid health," said Merv, stroking his clean-shaven chin. He had often commented to Jenny that he missed his beard, as stroking it made him look wise and gave him time to think without losing the attention of his listeners.

"So how soon can we get at least that much done?" Jenny asked, as the rest appeared to be still deep in thought. "I have to admit that the workout room isn't as comfortable as the gate office, and it kind of gives me the creeps to know that thing is in the office under my floor, to be honest, even if it can't affect me directly. I didn't get the disconnect with contacting the Earth guardians until I actually took it out and handled it, now that I think about it."

Lova cleared her throat. "I'm not a scientist per se, but I think, unless we find it can be harmful once it is shielded, maybe we need to shoot it out into space or something, into the sun so it can be burned up."

Burt broke in, "But we need to be careful about even that. We need to know where it came from and why it's here and whether or not it is somehow communicating with the Inseni. Is there any chance, for instance that some Inseni spy saw everything that happened in the gate office today? Or that they witnessed Jenny's failure to contact the other Earth guardians? What if they didn't realize it could do that? What if they found that out and decided to pelt the Earth with these things? If it could short out Lizziebot, what could a lot of these things potentially do to Earth's other tech? I, for one, don't want to see another repeat of the last time they shorted out every power source on our planet."

"Come to think of it," Bob said, almost bouncing in his chair in excitement. "Is there any chance that whatever was on the moon that caused that blackout last time might have been a similar technology? Do we still have the research that was done on that by the Alliance last time?"

"Just what we need right now," Arvid growled. "It isn't like we don't already have enough to go on with."

"I agree, old dwarf," said Tarafau, "But perhaps this is just the key we needed to figure out some other things. In the meantime, all of our military leaders need to know the possibilities of what they will be facing. After all, don't you think it would be a bad thing if one of these coins got stuck to one of our space vehicles and shut all systems down, without having a fix for it or knowing it was a possibility?"

Arvid made another wordless growl and nodded his head reluctantly.

"What about the Nanoites and the Mookookie?" asked Adele. "We know they have access to things that confound us."

"That's not a bad idea," agreed Merv, "But before we can involve them, in good conscience, we need to figure out how to test to see if they are vulnerable to these resonances at all. At some point we need to bring them into the conversation. They are both organic beings, after all, not robotics or machines of any kind.

I know that, because the Nanoites more or less invaded Fidget at one point, we originally assumed them to be some kind of cyber creatures, but the evidence says otherwise. And just because the Mookookie seem to be immune to just about everything except a direct physical attack like a bomb or being stabbed by something, it doesn't mean they would be immune to resonances we don't understand."

"Understand *yet*," said Cornelium firmly, emphasizing with draconic power the word *yet*. "This is just the beginning of the research on this topic, although I admit it needs to be given high priority. Let's not ditch the experiment before we even do the initial tests and research. The concept of resonance is complex, and the effects of different types of resonance are often not understood fully, even once we can see evidence of them. So, for now, first step is to determine a safe place to test our theories and answer all of Burt's many, many questions." He said this last with a draconic smile, showing all of his teeth and the pointed tips of his tongue. Jenny realized with a start that he was laughing at his own joke, and she couldn't repress a grin herself.

Chapter 15: Repercussions

Liliath's draconic eyes were slitted as she focused on Jenny's report of the recent meeting in Sanglarka and the revelations that had occurred there. She marveled at how much Jenny had grown into her responsibilities as the Gatekeeper of the entire Dimensional Alliance in such a short time and at such a young age. Miriha had chosen well.

She considered the evidence that perhaps there was more to the Earthly dimension than they had previously considered. Why this planet? Why all of the attention long before Jenny had become the Gatekeeper? Up until now, the consensus had been that this was just one more set of gates that needed guarding, but that the planet's inhabitants themselves were not yet at a place in their development that Earth could be considered for membership in the Alliance.

It wasn't that any of the current member planets were exemplary, by any means. She was painfully aware over her long service in the Alliance that there was no absolutely perfect culture, nor did the members within the Alliance agree on every point of law. The best they had ever been able to achieve was an agreement of rule by majority vote.

Each representative of the individual member dimensions had only one vote on any proposal or point of order. The ruling council, Liliath and her two councilors, didn't rule so much as organize and, if she admitted to herself, referee the discussions and issues that came before the council. In the final analysis, the best they could do was make decisions based on the opinions of the majority of their members.

The number of known gate-enabled dimensions was beyond their ability to "rule over." They made very few decisions without consulting the council, and those had to do with everyday operations. Alliance membership was all about the ability of a culture to accept the existence of alien beings and the willingness to "live and let live" without any desire for conquest or dominion, the very thing they were up against with the Inseni.

The ruling council was in charge of daily running of the agent training center, the day-to-day operations of the military and the space fleet, and interacting with the Gatekeeper to assist with his or her responsibilities, whoever was Gatekeeper at the time. In the case of Jenny, since she had been installed, Liliath continued to be surprised, with all she had already gone through. Not only did she keep operating at the top of her abilities, but her abilities continued to expand beyond the initial impressions or expectations the council had originally had of her.

"And so," Jenny continued, *"we will need help once again from the military forces of a humanoid nature in patrolling and monitoring the situation in the Amazon jungle. We will also need to work closely with all of the available scientists to puzzle out not only the original purpose of the little coin I found at the portal site, but also its potential danger for future purposes on both sides of the conflict.*

"In the meantime, we continue to receive reports from our Mookookie spies among many of the various dimensions currently held by the Inseni. In addition, we are exploring a new relationship between the Mookookie and the Nanoites. Both parties have agreed to join forces as needed to do anything required by the Alliance in this struggle, as long as it won't require them to kill or damage any organic life form."

Liliath sighed, a somewhat disconcerting action from the side of the observer. But by now Jenny was used to Liliath's moods and wasn't intimidated by them, although, admittedly, she wouldn't want to be on the receiving end if the dragon decided to become aggressive.

"Very well, Jenny. That is definitely enough to be going on with. Reports tell me that your mental communications network is working out very well. At this point only non-essential or non-sensitive communications are going out from the Alliance network. From all appearances from the Inseni side, it looks like we're going about our own business and ignoring their current status as aggressors and tyrants of the dimensions they currently occupy.

"We have located four new candidates to be trained as communications specialists, but before you get it into your head that this will be added to your plate, Fo has volunteered to train them with Amenia, continuing to use your mental fortress as a training ground, as you agreed when we began this. Your only responsibility will be to go with them in their first foray across your mental drawbridge.

"Also, I would ask you, before you do so, to consult with Amenia on how to make your mental space secure. The mental communications candidates should never have access to more than the communications training center. This is still your own mental space, and we don't want to impinge on its rightful use."

Jenny considered this. It hadn't occurred to her, but she knew she had been fooled in the past with dreadful consequences. How might this affect her if someone could just go in and take control of her subconscious? She shivered at the thought.

"Good counsel, Liliath. I'll talk to Amenia, and we will plan out the best way to make that happen. I think we should also make sure that our mental communications specialists understand that this is high security work and they are under contract to keep all communications strictly on a need-to-know basis, and that need would have to be determined by the high council in advance. The whole point of this exercise is to conceal our plans and intents from anyone who could create a leak,"

Jenny added. *"It would probably be a good idea to have Chidwi or another linkling vet the candidates for this training program.*

"I'll get with Amenia and report back as soon as I can. In the meantime, I will personally continue to coordinate information between the various Earth-based teams and their Alliance counterparts. Is there anything else?"

Liliath shook her great head. *"No, I think that is all for now. I will have new information to pass on in a day or two. Stay in touch as you need to, and recognize our gratitude for your commitment and diligence in this calling that came upon you so unexpectedly."*

Liliath faded from view and Jenny looked up to see Mynn, who was waiting patiently in the workout room for her to pause in communications. Jenny saw that either Lizziebot or one of the other bodyguards had left an ice-cold root beer on the desk with her favorite "ants on a log" snack. She often complained that if it hadn't been for her consistent workouts with the girls and Tarafau, she would have gotten very fat by now, considering how often she was provided with snacks and good meals without any effort on her part.

"So, what's on our list today?" Mynn asked with a grin. Jenny seldom saw Mynn downhearted or grumpy.

"I have to spend some time with Amenia, and then we need to get in touch with Burt and Elizabeth to see where they are in their process. I also need to talk with Cornelium's team regarding the new information of the buddy relationship between the Mookookie and the Nanoites. They seem to be setting themselves up for a new role in all of this, and I have a feeling it will be important to our final success with the least casualties possible."

Mynn nodded. "So, will I be riding along, or am I just on Jenny watch for today? I ask because if I am on Jenny watch, I want to go get the book I'm reading."

Jenny laughed at this. Mynn was definitely the intellectual of the group. She loved long discussions with Jenny at mealtime regarding the various tech and scientific projects they were involved in with all of the science teams. The other two would just roll their eyes and bear it in silence, most of the time, preferring to discuss one of the Earth TV shows they had been following or what they planned to purchase on their next trip to the mall or the Farmer's Market.

"Actually, Mynn, I think you should come along. We're going to be talking about the Nanoites and the Mookookie, and last time you had some interesting ideas to contribute. Let me finish my snack, and we'll get right on it.

Mynn and Jenny, with Chidwi perched on her shoulder, got to the lab via Jenny's talent, when all four of the team were in earnest discussion of their latest theories. With Cornelium, Bob, Merv, and Anela were a couple of Mookookie. In addition, Jenny surmised that multiple Nanoites were in attendance, though invisible to the naked eye. Jenny assumed they were attending with Fidget, who stood by Bob's side. Fidget often translated conversations to and from the Nanoites and the other attendees.

Merv had asked Jenny most recently to consider how she might have mental communications with the Nanoites to facilitate this and to let the Nanoites communicate with her directly rather than having to go through one of the bots. After all, they reasoned, some of the things they discussed could be critical and potentially urgent.

Jenny actually had come up with an idea of how this could be done since last they met, and she was eager to discuss it with the group.

After greetings all around, Merv spoke for the group, as he often did. "Lovely to see you two ladies," he began, with a wink for Mynn. "We were just mentioning you, to be sure. I understand you have something to share, Jenny?"

"Okay, folks, so how about this? I understand that Lizziebot's upgrades continue apace, most of the time without me having any idea of the improvements you continue to make to her. These usually take place virtually, across the Alliance network. What I'm proposing today will require some in-person meddling, perhaps for Bob to travel home to do it.

I was thinking that perhaps Lizziebot could host a Nanoite or perhaps more than one. I understand that Nanoites have the ability to communicate to one another directly, regardless of location, something like what we might call a "hive mind," similar to the Mookookie. I wouldn't ask for this merely as another method of secure communication, but also to allow me to begin to understand the Nanoite culture and the world around which their MDP pods orbit.

I also would like my Noony back, as you all have access to many Mookookie at this time. I want to see for myself the interactions between the two and also experiment with mental communication with them both.

In addition, I want to prepare for the tests we will run with the little bit of metal—call it a coin—which seems to want to toss a monkey wrench into our plans."

She stopped watching the faces of the four in front of her, who looked various kinds of stunned at the moment.

Merv finally laughed, shaking his head. "Just a few small favors then? I'll give you this much, Gatekeeper, you definitely seem to know what you want and why you want it. What say you chaps? Shall we grant the lady's request?"

Suddenly Noony sprang out of the arm of Bob's chair with a grin. "Noony come home to Jenny?" he said happily. "Play with the linkling and the cat?"

Chidwi chirruped excitedly, bouncing lightly up and down on Jenny's shoulder. "Yes! Mookookie must come!" she replied enthusiastically before anyone could respond.

"Well, why not?" Bob responded, his moustache twitching in amusement. "We've got a tribe of each here in the lab. Fidget, will the Nanoites agree to this?"

"Indeed, boss, they seem to like the idea. Shall we go now?"

"A bit eager, aren't you?" Bob countered ironically.

"I would enjoy seeing Lizziebot and spending time with Jenny on Infinity Loop. It is my origin, after all," the bot retorted.

"You can be a bit scary at times. Did you know that?" Bob replied to the smart-aleck comment.

"Okay," Jenny interrupted, knowing how Bob and his bot could get into it at length. She never knew how Bob had programmed this personality into the bot, but she had been continuously impressed by how "human" Fidget came across. If you couldn't see his robot body, you would never guess his voice didn't come from a smart-aleck teen or college roommate. "So as soon as I fade out, come on by, Bob.

"But first, please upload any notes or reports you might want to send to the Alliance to Fidget so I can relay the information to the appropriate people. I didn't want to stay long, as I know you all have enough on your plate to be going on with. I will want a discussion in the very near future about our scary little coin. It remains where we put it. I have some thoughts about some safe ways to test it, but that's for next time."

Before any of them could object, she waved cheerfully at them and faded into the workout room; and the moment it solidified in her vision, she and Mynn went straight to the gate office to receive Bob and his friends.

She had barely sat in her office chair with Chidwi bouncing up and down on the cushion of Tidbit's bed and Mynn standing at parade rest in front of the door that led into the house, when Bob showed up with Merv. Jenny hadn't expected Merv to come along, but she always enjoyed his company and respected his advice, considering his inexplicable age and the ages he had spent in various guises on Earth, the most notable being his time as King Arthur Pendragon's advisor and court magician Merlin.

They had barely cleared the office doorway from the gateroom when Noony popped out of Bob's armband, sprouting arms and legs and then, to Jenny's surprise and delight, encircling her with an enthusiastic hug.

"Noony has missed Jenny," he sent in a mental croon of glee. *Noony can stay?"* he added hopefully.

"Yes, Noony you can stay. I need your help, and Chidwi has missed you so much."

Noony relinquished his hold on Jenny and turned to find Chidwi waiting behind him, arms extended. Noony shrank his appendages to Chidwi's height, and the two of them embraced enthusiastically.

Merv and Bob grinned. "So where do you want to do this?" Bob asked, watching the linkling and Mookookie interact. "We need to establish some guidelines for the participants. Both Noony and the Nanoites we will be introducing into Lizziebot need to know the rules from the beginning. They will follow instructions willingly; but left to their own devices..." he trailed off, shaking his head and rolling his eyes.

"C'mon, chap, it isn't quite so bad as that..." Merv began, but Bob continued to shake his head ruefully.

"For instance, Noony needs to know what is *not* on the menu, and the Nanoites also need to know their boundaries. So far, we haven't noticed them interfering with the normal operation of our tech, and they would never intentionally hurt any of our equipment, but they have some interesting talents, and their understanding of technology is almost intuitive. So, why don't you call Lizziebot in, and we'll start in here, then, out of the way of unnecessary interruptions?"

Mynn nodded and rushed out to retrieve Lizziebot. Bob and Merv settled into two of the chairs in the semicircle around the desk. Bob invoked Fidget out of his MDP.

"We're going to introduce you to two of the Nanoites. Like humans or other beings you have met in your travels, they have names, personalities, and language. So far, we have been able to communicate with them in a form of mindspeech between them and Fidget.

We are in the process of creating a portable translation device that will allow them to communicate from outside the bots, and that will mean they will not have to remain inside the robotic structure. This will give them freedom to do other things besides just advising us regarding technology and a variety of projects we are currently working on," Bob said, pausing as Mynn and Lizziebot came back into the room.

Once Mynn settled into another chair and Lizziebot turned to face Bob and Merv, Fidget rolled beside her, and they waited for Bob to continue.

"Fidget, please introduce our guests," Bob said, like the host on a gameshow.

Fidget blinked and said, "Allow me to introduce Fagir and Gini, of the cluster of Memen. Fagir styles himself an engineer and Gini as a molecular physicist, or at least that's as close as we can come to a translation from their language. They have each volunteered for this project, and we have explained the risks and potential gains of the experiments they will be engaged in.

They are both ready to be transplanted to Lizziebot. Once they are settled, Lizziebot will be rebooted and an update installed. This will take about three hours from start to finish. They are prepared to begin immediately."

Jenny was a bit taken aback by how quickly this was all happening, but simply nodded and said, "Then let's get started. Thank them from me and our team for their willingness to aid us in this."

"They can hear and understand you, Jenny," said Fidget. "You may speak directly to them once they are installed in Lizziebot. Do not think of them as another piece of software or an app. They are intelligent beings and will give good service. As you wish to speak to them after their transition, simply address them by their names, as you would any other being."

Feeling somewhat embarrassed, Jenny said, "Gini and Fagir, I thank you for your help and will remember. Your type of being is new to me. I meant no offense."

Twin voices unlike Fidget's familiar tones replied almost in unison. "You are welcome, Jenny. Let us begin."

Jenny remembered what Burt had told them about the Nanoites being of a type of hive mind, but with individual consciousnesses, and she realized this might take some getting used to.

Fidget faced Lizziebot and held out his hand. Lizziebot extended her own palm, and at once her faceplate went dark and she stood like a statue.

"Not to worry, Jenny," Merv said, watching her face. "She is just rebooting and installing some new software. Perhaps we can now discuss where you're going with all of this. Something tells me it isn't just curiosity about that little farthing you found in Brazil."

"Not curiosity, so much as something that keeps nagging at me about it. I have a feeling that the Nanoites might be able to ascertain some things about it that may be helpful in not only protecting us from any potential harm it represents but also seeing if there is anything we can learn from it to help us in the upcoming conflict."

"Always thinking, our Jenny," Bob commented almost smugly. "That's one of the things I noticed about her right away. Right from the beginning, I could see how much she resembled Lizzie."

Merv nodded, and Jenny remembered now that Merv also had known her aunt. The amused set to his mouth made her wonder if that had been a compliment or not.

She chose to ignore it. "I wish she was here. I'm sure she would have probably figured this out before any of us; but for now, we will have to work it out ourselves. It occurred to me, however, that not only can the Mookookie, the Nanoites, and the bots communicate with one another, but they also see the cosmos much differently than any of us do. From their standpoint, solid mass is not what we think it is; and even the concept of time is so very different for them.

I also notice that so far each of them seems to be very puzzled by the idea of conflict. They recognize the importance of opposites and the idea that friction is a given in most things, but they don't seem to apply it to the kind of friction intelligent beings often inflict upon one another. The whole idea of conflict with the purpose of inflicting harm on another living being is alien to them."

Jenny noticed Bob and Merv nodding approvingly at her statement. "So, knowing that," Merv asked, his eyebrows raised, "what do you propose to do with the Mookookie and the Nanoites that relates to your own duties in the Alliance? And do you have some insights that may also help us in our own tasks?"

"I think so. I will know more as I proceed. The first stage is for me to see how the Nanoites and Mookookie interact and to have some actual conversations with them about what role they would like to fill. I know they agree with our aims to free those who have been invaded by the Inseni, but I'm sure they wish to find ways to do this that won't require any more harmful measures than necessary. I also have a strong feeling that there is more to both of our new friends than we currently understand. This could make a huge difference as to how we approach our current quest to free the enslaved dimensions."

Again, Bob and Merv nodded in agreement. Jenny felt a little sheepish about talking to these two experienced and learned scientists about something that wasn't her bailiwick at all. She had always had a certain level of curiosity and interest in the sciences but had chosen to focus instead on language arts and history in her university studies. Mynn had sat there the entire time after escorting Lizziebot back into the room, and Jenny could see her taking in every word, a look of awe on her face.

"Well, I think you may be on to something here," said Bob. "So far, we have been mostly focusing on MDP science, and I know you have been studying the Alliance MDP network as part of your gate-keeper duties. I think after we have had a chance to both pursue our current trend of thought, we should definitely take some time to consult with one another regarding our findings. I admit we all feel quite a bit of urgency in creating a master plan for our attempt to, once and for all, rid the dimensions of the impact of the Inseni plans for universal dominion. I think it's making us feel impatient."

After agreeing to get together again within the next three weeks, there was nothing more to do than to go out to the patio and hang out with some cold root beer and enjoy the beautiful garden, idly chatting while they waited for Lizzie to reboot. Bob assured her that Lizziebot would let them know when she was back online and that they could relax.

Mynn sat holding her root beer, silently taking it all in, but Jenny noticed that her eyes never stopped scanning around them. Even though they had been assured that the backyard was as secure as it was possible to be, it was clear that Mynn took her duties seriously.

Chidwi and Noony followed them out, and to everyone's surprise, Noony, after watching Chidwi scramble up Windsong's trunk into her branches, promptly sprouted limbs and followed her up, gazing with great interest down into the koi pond.

"You should know that Noony has already been given instructions about not eating anything without asking about it first and was told that you will be setting his boundaries. He has agreed to abide by whatever you say. We have found the Mookookie to be extremely honest and trustworthy; and all in all, they seem to be very enjoyable companions," Merv said as they settled down to watch Chidwi and Noony cavort together.

"Once again I will remind you that anyone peering into your backyard over the fence or even hovering over your house will only see some very happy squirrels playing in your yard, so you needn't concern yourself about letting them play outside."

So they chatted quietly, sipping root beer, until suddenly Fidget appeared, framed in the sliding glass door. "Come, we are ready," he said, beckoning them in.

Chidwi and Noony scrambled back down, and they all trooped back into the gate office, Tidbit trailing almost lazily behind them. Lizziebot stood there, looking no different than usual, her female robotic face watching them as they gathered around her.

"It is curious," she said, blinking her blue eyes, so much like Lizzie's. "I do not feel much different, although I now know much more about the Nanoites and the two of them who are currently residing inside me. I can see where we may be able to do some things that may resolve some of the issues you have been pursuing. Gini and Fagir are excited about the upcoming study and exchange of ideas. They also intimated that perhaps Chidwi may add additional insights, as they sensed her mind when they were first introduced here."

Jenny looked at Chidwi with surprise. It hadn't occurred to her to include Chidwi in this experiment, but she also knew she still didn't completely understand the full range of her linkling's talents or level of understanding.

"Well then," said Merv, observing Jenny's look of wonder and feeling like he could literally see gears turning in her mind, "we'll be off. Cornelium told us not to spend too much time socializing, as we are definitely in the middle of something interesting at the moment in the lab."

After Bob installed Fidget back into his MDP, Bob and Merv each reached over for a quick hug, and they headed out to the gate-room with a cheery wave.

Jenny sat there for a moment, staring at the closed door and then giving herself a mental shake. She looked up to see Mynn grinning at her. "Should we call the others in to brief them on this new wrinkle?" she asked expectantly.

"Good idea," Jenny responded. "I think the more brains we have working on this project, the better."

Chapter 16: Vibes

Jenny had always been in awe of the complexity of creation. Although science had not been her major in school, she enjoyed every one of the required science credits she had earned over her four years at the university. So even though this project added a lot to her already full daily agenda, she found herself looking forward to the time each day she had divided out to work on what she thought might be the answer to many of their issues at once.

The first thing she did, in the presence of her bodyguards, Chidwi, and Tidbit, was to assure herself in front of witnesses that she would not be taking advantage of Noony, Fagir, or Gini and their amazing abilities and knowledge.

After she briefed the three on the path of inquiry she wanted to pursue, she said, *"I need to know that you have the agreement of your dimensions' governing bodies and that you individually are completely willing to participate in this study. At any time, if any of the steps we are about to take make you uncomfortable or go against your beliefs or conscience, please promise me that you will tell me. I want to understand a lot of things, including your histories and cultures, as well as your sciences and natural abilities, but I won't go past the lines you set. Are we agreed on that?"*

Fagir, Gini, and Noony sent warm thoughts of not only agreement, but support of what Jenny was trying to do.

She exhaled slowly in relief. *"So, at this point I know that both the Mookookie and Nanoite communities have been communicating and have come to some agreements as well as sharing information about your abilities. I admit we underestimated the scope of what each of you understand and are able to do, so I think we should start with the first thing we learned about the Mookookie. Noony, what can you tell me about 'the spaces'?"*

Noony's eyes were wide and his smile, if anything, was as wide as Jenny had ever seen it. Considering it took up most of his wide face, that was saying something. Jenny could hear the pride in his mental voice, to be asked such an important question.

"Spaces is big," he began, sprouting arms and holding them wide to illustrate. *"Spaces is far and yet very close. All things has spaces. All things has many many spaces. Mookookie see spaces and go into spaces. Spaces is safe and quiet except for the spaces song. Spaces sing, each sings different, each sings joy, each sings life and light."* He paused and looked at each of the faces, apparently wondering if he had been clear.

Jenny knew that Mookookie thought very differently than most beings she had met, and Noony's mental voice reflected that, the grammar not corrected, as it normally would have been, into English the way she would have spoken.

"Can you tell me how you see the spaces?" Jenny asked, to encourage him to continue.

"Eyes, but not eyes, see the spaces. I look at Jenny," he continued, looking directly into Jenny's eyes and then scanning her from head to toe, *"and I see Jenny's spaces, many, many, many. But eyes alone cannot see spaces. Many things in me, see them all at once. With eyes closed I can feel spaces and hear spaces singing to me. Jenny's song is one of peace and delight, and also a burden which Jenny bears willingly."*

Jenny was stunned by this very personal revelation. She thought she understood that the "spaces" were the space between atoms in any given solid body but decided to ask instead of assuming anything.

"So are there also spaces in the air?" she asked, feeling a bit foolish about the question.

"Air has bigger spaces, and is wiggly, not still. Wiggles in air can be big or tiny, and spaces change. Spaces in different things are closer or farther. Mookookie don't try to go into air spaces... too wiggly."

Jenny didn't laugh, although she found herself amused at the creative way Noony communicated really big ideas.

"When Mookookie go into the spaces, how do they know how to go in and how to get out?"

Noony's face assumed a somewhat puzzled expression. *"All Mookookie know where they are and when they are, so this is easy. New Mookookie just know this, not learn, not teach, just know. Can't tell Jenny this thing, don't know it."*

To her surprise, Jenny sensed laughter coming from the Nanoites.

"Why is that amusing, Gini?" she sent.

"The Mookookie is right and smarter than we might think. Like a well programmed thinking device you term a 'computer,' they have this ability naturally. We too wondered about this. Our relative size to the Mookookie or any physical being we have encountered means that this is also a normal thing for us. We have trouble envisioning how it might feel to not be able to do this. It is what made it easy for us to penetrate the robotic being, Fidget, or to reside in Lizziebot.

"To us, the spaces are wide and obvious to our senses. We use the spaces, as the Mookookie name them, differently than they do; we have no need to hide in them, as a being that can detect us without specialized equipment is rare. Even now, the Alliance does not have any technology that can do this. The only reason you even knew we were in what you call the MDP pods is because we presented ourselves via Fidget's programming."

Jenny considered this. *"We know very little about Nanoite culture or history except that your communities were established on the MDP pods with the help of ancient Dimensional Alliance agents when your planet became inimical to your lives. Do I understand that in addition to living in the pods, you now also are able to construct new pods? And how do you traverse the space around your planet? These questions are a little outside the purview of our current project, but it might give me some insights about things I hadn't considered."*

Jenny felt more than heard the amusement in Fagir's reply.

"One of the things we are learning about Earthlings is to respect their nearly insatiable curiosity. Yes, we can create new pods. After your ancestors built the first of the pods that orbit our now-dead planet, we requested that they leave the plans for these for our engineers and scientists to review. We also learned the use of the equipment they employed to build the first one.

"We came to an agreement. Your ancestors harvested metals and other substances from our planet. In order to create the first pod, they had established a station in orbit and it then became a storage facility for materials and equipment when they were finished. The facility was vast, by our standards, and had also the ability to construct pre-molded components to build additional pods.

As we worked side by side with the Alliance engineers in the building of the initial pod, we collaborated on the idea of the MDPs. The power of the gateways that resided on our planet was extended to correspond to each pod. And, before you ask, no, we don't understand how it was done, but we know how to operate the equipment that establishes a new portal into each pod after completion. That equipment resides still on the construction station, and each time we construct a new pod, a new MDP coordinate is loaded to the entire MDP tracking system, which, as we understand it, you personally have access to."

Jenny nodded, almost numb with shock. This was so much more than she had expected already. She was glad Lizziebot had been instructed to record all of her sessions with the Mookookie and Nanoites and could envision the greedy looks of Merv and Bob when she sent this to them via Burt and Elizabeth, taking no chances to forward it through the normal Alliance network channels.

Fagir continued. *"As you now know, there are currently a few thousand of these pods. What you may not know is that our native planet is huge, when compared to even the largest planet in your galaxy. Its orbit can host thousands more of the MDPs, and we continue to create them. The benefit to the Nanoites is that each new pod gives us ample room to expand our own population, within reason, and the byproducts of the construction of the MDP pods give us the wherewithal to sustain life, as it serves as what you would call food for our particular form of life."*

Jenny was astonished, and for a moment stunned silence was all she had to offer. This was so much more than anything she had expected, and her brain was whirring with the implications.

Gini broke in. *"What this means to the Nanoites, the Alliance, and the Mookookie, is that we have a high incentive to not only be at peace with one another, but also to assist one another in the protection and expansion of the Alliance gate system.*

"For what may have been a few thousand of your years, for whatever reason, we lost contact with the Alliance, only continuing to build pods and communicate the coordinates out from the station as we had always done. Imagine our surprise and delight when Fidget entered one of our pods that day. The technology was different from what we were used to, but the identity of the bot as an Alliance servant was clear when we entered Fidget to investigate.

"One of the tasks the Alliance had initially given us was to guard the pods as well as to build, tend, and maintain them. This is something every new Nanoite knows from the first moment of sentience. Fidget passed our tests, and you know the rest.

"Now, for the first time in our memory, we also travel the dimensions via the gateways. The Alliance council has acceded to our request for membership, and we now have an even higher vested interest in continuing our stewardship."

"And now, do you see yourselves as continuing in your service to the Alliance and perhaps expanding it?" Jenny asked with increasing interest.

"Indeed, and it is fitting we should find our services under your personal stewardship, as, in a very interesting way, we are also Gate Guardians, wouldn't you say?" asked Gini in response.

"I hadn't considered that," Jenny admitted. *"So, in effect, it is appropriate that we work on this project together, since what we will be studying and testing could have a direct impact on all of the gates and, most especially, the MDP pods. Am I to assume that you and Fagir will be the Nanoite liaison with me as the Gatekeeper in a permanent position?"*

"Indeed," replied Fagir, *"if that is acceptable to you."*

It was hard to determine if that was said with a touch of humor or not. It was odd, not being able to actually see the Nanoites due to their microscopic size, so she had no facial expressions or body language to go by. It was a lot like texting with someone you didn't know, as she wasn't sure how much, in this case, the mental tone of voice was any indication of emotion or intent. This might be another thing she would want to explore once the current project was completed.

"You do understand there is a certain possibility of risk involved?"

"We were thoroughly briefed by Cornelium before coming here," Fagir stated, *"and we accept that exploring the makeup of that unusual piece of metal could prove both challenging and perhaps dangerous. As scientists of our community, we are not naïve enough to assume otherwise. When would you like to begin? As I understand it, part of what we will be doing is demonstrating our abilities and also how we relate to the Mookookie community."*

Jenny considered before she answered. *"I'm unaware of what accommodations you may need for rest and food. I know the Mookookie are very adaptable that way. Is there anything I need to provide for you? And what kind of schedule are you used to?"*

"Rest, as you conceive of it, 'sleeping' you call it, is not necessary for us. We live in fragments of time that may seem both tiny and massive to your species. Rest for us takes what you would term 'nanoseconds,' and we intake nutrients from the environment we live in, more specifically the intrinsic power that emanates from every solid substance. Not to worry about your bot in that regard. The nutrients we require would be considered byproducts of her power system and are so small that she will not notice it."

Jenny was relieved to hear this, one less detail for her to deal with. *"Then, Noony, tell me how you feel about all of this. Do you understand the potential danger of what we are about to do? Just because you and I are bonded, doesn't mean you can't choose to refuse my request."*

"Noony is happy to help. Jenny helped us fight the bad ones. Jenny wasn't afraid. Jenny gives Noony chocolate?"

Jenny couldn't help but chuckle at that. *"Yes, I will give you chocolate, even if you don't want to help."*

"Noony is happy to help," he repeated. *"Lizziebot told Noony what I can eat and not eat. Lizziebot told Noony he can sleep on the window seat or in it as I would like. Noony will help."*

And with that they began.

Chapter 17: Tingles

By the end of the next day, after interspersing her work with Noony, Gini, and, Fagir with her usual responsibilities, she was so glad to melt into her mattress, anticipating her various mental conferences and her time with Burt, but even more, looking forward to some real sleep.

Once she had drifted off, she reported to Liliath and then drew the science teams into their conversation. When all parties were settled, she began her report.

She looked around into every face, all of which were evidently rapt to hear what she had to say. As usual, she felt that tiny nagging reticence to be the focus of everyone's attention, especially now that she was in such an unanticipated position of authority. It still made her more than a little uncomfortable that all eyes were on her.

"We have only started our investigations, as you know, but already I am seeing some real potential in our study of the phenomenon caused by the little bit of metal we found at the Amazon portal.

"One of the first things we tested was the ability of both the Mookookie and the Nanoites to detect and identify various types of resonance, as it has been posited that it may be resonance on an unknown frequency or in an unknown form that caused the glitch in my mental communications that day.

"We discovered that both the Mookookie and the Nanoites are extremely sensitive to resonances related to expended energy of any kind we are aware of. We started with a tuning fork and proceeded to several

types of devices, electrical outlets, as well as the human voice, physical vibrations, and even something as difficult as the resonance exuded by the human heart and, to my great surprise, the human brain." She paused, taking in the faces before her and noticed that now she could almost see the gears turning in many heads.

Satisfied, she continued. *"Also, Fagir brought up the notion that we should consider whether or not the item was dropped intentionally or by accident, as that would make a difference in how we view the results of our experiments. The notion that it may have been dropped accidentally puts a new light on the potential of our results. It could be either a deliberate act of sabotage by our enemy or an accident that may be a huge breach of their own security.*

"Put in that light, we need to determine as many potential uses for this object as possible. For that reason, once the Nanoites, the Mookookie, and I have gathered as much data as possible, we will turn it over to each of the science teams to allow them to do their own research on any applications related to the device that may aid us at any point.

"I suppose I need not remind you that every bit of this is strictly on a need-to-know basis. There could be some unexpected breakthroughs, and none of those should be shared with anyone except Liliath and me until we can determine its disposition. Agreed?"

Every head nodded solemnly, but she could see than many of them were agitated, fingers twitching as if itching to get their hands on the data immediately. She would have laughed if they hadn't all appeared to be dead serious at the moment. She knew that this is what these inquisitive minds lived for—discovery, exploration, and experimentation—and they were like hounds on a new and interesting scent.

"Okay, so the next thing you should know is that although we knew the Mookookie could 'go between the spaces' as they put it, it appears that the Nanoites have a similar talent. It isn't quite what the Mookookie call it, nor is the process the same. The fact is that the Nanoites are so

miniscule that they don't fit their own molecules into the spaces between atoms. They can actually walk through those spaces, the same way we would walk down a garden path. In other words, the likelihood that any other being could see them with their natural eyes is almost nil.

"The Nanoites can detect any sentient being of any size or type, as far as we can tell. In addition, we discovered that although they approach it differently than we do, they do have the capacity to communicate, mind to mind, with other sentient beings."

There was an audible gasp at this, and Jenny was not disappointed to see that some of them had even covered their mouths, their eyebrows raised, and others were shaking their heads in disbelief. She knew that for these scientists, these revelations seemed pretty much too good to be true.

"Finally, as you may have already expected, Nanoites reproduce similarly to the Mookookie, by some kind of mitosis. They have complete control over this process. They also are not resistant to the idea that perhaps they might establish colonies in what is now enemy territory and would potentially be willing to stay beyond the conflict, with the agreement of the native population, to aid those communities in recovery and even potentially remain long term, as new citizens of that dimension."

Jenny almost laughed aloud at the even more agitated expressions on her listeners' faces.

"I think that's enough to be going on with for now. I will keep you all up to date. How often do you think you would like to meet?"

"How about every ten minutes?" Bob asked with a yearning voice. *"Maybe we can just watch over your shoulder?"*

"Don't be silly old boy," Merv chimed in, his arm around Bob's shoulder as if having to restrain him from jumping from his current dimension without a gate. *"We've got our own plate full,"* he chided good naturedly. *"What would you say to every other day, unless you have a breakthrough that's urgent?"*

Jenny nodded with a grin at Bob's enthusiasm, although she could see that the rest of them all had the look of someone perusing desserts at a bakery.

"I think we could arrange that. What do you think, Liliath? Does that sound reasonable to you?"

"I think it will work. We can always adjust that as we go. I know this will be an ongoing project, potentially even after the conflict has concluded. Let us then decide to meet in two days from now, shall we?"

And thus began what to Jenny felt like one of the longest uphill hikes she had ever been on. She almost felt like she needed a figurative backpack, pitons, and some strong rope to get her past the tricky parts; but, like all steep climbs, she hoped that the view from the top would be breathtaking.

Every day was a new breakthrough. Every day was a new challenge. The more she got to know the Nanoites and her Mookookie friend, Noony, the more she respected them. She began to see how truly diverse and spectacular the dimensions were.

She discovered that the Nanoites had a sense of humor, though a rather dry one, and it was sometimes difficult to tell whether they were serious or not.

Noony, on the other hand, was a completely different surprise. Noony had a very serious side and was not only studious but also fascinated by what humans called science. He was incredulous at how humans saw creation as complex and unfathomable, when he and his people saw it as simple, logical, and understandable.

His simplified linguistic skills were not therefore evidence of a lower mentality, but quite the opposite. He spoke simply because his people had spent their entire lives communicating via mindspeech; and since mindspeech communicated not only concepts, but also intent, the idea of using a lot of descriptive words and phrases was simply alien to them. They knew what they meant and assumed that anyone receiving their communication would understand them.

The issue for the humans and others who communicated with them, then, was the fact that Mookookie also assumed the things they all knew from birth. They were born with the group memories that passed through generations with very little distortion, as you would expect, for instance, from traditions handed down verbally from one generation to another in any of the human cultures.

This meant that the Mookookie didn't quite understand the need for schools, for instance, or the written word. Books were an alien concept to them, and it amused them to see Jenny and others consulting written accounts to discover or remember a concept or historical notation.

Nanoites had a similar culture, relying on the hive mind mostly for communication. They had figured out how to use Fidget to communicate with their Alliance counterparts, but although they were used to 'thinking' to one another, it hadn't occurred to them that they could do this with other sentient beings. Jenny's discovery that they could communicate with other beings mentally, therefore, was a big deal; and clear across the dimensions, the message was sent to the other Nanoites throughout the MDP network of this amazing new concept.

Fagir and Gini assured Jenny that this was an unexpected bonus for them and their community. Jenny herself continued to be amazed at the increasing effects of her own talent and was only beginning to recognize, as Lizzie had, what a balancing act this could be between what she could do with it and what she should do.

Now that she could communicate directly with the Nanoites, it became apparent that Lizziebot could be anywhere in the house and they could still work together, as the Nanoites could now also communicate with all the other participants in this study at once.

She had met the night before with the Mookookie old ones, who had told her that the entire Mookookie community was committed to helping the Alliance rid the multiverse of the Inseni threat, only drawing the line at anything that would deliberately harm any being. Jenny respected them for that; and to be sure, the Alliance had the same view.

They knew that it was unlikely that this goal could be accomplished without any potential violence, as the Inseni's views were not the same, and sometimes the only way to defeat an enemy intent on your destruction was to meet force with force when necessary. More than preventing casualties on both sides of the conflict, they were very focused on making sure that there was no collateral damage towards the unfortunate populations that had been already harmed by the Inseni invasion. The Alliance could call on large armies and high tech sufficient to utterly destroy the Inseni wherever they were, but they couldn't, in good conscience, take that approach.

This wasn't about domination. It was about reparation. Their aims were simply to remove the Inseni from the currently dominated dimensions and to prevent them from ever being able to commit the same atrocities in the future.

The next part of Jenny's process was the examination and evaluation of the little "coin" by the Mookookie and the Nanoites. They knew that the potential for disaster by taking a technological approach was high. They didn't know how it might be booby-trapped to potentially interfere with any tech they might use to examine it, or if it might trigger some unknown power. Small as it was, Jenny realized that, after spending so much time with the Nanoites, size was not necessarily a good measure of potential power.

They also needed to do their tests in a place that was neutral as far as gateways were concerned.

It was Noony who suggested they do it on his home planet. It was a very low-tech environment, and Elizabeth could transport them there with the coin and attend in environmental suits. If at any time the coin affected the environmental suits, there would be time for Elizabeth to transport her and Jenny back to safety. The Nanoites would be carried by Noony, who would be riding along in Jenny or Elizabeth's environmental suits.

Once they were all there, the Nanoites and Noony would probe the coin, entering inside it. This was the part that most worried Jenny, as she didn't know how this would affect them and didn't want to put them in danger of harm. However, the Nanoites and Noony seemed unconcerned and were willing to take the risks if it might give them a clue as to what danger, if any, the coin represented and what potential advantage, if any, it might signify.

Jenny would be doing a 'ride-along' with Noony as he explored within the spaces of the coin, something that intrigued her. When she had told Liliath of her plan, she had raised one eyebrow and had told her that Earthlings never ceased to amaze her and to move forward with the plan.

Jenny remembered a hike and campout with her hiking club, looking up at the stars and imagining what it might be like to have the technology to be able to explore the stars and travel among galaxies. This would be a lot like that, she thought. She had been immediately fascinated by the idea of experiencing the "spaces" the Mookookie spoke of.

She imagined doing the exact opposite of exploring the stars and instead, somehow being among some of the tiniest things in creation. She shivered in anticipation as she and Elizabeth donned their environmental suits.

Chapter 18: Inner Space

They shimmered into being on a planet Jenny had thought she'd never be visiting again. The directions Elizabeth had received from Noony had been clear. As far as Jenny knew, Noony had never set foot on his native planet, but the connection between all Mookookie across generations meant that he knew exactly where he was and what place would be best for this experiment.

They were far from any of the domed colonies of the humanoids who had initially been transported here by their now deposed Inseni masters. It was a wide plain surrounded by mountains. Little puffy clouds scudded across a nearly green sky, and the foliage all around them was low and somewhat sparse. In the distance she could see what might have been the beginning of a forested area that she guessed might have had a water source.

This wasn't quite a desert, but couldn't be considered lush by any human standard.

Before they had set out, Burt had brought them a small box with two-inch-thick lead walls to keep the "coin" in. Jenny had not stored this in her MDP, since she had no idea if the coin could still project some kind of radiation or some kind of resonance that might interfere with the function of the MDP, so she simply held it in her hand while they made the transfer between dimensions. Elizabeth had assured her that anything she was touching would transfer with her, just as her clothes and any jewelry she was wearing would have done.

Noony popped out of the pant leg of her environmental suit where he had been concealed carrying the Nanoites. Jenny had wondered what that would be like, but she felt nothing to indicate the pant leg was anything but the fabric it was made of.

Burt had told her that he could feel it whenever BaaGah moved through the fabric of his clothing, but, evidently, as long as the Mookookie remained still, there was nothing to feel.

Noony looked around with evident delight on his body-face.

"We are ready? We can begin?" he asked, looking up at Jenny and Elizabeth.

Jenny nodded and put the lead box on the ground before the little Mookookie.

"We will connect mentally, like I showed you earlier," she reminded him. *"This way I can see what you see and experience what you experience, and hopefully we will be able to talk to one another the entire time. Elizabeth will also be with me. Remember, we are looking for what the coin is sending out and anything that looks unusual.*

"Fagir and Gini, do I remember that you believe you can analyze the atomic structure of the metal and potentially identify what it is made from and any tech that might be embedded in it?"

"Affirmative," replied Fagir. *"As you have instructed, we will immediately report anything that may be inimical to organic life. We will also stay in constant mental contact with you and Elizabeth. If at any time you do not get a response from us, get out. Leave us to deal with the repercussions. We hope this will not be necessary, but our instructions from our own leaders as well as the Alliance council are that your survival is essential and your safety must not be at risk."*

Jenny knew about these strictures, but she still felt more than a little uncomfortable about it. Of course, she didn't want to find herself in mortal danger, but she also didn't like the idea of abandoning the Nanoites or her Mookookie friend, if it could be helped. She nodded, knowing her assent would be transferred to her companions, even if they couldn't see her.

One of the things they had learned from the Nanoites was that these beings had little to no concept of body parts. Although they seemed to have five senses, sensations didn't appear to be transmitted via body parts or organs; rather, they just sensed all the same things that a human could feel. They also had emotional responses and tended toward desires and hopes, the same as any other sentient being Jenny had yet encountered.

"Let's go then," she sent, and opened the lead box, exposing the coin. *"Do you think I need to remove it completely?"* she asked her companions. *"If not, it will be easier to shut it up, if something happens, to prevent its influence. On the other hand, I wonder if the lead lining of the box, even though the box isn't completely shut, will mean we will get exaggerated or corrupted readings. I need your opinions before we go forward."*

They all seemed to agree that the coin should be removed from the box, so Jenny, handling it as if it were a live adder, pulled it out and set it on the ground next to the box, close enough that they would be able to return it to the box quickly.

"Ready?" she sent, and received an affirmative reply from each of her teammates, for this was how she thought of them. *"Then, lead the way, Noony."*

Jenny had not been sure what to expect from this experience, and had anticipated it being something like being in outer space: blackness with many floating objects visible from far away. This was nothing like that.

For one thing, it didn't appear to be dark "in the spaces." Instead, there was a soft glow that seemed to illuminate everything as far as she could see. Objects she thought she recognized as molecules were close around her, as if she were hiking through a dense forest, but none obstructed the path Noony seemed to be following.

"Noony, why is it so light here? I thought it would be dark in the spaces."

"All things have light inside. Jenny did not know this? Light is in Jenny also and plants and rocks and everything you can see and many things you cannot see. Light is creation. Light is The Creator." Noony's mind voice sounded somewhat incredulous, as if this should have been obvious to her.

"So far, does this appear to be normal for a metallic substance?" she asked as they floated, as it appeared in her mind, alongside the little Mookookie.

"Yes, metal, but there are troubles around us, the light is different, twisted, and dull. Noony would ask Fagir and Gini the same."

Gini began, *"Noony is right, the molecular structure seems normal enough, but this is not a single piece of metal. It has technical components that Noony would not recognize, his people not having the concept of machinery or technology in their cultural traditions. Nanoites, by contrast, have been intrinsically involved in large-scale technological equipment for as long as our memory goes back.*

"Even before the Alliance saved us from the oncoming disaster that made our own planet uninhabitable, we were building machines and were traditional users of technology.

"This made the Alliance solution to our problem perfect for us. They introduced us to new technologies and concepts, and we shared our own knowledge and understanding with them and as a result, the MDP network was conceived and established, a solution that helped both parties immensely."

Fagir cut in, business-like as usual, *"which brings us to our current study,"* and his tone was somewhat chiding. *"This is not simply a piece of metal, but a machine, a device similar to your robot companions, but designed more to sense certain things and then create and send certain resonances. It isn't clear yet, what those resonances may be or their pur-*

pose, though what is clear is that this is much more complex than it appears on the surface."

"And what kind of resonances do you detect so far? And probably the most important question is what would be the safest way to test the abilities of the device?" Jenny asked. *"So far, based on experience, I know it can interrupt long distance mindspeech on a planetary scale, although, based on our current experiment, it won't interrupt mindspeech within close confines, one of the things that was important to ascertain."* Jenny sent, feeling excitement building, that perhaps finding and pocketing this coin was more than simple coincidence.

After all she had already been through, due to seemingly random events, she had a very strong feeling that this was so much more than it appeared and may actually be a key to solutions moving forward. But in the meantime, they still had a lot of work to do.

They continued to do what Jenny could only call "wandering around" among the various molecules as her three guides persisted in their exploration and evaluation of their surroundings.

Fagir had informed Jenny when they first began discussing the project that one of the abilities of the Nanoites was a photographic memory and the capacity to project the things they thought from one mind to another, including to record everything that was said and done and to send all of it to Lizziebot to allow her to put it into a usable format for the scientists to study.

"What else can you tell me about this device? Are there any other abnormalities or anything that seems to stand out to you? Obviously, I have never been in this type of environment before, and I am not sure what to take into consideration," Jenny asked her companions.

"This is different technology, but not necessarily new." Gini responded thoughtfully. *"It seems to follow general computative theory, not much different than the devices common to the Alliance, but not the same, either. I am recording the code, which will need to be examined by the Alliance techs. It also seems to contain data that will be useful.*

"Ordinarily, this would be difficult, as the code is in a language formerly unknown to us; but seeing it in the context of a programming language, Fagir and I have now translated it into a format that will allow Alliance scientists to divine its nature and uses."

Jenny was more and more impressed with the skills exhibited by the Nanoites. This would definitely speed up the process of determining uses of the miniature device of yet unknown origin, considering that the Inseni she knew about thought of science as "magic" and, when Burt had connected with them, were importing scientists from conquered dimensions. She assumed that the Inseni had stumbled across the portals they currently were using entirely by accident and had, at some point, commandeered "wizards" to create the devices they now used to target individual dimensions via the transport equipment Alliance troops had appropriated at the Amazon portal.

"Then, do you have any opinions about the safest way to go about testing the device?" Jenny asked. *"Or will having the code with which it is programmed be enough? Will the code require the exact metal this is made of to replicate the device if we need to do that? I'm sorry, I have many questions, and I am sure you have some of your own. Can we create an environment for our scientists to safely test this device? If so, what do you recommend?"*

Fagir replied in his usual gruff mind voice. *"For now, I suggest we retreat from inside the device, replace it into its shielded container, and go back to your office. I believe this will require a consultation with the other scientists, and we are still not sure what prolonged exposure to this alien resonance will do to us or the Mookookie."*

"I agree. Noony, let's return to the planet surface."

She found herself almost immediately fading back to her own body, still standing near Elizabeth, and looking rather forbidding in her environmental suit. She quickly replaced the coin into its lead-shielded box and closed the lid.

"You were only gone a few seconds," Elizabeth said in wonder, *"and yet I could understand your sendings even as fast as they flew by. Did you get everything you need, do you think? My dad will be surprised at how quickly we return."*

"Let's talk after you take us back to the gate office," Jenny recommended. *"We have a lot to do, and I get a creepy feeling that we have a lot less time to do it than we thought."*

Noony had already faded into the pant leg of Jenny's environmental suit, and she assumed that Gini and Fagir were safely with him. Elizabeth obediently put one hand on Jenny's shoulder.

As soon as they faded into the office, Jenny opened the floor safe and installed the little box, enclosing it securely.

Noony emerged from the pant leg of her suit, and Jenny and Elizabeth removed their environmental suits, restowing them into their MDPs.

Jenny had even more respect for her MDP as she had begun to understand that the fact that they had them at all was no less than an interdimensional miracle. She had to admire those of that ancient race who had instituted this amazing system and rescued the Nanoites from death and destruction on a planet that no longer would support life.

It also gave her a great deal more respect for those who took the stewardship of her own home planet seriously. She began to understand the necessity of mindfully cleaning up pollution and doing everything the human race could do to prevent further destruction of the limited resources that allowed life on planet Earth.

"Thank you, all of you, for your help with this," she sent to the group. *"I will make preparations for a mental council. Fagir and Gini, please transfer your report to Lizziebot, who will make it available to Fidget via direct, in-person transfer. Bob and Merv will see to it that the other scientists working on this project will get it by transferring it personally to the other labs."*

She got an affirmative sending from the Nanoites, and Noony left, taking them to find Lizziebot. Jenny looked at Elizabeth, who rolled her eyes.

"This is a lot more than we thought it would be, isn't it?" she asked with a mental tone that told Jenny she was only beginning to understand how big this all was.

"Indeed, Elizabeth, the issue with the Inseni was always bigger than we thought it was. There seem to be more layers to it than we had thought possible. I'm grateful that I don't have to be responsible for the entire thing. It's all I can do to keep up with my Gatekeeper duties and the communications network, much less trying to figure out what to expect next from the Inseni threat. I worry that Earth itself may be one of the essential targets of our enemies, and I don't understand why."

"Well, I'll give my dad a hug and report back to Burt to fill him in. I expect he and I will be paying you a visit in person later today. He misses you, you know. I can see it in his eyes every time your name is mentioned. I hope you will soon be able to be together more often. It is a lot like what my mother went through when my dad started working with the Alliance."

Jenny hadn't considered this. She knew that Tarafau and his wife, Amenia, were madly in love with one another. This was obvious whenever she saw them together. Once again, she recalled how her mom had often gone for weeks and even months without her dad when he was in the military. She now had much more respect for the strength this must require on the part of both spouses. Then she remembered Lizzie's journals and once again mentally relived that time in Lizzie's life when she had lost her love so long ago. It definitely put her own sacrifices into perspective.

She straightened her shoulders and gave Elizabeth a hug. *"See you soon then."* And Elizabeth faded from her sight. She hoped that she hadn't noticed the tears in her eyes. Now to report to Tarafau and Liliath and arrange for another meeting with her scientists.

Chapter 19: The Crux of the Matter

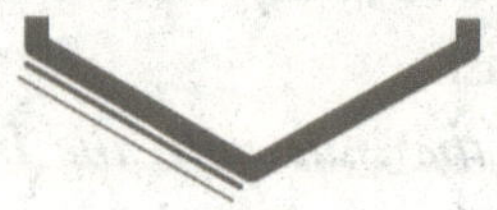

urt knew that Jenny was in good hands, with three bodyguards and the potential for immediate mental contact with a whole platoon of Alliance troopers who were constantly on alert and could come through the gate office in a matter of seconds if called. But he still worried about her.

Elizabeth had reported back and they would soon be meeting mentally in what Jenny called a "conference call," but it wasn't the same as his being by her side.

Even knowing they both had their part to play in this crucial mission, he still found himself longing to just take a break and spend some time with his wife doing something that didn't involve mortal peril.

Now he sat in the communications room in Sanglarka with the rest of the Earth guardian headquarters team. Lova sat perched nearly on the edge of her seat, and he knew that she too was concerned for Jenny and wished for this crisis to be over. Arvid sat next to her, his brows furrowed, and all were silent, including the Mookookie members of the team.

Burt wasn't sure what he thought about how many Mookookie were currently on Earth, both in the Sanglarka gate and the Switzerland gate under Adele's watchful eye.

They were proving to be very useful, and their Earth friends were careful to see that they didn't gorge themselves as they didn't want to create a huge Mookookie community. Their Mookookie friends understood this, and one thing Burt respected about them was their complete integrity. You could trust them to keep their word, as long as they completely understood their instructions.

He sat up straight as Jenny, Tarafau, Liliath, the Alliance science team alongside Liliath's councilors, the Swiss science team, Bob, Merv, and Cornelium all faded into view all facing in as if they were in chairs in a circle in a large room. It never ceased to amaze Burt how Jenny could bring them together like this, without any electrical devices across the dimensions to meet together in what appeared to be the same space, face to face.

Jenny looked around the circle and began...

"So, at this point, you each have received a visit from Lizziebot in person and received a transfer of the report from the exploration of the little circle of metal we are now calling Clyde. This way we can refer to it without concern of anyone having any idea what we are talking about.

"Clyde is definitely a concern, but for now it doesn't seem to have a direct impact on anything we are doing. The thing we need to determine is whether or not knowing what Clyde does will be a help or hindrance to ongoing operations. I think it's important, therefore, that we decide how much time and effort we should put into exploring those possibilities.

Merv and Tarafau both know, based on past experience, how a seemingly small thing can have a huge effect. Hopefully, we have learned some lessons from the past.

That said, I think we need to put a time limit on how much time we will spend focusing on what could amount to a red herring, meant to distract us.

Burt, now that we have removed Clyde from the portal entrance, what can we see at the Amazon gate?"

"There is pretty much constant traffic in and out. They don't stray from the gate entrance into the surrounding jungle. We haven't done anything yet to bar the gate, as we hope to get more intel that may help us know more about what they're up to.

"For instance, why do they need to come out of the portal at all? Why aren't they going directly from one portal to the next? It's like a layover in an airport for connecting flights.

"We're planning to capture a group of them sometime soon to interrogate and perhaps seize any tech they may have on them that will give us some kind of advantage and a clue or two of how best to track their future movements.

"It appears to be obvious, at this point, that the Amazon portal is somehow vital to their own system in a way that may be quite different from ours. It's almost like the Amazon portal is their version of the gateroom.

"Before we capture enemy troops, we have some intel-gathering strategies in place involving our Mookookie and Nanoite compatriots which will form the basis for our other efforts.

"After we have retrieved vital information through our Mookookie and Nanoite spies and have captured a few groups of the Inseni troops, we will block the gate as we did the gate on that planet they were invading before. We still have access to two of their portals that are not on Earth, via the Daringi's talent. But we really want to ascertain why Earth seems to be such a focus."

Liliath nodded. "Burt is correct. It surprises us that Earth became a focus so quickly. So far, the only reason we had considered is that the Gatekeeper is there, but we haven't noticed a recurrence of their surveillance on Infinity Loop or any attempt to attack the gate or the Gatekeeper since their last effort. Although it is true that they attacked Miriha's gate, which seemed to be a pattern with them, we thought we foiled this strategy, considering the seat of their main government was so totally disrupted.

"Engoza's rampage across the Inseni home world destroyed not only Gall and the huge capital city, but also thousands of Inseni troops. To our knowledge, the only remaining troops or officials were those who were in other dimensions they had previously invaded.

"Whether this is a renegade group or some troops continuing to act on previous instructions, we don't know. Whether there are any portals still in use on the Inseni home world, we don't know." She made a low growl in her throat, shifting in color toward the red spectrum, a small tendril of smoke drifting up from one nostril.

"There is far too much we don't know at this point. Even a supposedly small thing such as Clyde may be an important key to what we need to do, moving forward."

Adele nodded solemnly. "So, the work, as I see it, needs to be divided amongst the various teams. Perhaps the safest place to explore Clyde would be at the Swiss gate, as we have a lead-shielded room in the basement that was originally intended as a shelter in case of atomic bomb attack. I think we could safely examine and test Clyde here, if you think that would be okay.

"Perhaps Bob, Cornelium, and Merv could explore Clyde's internal programming based on the code the Nanoites retrieved, and the headquarters lab could coordinate the findings on both sides?"

"A good suggestion, Adele," Liliath agreed, having calmed herself and returned to her normal blues and greens. "I apologize for my impatience. It's just that this has been so much more than we originally thought, and I begin to wonder if there is more to it than we even suspect at the moment. For now, I believe what you have presented so far will be acceptable.

"Burt, continue with your plan. Gariel is ready with the appropriate troops when you are ready. The Daringi will be providing instantaneous transport for the troops and for the prisoners, once each mission is successful. We hope to repeat the success of the results of the Louisiana swamp mission.

"Speaking of which, do we have plans in place to reexamine the old Grogan camp there?"

"We felt the Amazon portal was a time-sensitive priority," Lova put in. "We are currently arranging for a team once we have completed the Amazon mission."

"Good enough," Liliath said. "So, for now, the Gatekeeper has her hands full as she will be doing some further training with her communications specialists. We have four new candidates, which should give us enough coverage to allow Jenny to focus on the main teams and allow her to actually get some real sleep from time to time."

Liliath's draconic grin made them all smile. It was common knowledge that Jenny did a lot of her work as she slept, and none of them were sure if time doing mental communication actually counted as real sleep.

"Then, if there is no further discussion that is necessary to the entire group, I think we have our instructions," Jenny said, looking from face to face. All nodded. "I wish you well. Take care." And once again Burt watched her fade from view, wishing he could fade with her to their little pond on the Merced.

Chapter 20: Teamwork

Since his time in the Desert Storm war, Bob hadn't felt so overwhelmed with concern as to how his actions would potentially affect the safety of others. He felt a strong sense of urgency, and yet here he was, in a castle fortress high atop a mountain range on a planet inhabited by intelligent dragons and humans who worked together in the same pursuits as every human on Earth.

He looked up from his monitor as Cornelium strode through the huge doors that opened into the lab.

"I think we need a construct to test this on," Cornelium grumped at the room in general. *"Bob, do we have a bot on hand that might work for this? I don't think we want to mess up Fidget. He is far too useful, and I think his resident Nanoites wouldn't appreciate it."*

"Yep, I was just thinking the same thing. A number of bots came off of the assembly line recently, of various types and sizes. I couldn't have assembled that many with my own resources on Earth, but several of the Alliance members have pitched in. By now, we have probably tripled our inventory since we went to attack the Inseni this past year.

"And Fidget is definitely off the menu. The Nanoites think of him as a hero, you know. They seem to think he is as sentient as they are, although I can't imagine that is so. I do believe, however, that something definitely changed when he was given mindspeech, and it had nothing to do with my own programming. He and Lizziebot are unique; and as far as I am concerned, for now they can remain so."

Bob had no desire to create a whole new species of intelligent life. The bots, as far as he was concerned, were nothing more than a convenience and had never been intended to be more than that. He had to admit, however, that Fidget definitely seemed to have developed what appeared to be a personality of his own, especially since he had become inhabited by the Nanoites.

Bob had intended that he appear to be intelligent with his own quirks and personality, but lately he had noticed that Fidget actually seemed to express emotions and even a sense of humor. He wasn't sure how comfortable he was with this.

But for now, he needed a way to test Clyde's programming, and a bot with an AI aptitude would probably make the most sense. He wondered how compatible his own programming of the bots would be with the code the Nanoites had retrieved from the little coin.

"I'll put in a requisition for one, then," Cornelium responded. *"In the meantime, we have our other project. I spoke with Adele's team through Jenny last night, and they think their work with the Mookookie and Nanoites as working teams may be paying off. We need that list of dimensions that we know have been invaded based on our information from the attack of the Inseni base. We were able to... erm... persuade some of the captured enemies to be forthcoming.*

"We also got some interesting information from those slaves on the Mookookie planet. They were happy to talk about their home worlds, and some even were able to use the portal at the palace to return to their own worlds. Some of those dimensions were still held by the Inseni; and, with the help of Alliance troops, the natives were able to take back their planets. But most of them stayed behind, as they knew their planets were currently beyond saving without severe casualties of their own people who were currently under Inseni dominion.

"We can use this information as a starting place. What we know already tells us that this project is bigger than to just go down a list and conquer one Inseni master after another. Adele and her team have come

up with a way to get the intel we need and perhaps prevent a lot of un-necessary bloodshed and destruction.

"Like when we conquered that Inseni base, I believe a combination of what the Earth team are working on and the use of bots of various types may be the key. There is a strong faction on my planet that are skeptical of the need for us to get involved in this. They feel we have already done enough by destroying the main governmental body of the Inseni. They are reluctant to continue to expend resources and lives in what they consider to be a potentially unending conflict with no hope of resolution." The huge dragon sighed, and Bob was once again struck with awe. A dragon's sigh was a sight to behold. His hair blew around his face with the huge exhalation.

Bob had also been aware that not all Alliance members were completely committed to this course of action. However, Bob felt, like Cornelium and what was currently the majority of the Alliance, not only that saving these other dimensions from Inseni dominance was right on a purely humanitarian basis, but also that the gate network the Alliance had been established to protect was also in jeopardy if the Inseni portals weren't discovered and deactivated in some manner.

Regardless, once again he found himself on the front lines, but not like his time in the Army. It was unlikely he would personally be under fire this time. Instead, his team's projects would hopefully prevent as many casualties as possible in this conflict, and he definitely preferred that to what he had done in the military.

Merv popped his head around the lab rest-area door. "Hey, mate, take a bit of a break? Well... not really a break, but we need to talk. Hey, Cornelium, you up for a chat?"

They both nodded and after they had seated themselves in the spacious break space, Merv grinned insolently. Bob was still in awe of the fact that Merv had been the ancient Merlin of Earth legend, but he had never pictured Merlin without a beard, dressed in jeans and a t-shirt. True, his hair was white, but it seemed to be the only indication that he was thousands of years old.

Merv never spoke much about his origins, but Bob still hadn't figured out how he, Bob, had ended up in such illustrious company: a wizard (by reputation, if not in fact) and a dragon scientist. Mentally shaking himself, he reminded himself to pay attention.

"It's like this. We're really close to several breakthroughs, but I don't want us to get too scattered here. Cornelium, I know this is your lab, and we appreciate a secure space to work on these projects. But, at least for now, I'm the team leader, and I say we need to focus on just two things instead of all of the vast possibilities. Bob, you are our bot specialist, but one of the main reasons we brought you here is your innate creativity. You see things much differently than either Cornelium or I do... or any of our other scientists in the Alliance, I daresay.

"But it all comes down to where to place our attention, and I see it that we need to get cozy with the Nanoites. They may have some keys we can use to see this whole thing in a different way. This species is unique in the multiverse, neither humanoid or any other kind of life as we understand it. They are thinking, intelligent beings, scientists and engineers, and somehow they managed to become so and still keep the virtues of a giving and kind heart.

"As far as we can tell, they have managed to be organized without any discernable politics, and they have a strong concern for the preservation of life and the right to choose. The concept of destruction of any kind is anathema to them. These high values mean that preservation and creation are their only goals. They have informed us in no uncertain terms that they will not participate in any action that might harm another being.

"We respect that, and it is something we can work with. The other thing we know about them is that they work well with the Mookookie. Both cultures have similar views, and both want to help rescue those who are under the Inseni thumb. I believe, with the help of the Earth team, we may have come up with their proper role. Adele agrees, and she is currently in contact with both the old ones of the Mookookie and some representatives of the Nanoites.

"This means that although we need to be aware of this project, it is no longer on our proverbial plate."

Cornelium was atypically silent. He was in what Bob recognized as his contemplative state.

"So," Bob put in, "we focus on the Clyde issue and what?"

"We need your creative brain to take a huge leap. I believe the Nanoites can play another important role and you can make that happen. You see, the Nanoites have this unusual ability to be able to see and interpret DNA strands. Unlike you and I and pretty much every other scientist I've ever met, they see DNA like we see someone's face. They recognize the differences between one person's DNA and another.

"I feel like this may be a key to potentially ending this conflict with as few casualties as possible. I honestly can't say why. It seems a big leap, but I wanted to charge your ultra-creative Earth brain and see what falls out."

He grinned an almost evil grin at Bob's stunned expression.

Bob almost uttered the thought that hit him like a thrown brick: *Why me?* but before he could say anything, Merv shot him a wink and said, "Because it's why you're here."

Bob shook his head. Merv couldn't possibly be reading his mind, could he?

...

Liliath stalked down the corridor to her apartment high atop the Dimensional Alliance headquarters building. As she entered her lair, she slammed the door behind her so hard that the paintings on the walls rattled. She was red and purple with rage, and smoke swirled from her nostrils.

She shook her head. She needed to calm down, but that brother of hers would be the death of her, or potentially himself. He had stormed into the council chamber past the protesting receptionist, unannounced, and proceeded to accuse her and her councilors of prejudice and unfair dominion of the Alliance general council.

He had demanded a dimension-wide conference on the grounds that she and her "minions" were forcing the Alliance into a potentially unending and unnecessary war that would accomplish nothing in the end but waste lives and resources.

How dare he? How dare he accuse her of prejudice of any kind? She had spent her entire life teaching and working with beings of every culture across the dimensions. She had devoted all her time and energy to preserving the rights of beings across the multiverse to choose their own lifestyles and cultures. She had seen companions in the cause die from the infringements of those rights.

She sincerely wanted to flame something, but that wouldn't solve anything; and even though her apartments had been flame-proofed, as were all of the draconic apartments in this floor of the complex, she hated giving in to temper when what she needed at the moment was calm logic and presence of mind.

So, instead, she walked to the balcony doors, opened them out onto a view of the city, and launched herself into the air, soaring high above the tallest buildings, over the city streets and out beyond the hill where the headquarters portal stood. The rush of the wind over her wings and the cooler upper atmosphere was indeed calming, and she began to fade from deep reds and purples to her usual greens and blues.

How could she have let his rants upset her so? She had been aware of the minority group in the Alliance that just wanted to be done with the whole Inseni issue. They saw it as finished.

However, while it was true that much of the Inseni government was devastated by Engoza's attacks, they still had strong footholds on planets and in dimensions that were not their own. Reports told her that this was not a benevolent rule, but that the populations of the planets they had invaded were cruelly enslaved and tormented by their captors.

These were nothing but glorified dimensional pirates, focused only on pillaging the planets they conquered and moving on after they had exhausted all the available resources. They sent their slaves to other planets, including their own, to use as forced labor, separating families and grinding them down as effectively as they could.

The Inseni usually chose cultures that were peaceful and unequipped to fight back. Like all bullies, the Inseni never took on a challenge where there was any chance they might come off the worse for it.

As she soared, she noted the two suns, both in the sky at this season. She missed her own planet. The planet that hosted the Dimensional Alliance government headquarters was so very different than her home. She missed the craggy mountains and deep valleys of her homeland and her family and friends.

She smirked. Well, except for Gighil. They had never gotten along. He had hatched long after Liliath was an adult and already preparing for a career in teaching. Somehow, he had taken the fact that Liliath was well-liked and honored by others of her kind for her diligence and intelligence as a challenge rather than an inspiration.

From as early as before he had fledged, he had developed a firm dislike for his older sister and had gone out of his way to demonstrate his disdain. Fortunately for both of them, Liliath had gone on to work with the Alliance, which took her far away from her home world.

Now here she was, dealing with a fully grown, arrogant, and challenging brother during the least convenient time of her career. She would only serve as the Chief Councilor for five years, but it seemed somewhat ironic that after hundreds of years of nearly uninterrupted peace, she would be handed the reins of the Alliance government now.

She glided for a time, riding the currents and continuing to calm herself. She couldn't afford these fits of anger right now. She needed to be calm and in control of her emotions. Where had that control gotten to? She had noticed in the past few years that she no longer seemed to have the continual poise that had typified her work in the past. Was this a sign of age, or was it just that lately the stress had been building ever since Ingot's violent death?

She shook her head and turned back. There was work to be done.

...

Burt and Elizabeth emerged from the Sweden gate into the basement of the Swedish observatory high in the Swiss Alps. Adele was there to greet them, waving for them to follow her to the elevator. They didn't use the elevator much in the observatory, since the sedentary nature of the study of science had its physical drawbacks, so generally, unless in a hurry or transporting something from floor to floor, they took the stairs to the various levels.

Today, however, it was obvious that Adele had something to show them that she was excited about. She didn't speak, which, in and of itself, was unusual.

Burt decided to allow her to hold onto her secret a few moments to give her the opportunity to do a big reveal.

They walked into the main lobby, a brightly lit area with many conversation area groupings of chairs and end tables, designed to give the scientists who worked there a casual place to hold deep discussions about whatever project was in the works.

To his surprise, the room was full, not only with all the scientists working on the various Alliance projects, but also all the Earth gate guardians and the entire observatory staff. In addition, each human was paired with a Mookookie companion, all of whom seemed a bit agitated, as they had all sprouted limbs and were doing some kind of animated dance to music only they could hear.

Adele paused for effect, turning to Burt and Elizabeth.

"We're ready!" she sent at nearly a mental shout of exultation. *"We have twenty Mookookie prepared for duty with an accompanying Nanoite pair! You can begin to send them out as soon as you're ready. Do I remember that you plan to send the first ones out with some of those Inseni going through the Amazon gates?"*

Burt gave a low whistle. *"Wow! That was fast! Do they understand that they are to report to the 'old ones' with coordinates and as much information as they can gather? The Nanoites will gather DNA, soil samples, and any other scientific observations they can obtain? Is it understood?"*

Adele nodded enthusiastically. *"Indeed, and they are excited to be able to explore alien cultures and dimensions. The Mookookie have been given instructions that they will be given a signal to eat as much as they would like at some point and begin to multiply on each planet, with the understanding that when the conflict is over, if the natives don't wish them to stay, they can either return to the Mookookie home world or we will find them a new planet to settle on and multiply as they wish.*

"By the time we are ready to press forward with our strategies, we will have an entire army on every rescue planet, ready to devour the enemy's weaponry and tech. They are also aware that this may mean some casualties on their side, but they are willing to make the sacrifice to save the unfortunates currently enslaved by the Inseni. They bear the Inseni no good will, considering what they did on the Mookookie home world.

"Even then, they refuse to participate in any violent maneuvers, preferring to do their part to protect innocent lives and give us the edge we need to minimize casualties and still eliminate the Inseni threat.

"Their human trainers have worked with them one on one and report that all has been received and understood."

Burt considered this. He was certain there was no perfect solution to this dilemma, but he too, hoped to find ways to remove the threat without significant loss of lives or damage to the various planets the Inseni had invaded. In the meantime, he appreciated the hard work by the entire Earth Alliance guardian community to pitch in on this.

"Congratulations. We will begin part one of the operation this coming week. We need five of the most adept Mookookie and Nanoite pairings to transport with us with Daringi assistance to the Amazon portal, at which time they will be given specific instructions for this part of the plan. This coming week we will be transporting several pairings to the Inseni home world.

"In every case, we need to emphasize that each pair is to report daily to the old ones, who will then report to the Gatekeeper. She alone will determine what information gathered by our spy network is released and to whom. In the meantime, we will likely need more Mookookie-Nanoite teams in the very near future. Please continue your excellent work. I have to say I am very impressed."

Adele practically glowed with this praise. The Mookookie assembled with their trainers danced and cavorted with obvious glee. Burt sighed. He was glad for this little celebration but was all too aware that there would be days of mourning ahead as well, and he did not look forward to that.

One of the benefits of the Mookookie hive mind was that they could communicate with one another across the "spaces" and quickly seemed to pick up languages, both mental and verbal. That is, they understood a verbal language without making an effort to actually speak it. This suited their plan perfectly. The Mookookie were not being sent as ambassadors.

They would use their ability to hide in whatever was close at hand, such as a pant leg, a tabletop, a tree, or a piece of paper. The size, shape, or density of the object didn't seem to matter. This made them the perfect spy, as they were essentially invisible to those around them, but they could still hear conversations both mental and verbal in the vicinity of their hiding place.

The Nanoites would be carried by the Mookookie into whatever hiding place they chose and could, from that vantage point, scan the area around them and not only gather much needed information about the organic beings nearby but also catalog technology, weapons, and communications equipment, with a full analysis of how it worked.

Burt had to smile at that. He knew his friends on the various science teams would be absolutely gaga with all of the new information that would now be available to study. While Burt was also very interested in what he called "sciency stuff," he would leave the in-depth study to the guys in the labs across the dimensions. This always seemed to benefit him in his own work, as it was easy to get the latest gadget right off the assembly line, due to his good graces with the scientists throughout the Alliance.

He often kidded Jenny and Bob about "dastardly alien tech," to the point that they had simplified it down to "DAT", something that usually got a chuckle from those who knew what that was.

"*Okay*," he said to the crowd at large. "*Is it lunchtime yet? I'm starving.*"

This got a laugh, and they all gladly trooped off to the dining hall.

. . .

Tarafau heaved a deep sigh, his arms snugged around his sweet wife, his face buried in her hair. "I will come again when I can," he whispered. "I will be sure to give Jenny your love. Things are about to get very intense, and I may only be able to visit once or twice a week, and sometimes not even that."

"I understand, old cat. Just remember that I don't just miss you. You are my heart. Without you, time passes like the gradual erosion of a boulder."

He looked deep into her eyes, which changed colors depending on her mood. Today they were deep green, the pupils wide and dark as she leaned back to view his entire face, as if memorizing it.

"I think, after we settle this issue with the Alliance, it is time for us to focus on something new. Not sure what, as long as we can be together for a while. Since Burt married Jenny, I have thought that perhaps his skills might be best used as her Guide. It would be appropriate, don't you think?" Tarafau asked with his catlike grin.

Amenia laughed heartily, her rich alto voice that he loved so much filled with joy and mischief.

"This sounds like a nice solution to a pressing problem, my love, but I think we won't see the resolution to this particular issue any time soon. In the meantime, please stay as safe as you can. Even if I can only get you for a few hours at a time, I'll take whatever time is allotted me. I agree that your work with Jenny is essential and, as we consider her a daughter, I am grateful she has such amazing support from you and those the Alliance have given to her. I don't begrudge your commitment to her and to the cause you have espoused. You know that."

He kissed her fervently in response and, with a regretful last hug, faded from her view.

Chapter 21: Revelations and Reflections

Burt was almost painfully aware of Jenny, riding along mentally on this crucial mission. He tried hard not to feel a bit of resentment that she couldn't be here in person. For one thing, he realized she felt a bit isolated from the action, even with her ability to attend mentally. It wasn't quite the same as being in the middle of things. For another, he just missed her... missed holding her hand, hugging her, and being able to look directly into those intense blue eyes as she gazed so very lovingly into his own.

But he wouldn't trade her safety for his own selfish longings, and he certainly felt it was worth a little frustration on her part to keep her safe.

For now, he looked across the clearing at the very visible Inseni troops coming and going from the invisible portal and couldn't suppress a knowing grin. In the night, the flying nanobots had deposited some jungle foliage over the path in and out of the portal, as if it had blown there.

The various Inseni ignored it, trampling across it, to Burt's great satisfaction, as each of the leaves and branches they stepped across or flattened bore Mookookie, who transferred to their boots without anyone noticing. Each time, the Mookookie sent an acknowledgment to Jenny, mentally noting their success.

Burt had to suppress a hoot of triumph as he watched the Inseni carry their little stowaways through the portal with no clue as to what this might lead to or that they had been invaded by the little foreigners. As they had planned, each Mookookie carried a couple of Nanoites along. Between the two creatures, they had the means of not only tracking the Inseni across dimensions, but also over-hearing conversations and analyzing their surroundings through the Nanoites' acute observational skills.

At least this part of the plan seemed to be going off without a hitch. He could only hope that it gave them the edge they would need and the information their scientists required when designing the technology to keep the violence, damage, and potential casualties at a minimum.

He glanced to his right at Elizabeth, who watched the whole procedure with interest and more than a little satisfaction written plainly on her face.

She had been a delightful surprise when Liliath had assigned her as his personal Daringi escort. Only a few agents had the advantage of traveling the dimensions Daringi style, without the use of any gateways or portals, but Burt's active role in the tactics and strategies necessary to oust the Inseni from their strongholds had qualified him for this special dispensation. The fact that she was also Jenny's "adopted" sister only added to his satisfaction.

Elizabeth was devoted to her part in his mission and would do nearly anything to see to Jenny's protection. She was easy to work with, and he never heard her complain about the long hours they put in, traveling all over the dimensions to get the work done.

"Well?" he sent to Jenny and Elizabeth. *"Do you think we're off to a good start? I'm trying to think of what can possibly go wrong and the fact that I can't think of anything is actually a bit worrisome. I don't want to say the typical 'I've got a bad feeling about this,' but I always expect to find a monkey wrench lying around when things appear to go this smoothly."*

Jenny sent a mental chuckle. *"Always the optimist, my Burt. Elizabeth, you might want to give him a kick in the pants for potentially jinxing this operation, would you?"*

Elizabeth sent back with a smirk, *"Actually, I was just thinking the same thing. I've been nearly holding my breath, waiting for something to go wrong."*

In Burt and Elizabeth's mental vision of Jenny, they saw her shaking her head. *"Ganging up on me, you two?"* she sent with a wry twist to her mouth.

"You know we would never do that, sweetheart," Burt sent, putting on his most innocent face.

"Of course not," Elizabeth agreed, rolling her eyes.

"How many do we have left?" Burt asked Jenny, who had been keeping track of the Mookookie spies who had hitchhiked on the various troops coming in and out of the gates.

"We are down to two. Eighteen have already arrived at various destinations. I will be getting a detailed report this evening from the old ones. We should know by morning how successful the various Mookookie-Nanoite teams have been in getting to anyplace significant to our project. We will also discover how detailed the reports will be, remembering that Mookookie communications tend to be fairly simple.

"All of the Nanoites are assembling reports as well and they will transfer their reports to Fagir and Gini, who will then send the information mentally to the Nanoites currently working at Alliance headquarters."

Burt nodded and sighed. *"It's hard not to be impatient with the process,"* he said, looking thoughtful. *"I keep thinking of what I saw on Peril's planet and wishing we could hurry the process somehow. Even so, I suppose the invaded dimensions have been dealing with this for a lot longer than we have known about it. Hurrying will only lead to potential mistakes that may make the situation worse than it already is. I just remember the dead look in the eyes of those children in what the Inseni passed for 'schools' and wish we could move faster."*

Jenny smiled tenderly at her husband. It seemed as if he should be able to reach out and touch her, but he knew better. Nevertheless, he couldn't help but want to hug her close for understanding his dilemma.

"The last two just went through the portal," Jenny announced. *"Is there any reason we need to stay here at the moment? If not, maybe some lunch out on the patio?"*

Burt grinned at the thought. *"What do you think, Elizabeth? Root beer and peanut butter and jelly sandwiches?"*

Elizabeth nodded enthusiastically and placed her hand on his shoulder, and they disappeared from the jungle into Jenny's backyard.

Lizziebot had already headed for the kitchen when they seated themselves on the patio. Tidbit lay lazily observing the koi in the pond while Chidwi crooned in the yew tree above him. Burt loved the little garden area as much as Jenny did and whenever they ate at home together it was usually outside, California weather being what it was. There was generally at least one bodyguard in attendance, but today it looked like they were all there. Evidently, they had been indulging in some type of game similar to badminton but without the net you would expect.

Jenny had done her mental visit with Burt outside today. Burt seldom worried about her safety anymore, except for her potentially exhausting herself with her strict schedule of heading up the communications aspect of the Alliance efforts to eliminate the Inseni threat, along with continuing to educate herself about her normal Gatekeeper duties and expanding her mental abilities.

He continued to be amazed at how she managed to work it all in and not be completely burned out already. He had seldom met anyone with such ferocious tenacity to a task once she had committed herself. It suited him well, as he was also known by his compatriots as tenacious and dependable when assigned a mission.

When he contemplated a hopefully long life together, he had a hard time imagining them as a retired couple. He was pretty sure that if they survived their various duties in the Alliance, they would probably "retire" to Sanglarka to continue their work with the Alliance in a more casual capacity.

But first, there were the Inseni to deal with, and hopefully afterwards they would both be very involved in the more enjoyable aspects of their roles in the Alliance. Burt certainly wasn't averse to an occasional adventure, but this business with the Inseni was stretching it a bit more than he liked, especially when it meant he hardly ever got to spend any time with Jenny.

So, they ate and chatted and afterwards their company—Elizabeth, Jenny's bodyguards, and even Chidwi and Tidbit—somehow almost evaporated into the house to allow Burt and Jenny some private time. They stood before the koi pond under the old yew tree with their arms around one another, not speaking, just looking into one another's eyes for a long time. Finally, Jenny said, "Will it ever be 'normal' for us?"

"I hope not," Burt replied with his usual cocky grin. "We aren't normal at all. We're exceptional. But if you mean do I think we'll ever get to be together like any other couple who are madly in love with one another? I hope so. But will it be the end of adventures and big bumps in the road? I don't think any couple in the multiverse ever gets that kind of normal. That only happens in storybooks, I think."

Jenny sighed and nodded. "You're probably right," she agreed with a reluctance in her voice. "However, if absence makes the heart grow fonder, we are going to be the most loving couple ever. I suppose though, it isn't much different than my mom being married to a career military man. It's just that I miss you so much. Never thought that would ever happen to me."

"Well, at least we have our pond… never need to miss a night there." And he kissed her so fervently her toes wanted to curl.

As they drew apart, a new voice came from the patio doors. "You two at it again?" Bob's voice came across the yard with a chuckle.

They all laughed.

"What are you doing in our neck of the woods?" Burt asked, still keeping one arm firmly around Jenny's waist as they turned to see him striding across the lawn.

"A bit of a breakthrough, and I wanted to tell you in person; and I brought an upgrade for Lizziebot, as we can't afford to send them through the Alliance network until we've figured out how to secure it."

"Oh, really?" Burt replied. "I can stay long enough for you to brief us, and then Elizabeth and I have to skip out to report to Sanglarka and the Sweden gate team. Is it all right to bring the girls all back for your report?"

"Absolutely. Tidbit and Chidwi went to get them. They had retreated to their apartment."

And like a bunch of genies emerging from a lamp, they all appeared framed in the French doors. Burt noted the looks of anticipation on every face. Even the cat had that curious look that only a cat's face can express.

"Well," said Bob, even before all of them could seat themselves around the patio table, "it appears that the Nanoites have the ability to create something out of almost nothing. Remember the science fiction premises that talked about something called a 'replicator'—a machine that could use common materials and assemble them into anything, including food and equipment of various types?

"The theory was that you give it the common atomic building blocks and input your requirements, and out pops the thing you asked for."

Everyone sat up straight in their chairs a picture of anticipation.

Bob held up both hands. "Okay, don't get too excited. It isn't perfect science, and they do have limits, but in theory Nanoites can create a lot from a little in a very short time. We've only tried a few things, but it appears, based on the report by Fagir and Gini, they were able to replicate "Clyde."

I tried to describe a DeLorean, but so far, no luck," he added with an evil laugh. He continued, grinning at the look of total astonishment on every face surrounding him, "it might mean that we have some new options that never came into our calculations before. It is vital, however, that we keep this latest development to ourselves at the moment. Jenny, only let Liliath know. Not even the other scientists should be told, as it would likely distract them from their current projects. Got it?"

They all nodded nearly in unison. Burt could see the wheels turning furiously in every head, and Tidbit's tail was twitching agitatedly, his ears twitching back and forth almost in the same rhythm as his tail.

"The repercussions of this could be vast on both the good and bad side of the spectrum," Jenny commented, shaking her head. I can see it being used for both good and bad purposes. I will definitely not share this with anyone besides Liliath at this point. One thought that occurred to me: How much energy does this take? Do the Nanoites generate it themselves, or does it need an outside power source?"

"Actually, the Nanoites are somewhat confused by that question, Jenny. You see, they consistently draw energy out of the air around them. They consider it an unlimited supply that exists naturally in the cosmos. The idea of running out of energy or having to generate power is a completely alien idea to them."

There was a stunned silence. Then Mynn broke in excitedly. "This has long been theorized by the scientists on my planet, and we know there are beings who actually generate so much electricity in their being that they are somewhat dangerous for other organic life forms to touch them."

Jenny nodded. She remembered one of Lizzie's podmates had been just such a being. Once again, she marveled at the incredible diversity of life in the cosmos.

"So, what does this mean to our mission?" Burt asked, excited by the information but trying hard to keep his focus on the task at hand.

"Well, for one thing, since they already inhabit every one of our MDPs, not only can we count on the supplies we currently store in them, but in future, perhaps not too far into the future, we will be able to have them manufacture things for us at need. It is amazing how fast they were able to re-create Clyde. And that was just a few of them working together.

"If I understood them correctly, it turns out that every single MDP pod is inhabited by billions of Nanoites. They expressed a willingness, on a need-by-need basis, to aid the Alliance in this way and to work with our scientists to determine how best to utilize their talents. Turns out they are ready for what you might call 'new frontiers' for their abilities."

Burt gave a low whistle. "Okay, so that's for the future, as far as I can tell. In the meantime, let's give it some thought as to how this could give us an edge against the Inseni. I was thinking about something in the nature of what we have previously discussed about the Mookookie sabotaging enemy weapons?

"That would prevent casualties, and if the Mookookie were to eat anything the Inseni could do damage with, that might solve a lot of issues. At the same time, we need to be careful not to take advantage of the Nanoites or the Mookookie just to save our own hides. I think we need to give this careful thought and confer with both groups regarding their own willingness to help beyond what they are already doing."

Jenny nodded, and Burt noticed every other head in the group, including Bob's, was also indicating agreement.

"Okay, then, is there anything else I should know before Elizabeth and I head out? What is the Lizziebot upgrade about, and when do I get my own bot?" he asked, not quite kidding.

"Actually, I wanted to talk to you about that," Bob replied with a twinkle in his eyes and a twist to his salt and pepper mustache. "It turns out I've been working on a new iteration of Fidget and Lizziebot, only smaller, with the same power and abilities. What do you think about that?"

"So, where's mine?" Burt shot back.

"Well, actually..." Bob held out his hand, and from his MDP appeared out of apparently thin air a small robot about twice the size of a cellphone that could have been the action-figure version of Fidget.

"Cute." Burt laughed. "So where is it really?"

"No, you don't understand... this *is* the new bot. Rebus, say hello to your new boss."

"Hello, Burt. I understand you are my new employer. How may I serve you today?" The voice that came out of the tiny bot was clear and a deep bass, which contrasted with its tiny size.

Burt's eyes went wide and he held out his hand. The little bot walked confidently onto his palm and looked up at him. "Rebus is it?" Burt said. "Well, Rebus, I suppose you have some features I should know about. Let's have a nice chat after I've had a chance to brief the scientists at Sanglarka and the Sweden gate about the Amazon project, and then we'll go from there."

"Yes, boss. You should know that Bob took me to the Amazon portal with the help of a friendly Daringi from headquarters, and I downloaded all the information from the Amazon patrol bots for use in your presentation. Will that be helpful?"

Burt grinned and grabbed Bob in a hearty hug, one hand still clutching the little bot.

"You never cease to amaze me, you old duffer. I hope you live forever."

He and Bob grinned at one another like a couple of school kids, and Jenny couldn't stop smiling at the two of them.

"Okay, now we really do need to get out of here, Elizabeth, before I start to cry." And he wiped some imaginary tears from his eyes.

She just grinned, hugged Jenny, and placed one hand on Burt's shoulder. Burt never stopped looking at Jenny until she faded from his sight.

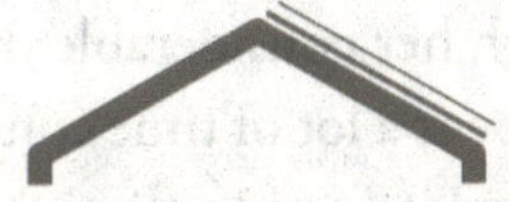

Chapter 22: Between a Dragon and a Hard Place

Tarafau sent another blow directly towards Jenny's head, and she adeptly countered with a loud crack of her staff. Chidwi cheered from her spot against the wall, and Jenny pivoted to intercept a blow from Lyra towards her midriff. In the back of her mind, Jenny could barely hear the clack, clack, clack of the staves of Mynn and Nona. It was two on one today, and Jenny was grateful for the chance to completely disconnect her brain from all the things that had been consuming her lately.

As they exchanged blows in rapid succession, it was all she could do to focus on her two opponents. Lately it seemed things were both speeding up and slowing down. On the one hand, she felt an urgency to bring the Inseni threat to what she hoped was its inevitable conclusion: freedom for the enslaved and a final end to the Inseni's access to other dimensions.

Like the Alliance, she didn't wish to keep the dimensions from being allowed to make their own choices as to how to live, but she drew the line when a dimension attempted to force others to do their will. Like her father, who had always considered his job in the military as about protecting the liberties of the people he defended, Jenny had no thoughts of dominating others or forcing them into her own ideas of right and wrong.

This is why, although her considerable duties as the Gatekeeper were pressing, she still spent a lot of time considering what she could contribute to the Alliance's efforts to eliminate the Inseni threat.

She was well aware that they couldn't solve all of the issues in the multiverse, but this one in particular had such far-reaching consequences that it couldn't be ignored.

But, for now, she was completely absorbed in keeping the two staves from adding to her bruises. She was so focused on what she was doing that it came as a jolt when Tarafau sent, *"Enough!"* to the group.

The clacking ceased, and each rested their quarterstaffs on the floor of the workout room. They had recently removed the makeshift desk from the room, as Clyde was no longer on the premises. The fact that it had been replicated was somehow worrisome to Jenny, as they still weren't entirely sure of its function or what additional threat it might represent.

"Okay, you four, same time tomorrow," Tarafau sent. *"I see some improvement lately in your timing and reaction speed. Tomorrow we will do three on two: Jenny and me versus the three of you. Agreed?"*

Heads nodded, and they exited the workout room into the gate-room. Jenny, with Chidwi crooning happily on her shoulder, looked down at the cat now sauntering into the gate office, his tail upright like a banner behind him. Her bodyguards were at her back. She couldn't help but smile. Even with everything else happening so intensely around her, she was surrounded by caring beings and felt confident that with their help she could accomplish so much more than she had originally thought possible.

As soon as they entered the gate office, they found Burt and Elizabeth standing there. Elizabeth grabbed the cat and hefted the large tabby into her arms and he began to purr that rumbling purr that sent vibrations of contentment towards everyone in the room. *"Hey, Dad. I've missed you. Mom said to give you this hug from her."*

Burt did the same, grabbing Jenny in such a way that seemed to include Chidwi, who crooned agreeably at the gesture. The "girls" stood there grinning and winking at one another. They seemed to find a great deal of delight in seeing Burt's obvious affection for his wife.

"So, we were on our way to visit with the Daringi Council and decided to drop in just for a minute. We've been using Daringi escorts for a while now, and they want to evaluate how far they want to proceed with their involvement in Alliance affairs. There is a minority who are beginning to feel like they have more than fulfilled their initial promises for support and are considering either withdrawing or at least receiving some kind of compensation for their participation.

All in all, it sounds to me like a fair consideration, but I've been assigned to deal with this at the moment. I was wondering if you had any suggestions, Mr. Cuddly Cat."

Tidbit peered intently at Burt to the point that Burt actually began to squirm a little. Jenny loved the repartee between these two. It reminded her of the times she had listened in on the banter between Tarafau and Arvid at Sanglarka.

"Well, my main suggestion is to remember that their concerns are real and the Alliance is known for its fairness in dealing with this sort of thing. As a representative of the Alliance, you know very well that the resources of the Alliance are vast, but that on my world we have no gateways, so it may seem to some that this doesn't really concern us in particular.

"Make sure not to make any hard and fast agreements; rather, take their offer, whatever it may be, into consideration and then take it to the Alliance Council to decide. The beings on my planet are known to be patient; but consider that as we use our ability to escort various agents of the Alliance, it still puts the escort at a certain amount of risk. In

the final analysis, it will be for the majority of our population to decide whether it is worth the risk or not.

"Be sure to give them the facts, as we know them, regarding what the captured dimensions are facing due to the Inseni incursions. I think if you appeal to their better natures, you will find they will be reasonable in their requests."

Burt nodded. "Thanks, Tidbit, I kind of thought you might say that, but I wanted to make sure I didn't miss anything. So, now that we've had our hugs for the day, we'll be off. By the way, Elizabeth has been more help than you can imagine. She has a cool head and continues to remind me that what we are doing affects so much more than we realize sometimes. I wanted to thank you and Amenia for trusting her to her service. She is becoming a very competent and admirable agent."

Elizabeth put her dad, the cat, down with a final pat on his big head, and put one hand on Burt's shoulder; and as they both waved, they faded from sight.

Jenny sighed and turned to her guards. "Okay, it's time for me to get to my meeting with Liliath. Whose turn is it for Jenny watch?"

Lyra raised her hand, and the other two ambled out of the gate office without a backward glance. Evidently there had been a bit of a tiff amongst them, with Lyra in the middle of it. Jenny tried to stay out of these occasional bouts of friction. They were capable of resolving their issues themselves, and it was a lot like siblings, the way they dealt with one another.

Her meeting with Liliath today was basically a ride-along, as she would be present but not visible to anyone but Liliath. The dragon councilor was at issue with her brother Gighil, and she wanted an outside viewpoint, as she felt she was too close to the situation to be unbiased about his position. Jenny would basically be an observer, but even then, the idea of a confrontation between two very opinionated dragons was more than a little scary.

Lyra settled into a chair in the gate office as Tidbit wound himself into a ball onto his cat bed and Chidwi crooned quietly from her usual perch on the back of her chair. Jenny knew that the croon was Chidwi's way of preparing her for the peace that was necessary for producing the REM state that would allow her to mentally cross dimensions.

As she quickly discovered, Jenny's timing was far from perfect. She faded into Liliath's apartment sitting room to hear the dragon screeching, her wings extended and her neck arched towards her brother, who was sprawled negligently in the chaise across from her. Her coloring was reds and purples, and trickles of smoke drifted up from her wide-open nostrils.

If she hadn't known that she wasn't really in the room, her first instinct would have been to run. She took a deep breath, however and timidly called out mentally to the dragon. *"Liliath, are you all right? Should I get help?"*

Liliath shook her huge head, folded her wings to her back and lay back onto her own chaise with a heavy sigh. *"It's okay, Jenny, please stay. My baby brother has already managed to pull my chain, and he is very good at it. I'll try to stay calm and keep to topic. He doesn't know you're here. If for any reason I actually need help, I'll say something like, guard or guarding in a sentence, but I doubt I'm in any danger, other than maybe committing fratricide."* This message took only a couple of seconds to relay, but it did seem to calm Liliath, as she even chuckled softly at her own joke.

"Sister mine, I don't understand why you are so upset. You have to admit the council is a joke by any measure of logic. They follow your lead and give in while they are otherwise thinking things behind your back that would make you cringe.

"Why, just the other day, one of the dwarven reps said... well, I won't repeat it, but the point is that not all your supposed supporters are totally satisfied with the task the council has laid before us. The deple-

tion of time and resources, and the potential risk of lives and perhaps even the security of the entire gate system have to be taken more seriously." The arrogant satisfaction in his voice seemed to be deliberate on his part, attempting to refuel Liliath's angry response.

"You don't think we are taking this seriously? Really? You don't think we haven't taken into account the fact that this system we have been protecting for thousands of years is in danger? That's the one major reason we continue to oppose the Insenium. Even after their main governmental structure has been seriously compromised, it obviously doesn't stop one of these entities who have control over devices that allow them to invade other dimensions outside of our system from compromising our own gate system, which would put every single dimension we represent in potential danger."

"Ah, but Liliath, don't you get it? Many would rather take the risk of fighting the Inseni on their own turf than expending lives and resources pursuing them into alien lands, most of which either aren't members of the Alliance or don't have an Alliance portal on their planet. How do we owe any allegiance to beings in the multiverse we would not have otherwise even known about, if it wasn't for the greed of a small minority in a vast cosmos?

"Put this into some kind of perspective. Are we the guardians of the entire multiverse? How is such a thing even possible? What can you be thinking? I personally think power has gone to your head and you may be no better than the Inseni. You only wish to be in control of what others do and think..."

"YOU GO TOO FAR!" Liliath roared at her brother before he could continue his diatribe. *"How dare you? Do you think I have any desire to pillage, destroy, or harm another soul, regardless of where they live? Do you honestly believe I would risk everything for a few baubles or to enslave another being?"*

Gighil bowed his head, almost looking contrite at her reply. He held up both clawed hands before him as if to shield himself from a physical blow.

"Ah, well, I suppose that was stated somewhat too forcefully. I didn't mean—"

"You didn't mean to call me a tyrant? A besieger? A warmonger? It certainly sounded like that to me." Liliath was seething, mind and body. Jenny had often wondered if dragons could cry, and now she had her answer. Tears streamed down Liliath's face, and her coloring had gone pale as if diluted by her tears.

"I know we haven't spent much time together, as far apart as we were hatched, but I thought you would have known better of me. What motivates your treatment of me? What have I ever said or done that would make you think such things of me?"

Jenny felt somewhat embarrassed to be the witness of this outpouring of emotion between a brother and sister. She had felt close to Liliath during all her training by the beautiful dragon councilor, but not so close as to be listening in on what appeared to be family secrets.

She could feel Chidwi's tiny hands patting her shoulders and knew that the little linkling was doing her part to soothe and comfort her. She squared her shoulders mentally and stayed put, knowing that Liliath could also feel her presence and might take some comfort from her as well.

Gighil rose from his chair, affecting an aura of offended dignity. *"I did not intend to offend, but sometimes the truth is uncomfortable. But I do intend to support those who feel their rights as members of the Dimensional Alliance are being trodden upon. I have presented their case. I assume your answer has not changed. I will return and report. Good day to you, Liliath."*

When Liliath did not reply, he turned and exited the apartment, his tail swishing out of sight as he closed the huge door behind him.

For a few minutes neither Liliath nor Jenny said anything. Finally, Liliath turned to her. *"Well, Jenny? Have your impressions of my brother changed at all? Am I indeed being unreasonable in this thing? Should I handle this differently? I am at a loss. Even if the detractors of the plan to disable the Inseni's ability to invade other dimensions would come to me or communicate their objections in some way that didn't involve my brother, my answer wouldn't change.*

"The majority of Alliance members agree with the council, that we need to take action and sooner than later. Can we afford to let a very vocal minority make our decisions? Can we afford not to take into account the opinions of the minority? Is there any middle ground that would be acceptable to both parties?"

Once again, the dragon sighed heavily, trails of her tears still evident on that scaled face that had become dear to Jenny's heart. Jenny shook her head, grateful that Liliath could see the concern and sympathy on her own face. Even with the clarity afforded by mental speech, nothing really seemed to be able to take the place of facial expressions and body language.

In Liliath's case, it had taken Jenny awhile to learn to interpret emotions in the huge reptilian face and body, but she could see a certain amount of defeat and definite sadness and frustration in her friend and mentor's face and posture.

She wanted to go over and hug her, but she had to keep reminding herself she wasn't really there.

"Well, Liliath, you know how strongly I feel about this whole thing. I've seen only a fraction of what these beings are willing to do to gain dominion and ultimate control of every other world they can get their hands on. For myself, I don't wish to quit until I have done everything within my power to repair the damage they have done to so many. I know you feel the same way.

"Regardless of what you and I believe, what I heard your brother say was that they are all afraid—afraid of loss, afraid of sacrifices they

might have to make, and afraid of making a vast mistake that may affect the gate system and defeat the whole purpose of what the Alliance was organized to perform. I know he was extremely arrogant in his presentation, and his accusatory attitude would have offended pretty much anyone with a heart, but I think he was sincere in his point of view."

Liliath sighed again. *"Jenny, you're probably right. He does believe in what he's saying, but he doesn't seem to grasp the idea that this isn't just about the ethics of helping those downtrodden cultures who have been invaded by the Inseni. It's about saving the thing he claims to hold most dear.*

"I'm pretty sure he would be singing a different tune if the Inseni were attacking our home planet or trying to take over the Alliance gate system, which we believe is their next project. I don't know what else to do but to move forward as we've begun; but I would give much to help him and those he speaks for to see our side of this issue."

Jenny thought about this. *"You know, Burt is on assignment to speak with the Daringi and their fellow beings today as well, regarding a very similar topic. Their outlook is somewhat different, but they still have detractors regarding their own participation in this effort—and for good reason, considering they don't have any kind of portal on their planet, that they are aware of."*

Liliath considered this quietly for a moment, visibly beginning to calm down. Her color had begun to return, and she had wiped the tears from her face.

"I am so glad I invited you to come and witness this, Jenny. Not only did you probably save my brother's life, but you just gave me some perspective on the whole thing. It is hard for me to understand the position of the detractors, but that is why we have a council and not a dictator or emperor of the dimensions.

"If we are going to give people the right to choose how they act, what they believe in, and what they wish for, we must be prepared to not nec-

*essarily agree with the choices they make. Thank you, Jenny. Thank you
so much. You have done a greater service than you can possibly imagine."*

Jenny blushed to the roots of her hair. She still felt more than a
little amazed to find herself in a position of responsibility and respect
from other people, especially considering her age and lack of experience. The praise of beings like Liliath always took her by surprise,
and she had trouble seeing how she could possibly deserve it.

*"I know you have much to do, Gatekeeper. I appreciate your time
when I really needed the support of someone outside of my own consciousness. Those amazing gifts of yours couldn't have come forth at a
more opportune time. Your generosity of using it in such a good cause is
commendable and inspires us all. Speaking of which, your new trainees
are coming along well with Amenia, and she will be turning them over
to you to complete their training next week.*

*"Also, you should know that the first reports have begun to trickle in
from our Mookookie-Nanoite intelligence service, and you may be surprised at what they are already beginning to reveal. But that's for our
regular report later tonight. In the meantime, once again, well done
and thank you."*

Jenny simply nodded and waved goodbye and in an instant, she
was back sitting in her chair in the gate office, Tidbit peering over the
top of the desk expectantly and Chidwi crooning behind her as Lyra
looked up with interest.

"How did it go?" she asked.

Jenny shook her head and barely stopped herself from rolling her
eyes. "I think we need to get together so I can tell you all at once," she
said. "I'm still kind of processing, but there is definitely more to any
of this than it seems."

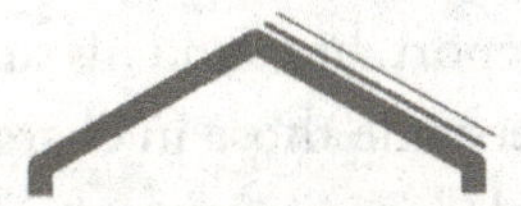

Chapter 23: Intel, Mookookie Style

Glart wasn't having a good day. It had started out well enough. He and his troops had come through that dratted magic portal into the jungle area in... what did they call that pestilential planet? Ert or something? Anyway, they were immediately attacked by an enemy they couldn't see. Some kind of insect that liked to bite. His men were jumping and slapping and itching, and he had a hard time getting them under control to get them back through the portal to their intended destination.

He had no idea why they couldn't go straight from portal to portal, but the protocol said go to Ert, then to your final destination. And if there was one thing Glart did consistently, it was to follow orders.

As instructed, he had returned to report the not-so-great news from his reconnaissance of the current Inseni headquarters, far from their home world. Those who had seized the reins of government after Gall's demise were still terribly disorganized and didn't seem to have a clear plan of how to proceed going forward, something which Glart despised.

Order was his life. Having worked his way up through the ranks as a sergeant of the Inseni army and having spent most of his life in the military, he found himself unimpressed with the civilian leaders who had taken over after the complete disarray of the Inseni government.

Now, returning to report, he found his superiors disdainful of his efforts to attempt to persuade those in charge to turn over the government of his current planet assignment to the general who was currently the acting governor… like he was some kind of diplomat or ambassador with any kind of training? How was it his fault? The dressing down he had received in front of his troops was bad enough, but now his unit was going to be reassigned to some backwater village with nothing to do but stand over the civilians and get them to produce more food.

He had entered the little inn where he frequently ate and drank and found one of his army buddies to commiserate with, knowing that Mink also was having a hard time with the current regime.

"Who's the big boss now?" Mink asked, looking curiously at his friend, who seemed to be dancing in his chair.

Glart couldn't stop scratching the itch from those pesky bugs and didn't much enjoy his meal as his companion was as gloomy as he was, but it was comforting to know he wasn't alone in his disgruntlement. They spoke at length about their last assignments and the details that only a fellow military man could appreciate.

"I'm not sure any one of the hare-brained fiddlesticks in the command center has any idea of what's going on or what to do about it. They keep sending me to different places, only to get back twaddle like 'Carry on' or 'You have your orders.' I bring back those messages and get torn into shreds in front of my troops. If they're so blasted sure they can get a different answer, I'd be more than happy to escort them wherever they'd like to get the answers from, in person. In the meantime, looks like me and my troops are out of it for now. I don't expect to see you again any time soon."

Glart's disgruntled face faded from Burt's sight, and once again he was seated next to Jenny at their mental escape near the little pond on the Merced. Before them perched three of the Mookookie old ones who had just ceased to transmit this snatch of conversation from the Mookookie stationed in Glart's boots. Bob and Merv were also attending via Jenny's talent from Cornelium's lab.

Burt had known that his little nanobot 'bugs' wouldn't transmit across the dimensions, but they had proven a handy distraction as each group of Inseni had emerged out of the Amazon portal, assembling themselves as they prepared to go back through to their next destination. It was all he could do not to laugh out loud from his shelter beyond the clearing when the Inseni began to dance, swatting at something they couldn't see, while the assigned Mookookie had clambered easily into Glart's boot.

"We seem to see a pattern here," said Finny, the largest of the three Mookookie, *"don't you think?"*

"Indeed, Finny," Burt sent. *"Every one of your reports has shown some definite disarray; and yet there seems to be more going on than even the ranks of the Inseni understand. This smells too much to me like there is someone pulling the strings who does not wish to be revealed. I'm guessing they are concerned about what happened to the last big boss of the Inseni and are trying to avoid a future recurrence of that rather nasty incident. I don't necessarily care for Sam's methods, but you have to admit they were effective. We're hoping to avoid that kind of carnage probably as much as the current Inseni mastermind does."* And Burt squeezed Jenny's hand, forgetting she couldn't feel his touch in this place.

Jenny nodded somberly. She tried not to think about Sam as much as possible. Though she had forgiven Sam, the hurt of that betrayal might never fully go away.

"So do we continue this fact gathering mission, or do we move to the next stage?" Bob cut in. *"I think it will be important to keep a flow of information coming in, but by the same token, I don't think we are getting as much out of this as we'd like. We did manage to get one of the Nanoites into the latest iteration of the portal navigation devices yesterday, and we expect a report at our next meeting tomorrow night. How-*

ever, getting the military grunts of the Inseni near any sensitive equipment is proving to be more difficult than we had assumed."

Merv nodded. It felt a little weird to Jenny to have such a crowd in what she considered hers and Burt's special place, but it was one place that few people knew about, and she was still more than a little paranoid about being overheard during these crucial conversations. The last thing they needed at this point was to 'blow their cover,' so to speak.

"You know, mate, don't you think we can continue the current surveillance and begin project 'where's my stuff?' If we can get enough Mookookie safely through the known portals and things just started to go missing among the Inseni elite under circumstances that would not make them suspect their slaves, wouldn't that create enough of a distraction to shake them up more than a little? Especially if we could do it in a way to shed suspicion on their fellows?"

"Or even better," Bob agreed, with a deliberate smirk in Merv's direction, *"if they thought it was 'magic' of some kind?"*

Everyone but the Mookookie elders laughed. Which really wasn't surprising, as the concept of magic was foreign to them. They were generally good humored, but they found more fun in slapstick than in any kind of subtle joke.

"That will require a lot more involvement on the part of the Mookookie." Burt said seriously, looking significantly at the Mookookie elders sitting calmly before them. *"Are you sure you are willing to undertake the risk? Even though it will not involve any violence on your parts, there is some potential at some point that one of our Mookookie friends will be caught munching on something crucial to the Inseni cause, and you know they won't take it lightly."*

"As you say, there is some risk," conceded Finny somberly. It seemed odd to see the Mookookie so serious, as Burt generally considered them cheerful and somewhat clueless about the seriousness of some things.

"That has been taken into consideration. However, we feel deeply for the sorrow and difficulty of those who have been oppressed by these Inseni. If the Inseni would stay within their own domain, they could do as they will. Nevertheless, as they continue to seek dominance and enslavement of others, we will not retreat from helping the Alliance to remove this serious threat.

"Therefore, at your signal, we will gladly send the message for the Mookookie currently stationed on the various planets to begin to consume everything that could be essential to the Inseni plans without harming the native population. Will that suffice?"

Four heads nodded solemnly in unison. *"Thank you,"* Jenny replied simply. *"We have no way to express how grateful we are for your help. This means we can begin to plan the next stage. Bob, how are we coming on the improved nanobots project?"*

As the four humans continued their discussion, the Mookookie elders faded from view. Jenny was only beginning to realize how far they had come in these few minutes and how far they yet had to go.

Chapter 24: About Those Bots...

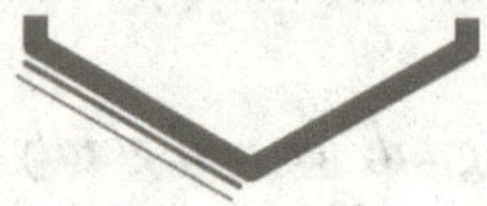

B ob sighed. "Fidget! Where are you?" he called in frustration.

The little bot had recently taken to circulating within the confines of the lab, apparently deep in conversation with the Nanoites that now resided in his robotic body. It seemed to be the robot version of a human pacing in thought.

"I'm here, boss!" Fidget replied. "What can I help you with?"

"The new production line of nanobots is ready, and I'm going to the production facility to receive them into my MDP. The question is, will there be enough Nanoites within the MDP to populate the Nanobots without leaving the Nanoites in my MDP shorthanded? And do we have those coordinates for the intended destinations yet? Burt wants to send them through to the conquered Inseni planets during the next quiet phase of the Amazon portal."

For only a moment Fidget paused, and Bob knew he was consulting with his resident Nanoites. "Yes, boss. All is in readiness. The Nanoites reiterate that all commands are available for the bots, as long as they do not involve any violent actions on the part of these nanobots or the Nanoites residing in them. They only await the coordinates that Burt will download to them based on the reports currently in the hands of the Sanglarka team."

Bob nodded. "Of course. The whole purpose of the Nanoites' involvement is to prevent having to use violence. They will provide instantaneous undetectable communication across dimensions that will be irreplaceable if we are to carry this off with the least possible

228

damage or casualties. I cannot, however, guarantee, as we have said, that no violence will be aimed at the Nanoites or any of the others engaged in this plan by the Inseni. It is the risk we all take to rid the multiverse of this threat."

Fidget nodded, a mannerism he had acquired after so many hours of human interaction. Bob had to grin at that. Every day, this bot seemed to take on more characteristics that implied intelligent life. He actually found himself wondering if there was more to this construct of metal and plastic than he had originally designed into it. Regardless, Fidget was a pleasant companion, and so useful in his work.

Actually, had it not been for Fidget, they might have never made contact with the Nanoites, who were proving to be very useful and willing to aid the Alliance in their current dilemma.

"Well, then, we have a dragon waiting for us to take us to the gate." He held out his MDP, and Fidget faded into it like a crumpled aluminum soda can.

The dragon waiting for him at the entrance to the castle was a young dragon he had flown with before, already equipped with the seat and straps that kept passengers safe. Festal was nearly white, with blue undertones, and not nearly as large as Cornelium, though perfectly capable of flying a puny human to his destination.

The diversity of the draconic species on this planet never ceased to amaze Bob. Some were as small as crocodiles of Earth, and many were nearly the size of a cruise ship. They lived in all the different climates, and even in the oceans of this world.

At one point, Cornelium, responding to Bob's curiosity about dragon-kind, had taken him on a three-day excursion to visit dragons in all their various environments.

He had delighted in Bob's pleasure and awe, and their own relationship had deepened as Cornelium expressed in return his own appreciation for the incredible diversity of humanoids in the multiverse, and especially how much easier it was to work with them than he had ever expected.

"How long do you think you will be?" Festal inquired congenially as Bob mounted below the shoulders between the nearly translucent white and blue wings.

"I don't expect it to take more than an hour, by the time we speak with the foreman, and Fidget and his Nanoites verify that the specifications were met. Adding them to the MDP takes almost no time. I don't want you to have to wait around for me, however. I will send a message via the network to Anela when we are ready to return. Will that work for you?"

"That will be fine, Bob. Although, I must say, I do enjoy the view from the gate, and it is a good place to just sit and think," Festal replied as they landed by the gate.

The trip adragonback was a short one and pleasant, now that Bob had gotten used to traveling this way. He dismounted and headed directly into the portal, not waiting for Festal to take his leave, as the wind from his wings could be a little unbalancing in the tight quarters of the ledge whereon this particular portal resided.

Bob pondered anew the questions he continued to have about what caused the various gateways to appear wherever they were on any given planet, or even out in space in the dimensions represented by the Alliance gate network. They obviously weren't unique in the multiverse, as evidenced by the portals now being used by the Inseni to plunder and ravage dimensions the Alliance hadn't even been aware of, up until the last hundred years or so.

But his thoughts were cut short as he emerged from the dimensional gate near the city, where the robotic factory was currently churning out various sizes and types of robots for the Alliance, all based on Bob's design. In no way could he have been able to do a project of this size on Earth. The price alone would have been prohibitive, not to mention the resources it would have taken to produce bots at this level and in this quantity.

As had been arranged in advance, a vehicle was waiting for him at the gate to take him to the factory site. The foreman and chief engineer was a mostly humanoid being, somewhat violet in color with an extra eye where an Earthling would have had a nose, with nostrils on either side of the eye. His name was Quix, and his smile seemed almost a fixture on his broad face.

"Your order awaits in the outer courtyard. Did you also wish to pick up the defense droids while you are here?" he sent jovially.

"Actually, Burt will be here with a team to pick up that order sometime in the next day cycle. I'd love to look at them, however, before I stow the Nanobots."

Quix nodded and led the way into a large storage room with what could have been described as a formation of military troops. Close to a thousand bots in each section, they were about four feet tall and were arranged in ranks, shining with the newness of having just come off the production line.

"By the way, those Mookookie who you sent us are working out well. They have allowed us to increase our production and reduce production time significantly. Many of them recently approached us to request they be allowed to colonize here. They seem to really enjoy the work, and they have taken care of our disposal issues. Whenever there is excess or anything that we would have previously thrown into a dump or had to recycle, now the Mookookie gobble it up."

"You are aware, Quix, that when you feed them over a certain amount, they will multiply?" Bob asked, concerned for the consequences that might imply to this world.

"We are aware and have counseled with them. The current arrangement is that they will keep their numbers to what we have both agreed upon as a manageable level. If anything, a large population of Mookookie will be very useful. They have already agreed to become part

of our waste management team for this area and potentially for the entire planet."

Bob considered this. It was good to see this working out so well for them here. It had occurred to him more than once how useful the Mookookie could be on Earth. Only his agreement with the Alliance as a qualified agent kept him from bringing not only the Mookookie but also several useful types of tech home with him for Earth scientists to replicate. It was one of the hardest parts of what he currently did, keeping all of that to himself.

"This lot looks very nice indeed. Did we add the camouflage programming routines to their software? They're beautiful as they are, but they might stand out in a combat situation."

Quix puffed out his chest in pride at those words. *"Indeed, as beautiful as they are, we did as requested. The bots should be able to blend into nearly any surroundings, with the exception of a complex moving environment such as a city street, and even then, we can make them less obtrusive by toning down the current bright white of their outer skin."*

"Sounds good. It has been a pleasure to work with you. The Alliance council has instructed me to tell you that the requested supplies and personnel will be delivered in the next moon cycle to reimburse you for your time, trouble, and willingness to serve. Of course, if there is anything else you need, you only need to ask."

Quix nodded and gestured for Bob to follow him out to the courtyard, which at first glance appeared to be unoccupied. However, when Bob squinted, he could see the slight shimmer in the air that indicated the presence of thousands of tiny bots hanging in the air around him. Each of these bots not only had been programmed to follow the commands of the Nanoites that would inhabit them as soon as they were installed into Bob's MDP, but also could respond to mindspeech by authorized Alliance members. Only a select few of the various tactical teams who were in the know about this project would be given that authorization.

Now, Bob sent his command to the apparently empty air around him and the shimmer increased as the Nanobots dutifully presented themselves to be ingested into Bob's MDP. When he sensed they had all entered the miraculous little black band around his wrist, he disguised the band once again with the little flesh-like sleeve that covered it.

Burt had given the Alliance scientists the idea to create these little flesh-like coverings early on in his duties as an agent, and they had since adopted them for every Alliance agent, creating them in a variety of sizes and flesh colors, as well as for gate guardians who worked among those who would not understand the meaning or the function of the MDP bracelet.

The bracelet itself was unobtrusive and had the ability to make people want to not look at it if they didn't know what it was; but some people with especially strong minds could still notice it. This was just one more little bit of security evinced over time by unfortunate experiences of agents over the centuries.

Merv had once told a tale of his time when he was Merlin of old Earth and how the bracelet had almost gotten him in trouble. Fortunately, he had been able to just put it down to the "magic" of a powerful "wizard" and thereafter wore long sleeves under his wizard's robes to cover the little device. This had only seemed to add to his reputation as a wizard of powerful magical means, not something that most agents could use in their own roles as ambassadors and diplomats on worlds unaware of the Dimensional Alliance and their work.

"Thank you so much, Quix. And now I must be off. I look forward to taking the new battle droids for a spin as soon as Burt picks them up. We're hoping that what we're doing with the Nanobots will mean we won't have to use most of their most impressive battle skills, but for now we aren't taking any chances. We need to have both sides of our tactics

covered in such a way as to hopefully ensure success and free those people as soon as may be."

"*We wish you good fortune in that endeavor,*" Quix sent back solemnly, for once his smile not apparent. "*No being should have to endure the dominance of another. Within the constraints of an individual dimension, it is necessary to have each see to its own affairs, but when it comes to one dimension's having the ability to reach into another to pillage, destroy, and enslave, at that point we must support whatever measures are necessary to stop that before it becomes commonplace.*

"*Perhaps we will come up with technology not only to locate these unusual portals but also to guard them against intrusion by unwanted visitors? Put your amazing Earthling mind to that for us, will you?*"

Bob chuckled. "*I appreciate your confidence in my abilities, Quix. I'll keep thinking about it, I promise.*"

With that, he exited to find the waiting taxi that took him back to the gate. It still amazed him that the little black band on his wrist could potentially hold the solution to a dimension-wide issue. It seemed like it should somehow be weighing down his arm like an anvil or large boulder. That was a thought for another time, but for now, he had work to do.

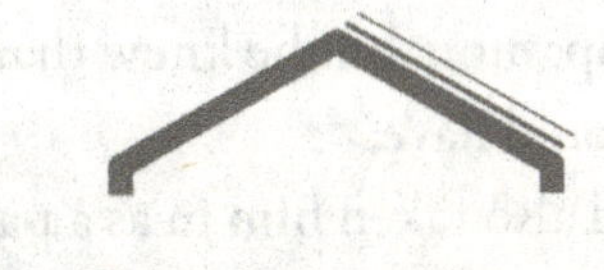

Chapter 25: War Games

Burt walked out onto the huge courtyard behind the Switzerland observatory, trailed by Elizabeth, as he paced along the rows of waiting bots. For now, they were resting like an army at attention before an inspection, until the "war games" they would be putting on in the valley just below the observatory began. The objective was to put them up against troops in mock combat in various terrains to test their ability to do covert operations as well as to counteract any war tech the Alliance was currently aware of that might be used against them in the coming conflict.

Later today, Bob would be joining him to double-check all the potential programming issues and run them through their paces outside of a combat situation.

He glanced over his shoulder to look at Elizabeth. As usual, she was focused on the task at hand, gazing thoughtfully at the ranks of bots before them, no doubt mentally going through their earlier briefing. She knew that Jenny would be doing a "ride-along" several times over the next couple of days, and she had already expressed her relief that Jenny wouldn't be exposed to any potential danger in the process.

Burt loved Elizabeth's devotion to his wife. He hadn't had much of an opportunity to spend time with Jenny's natural family, but if he could have chosen a sister-in-law, he couldn't have found a better one than Elizabeth. She was not only smart, fun to be around, and a reliable and dedicated companion, but he knew that she treasured Jenny as much as any sister would have.

Tarafau's family had also taken him in as a part of the family after Burt and Jenny had gotten married. Jenny's parents had accepted him kindly as well. For the first time in many years, Burt felt like he was part of something more than just the career that had basically chosen him, rather than the other way around.

Now, as he scanned the ranks of waiting bots, he realized that there was so much more at stake for him in this mission. He had never felt more determined or dedicated to a cause than he felt at this time. For him, this was not only vital to the cause of freedom, but he had the strong impression that it was more crucial for Earth than they had previously thought.

"Do we know which units of troopers will be attending our tests today?" Elizabeth sent. Although her English had been improving immensely, she was still a bit shy about vocal speech, as one of "the girls" had joshed with her about her accent. Not that they had any room to tease; most of them had adopted an indistinct Southern drawl to compensate for their own accents.

"I think Gariel is heading up the same group that came through for the Amazon expedition. I think he figures they are more used to Earth gravity and would have the best chance of giving the bots a realistic evaluation." Burt replied. *"Personally, I think anything we put them through here on Earth will be somewhat inexact, regardless, since we have no idea of the final conditions they will be dealing with."*

"I heard they even have underwater capabilities," Elizabeth sent with some enthusiasm. *"Do you think the Inseni have invaded any of the water planets?"*

"Hard to say. I'm still trying to figure out why they started doing this in the first place. The Inseni planet, as I understand it, is plentiful in resources, and they haven't even begun to expand the population so

far as to overrun the amount of arable and sustainable land on their planet."

"My dad says it's just plain and simple greed for power and domination. Evidently their leaders are so aggressive and so full of themselves that they think the entire multiverse should be under their watchful eye. I don't understand the idea of 'enough' not being 'enough' for some beings."

Burt nodded. *"We have similar problems on Earth and have had for centuries. I really don't get it myself, either. I do understand the desire to explore and the driving force of curiosity, but that doesn't require you to 'own' something or someone; it's just about seeing what's out there."*

Elizabeth nodded, but Burt could tell she was still more than a little confused. He didn't blame her. As much as he loved exploring and being engaged in a lot of interesting and different cultures, he still couldn't understand why anyone would want to take away what someone else had or believed and attempt to replace it with their own idea of what was normal or right.

True, he didn't always agree with the way things were done in places he went, and sometimes he was so grateful to get away from a place or group of people because they made him feel uncomfortable or even angry sometimes; but when it came down to it, he agreed with the Alliance philosophy of "live and let live," and he was willing to do whatever was needed, to defend the rights of people to live as they chose or believe what they wished to believe.

Besides, he thought, the cosmos would be an infinitely boring place if everyone was the same and every place you went seemed like a clone of the place and people you had just left. As it was, Burt's life up until now had been one surprise after another, including meeting Jenny and finding his heart of hearts.

The bots glistened in the light enfolding the Swiss Alps, reflecting into one another, as if to multiply them before his eyes. He began to see how such a force could be employed by their enemies as well as them and wondered how they might respond. Fortunately for the Alliance, the Inseni had never been technologically advanced or interested in the sciences, considering it all just hocus pocus by their supposed "wizards," people they had captured and enslaved due to their accidental discovery of portals.

For now, this worked in the Alliance's favor, but the big question was, how would it affect the cultures of those they were trying to free from the Inseni enslavement? The Alliance was dead set against technological pollution of a culture, but these various cultures, regardless of their current tech could be exposed, in the process of freeing them, to tech far above their current reach.

The one thing Burt had noticed seemed to be common to most cultures was curiosity, as well as the desire to make things easier in their lives. This was a drawback when these cultures were exposed before they were ready to technology that would spark that curiosity.

He sighed. There was nothing to be done for it. The fact was that the only way they would be able to significantly reduce casualties and destruction in ousting the Inseni from their current strongholds would be through using tactics that hadn't been used before, and that would mean that from time to time those the Inseni held captive might be exposed to technology they weren't ready for.

"Worried?" Elizabeth inquired, nodding towards the ranks of waiting bots. *"I am sure they will perform well. Our techs and scientists have come so much farther in this process than we ever imagined they would. Of course, robots and cybernetics aren't truly new tech, but, if I understood our briefing correctly, these will do things we've never considered possible for a robot to do, and this has the potential to save so many lives."*

Burt nodded, realizing that Elizabeth was right. Until they tested these, even in mock combat, they couldn't be certain of their success, but they were the best chance they had at this point. Most of the Alliance members had no idea any of this was happening in preparation for the upcoming conflict, but those in the know seemed relieved that there might be an alternative to outright physical combat.

Resigned, he asked, *"Do we have the operators standing by?"*

"All is ready. The troopers should arrive momentarily and will send us a signal once they are dispersed throughout the designated area."

In one of the labs of the observatory, a similar troop of Alliance agents were seated with headsets specifically designed to allow them to see through the eyes of the bots they were assigned to. This was a different type of army, their bodies not in danger even when immersed in combat. They had been practicing and rehearsing with smaller versions of the bots for the last few weeks. All these agents were experienced in hand-to-hand and armed combat; and they ranged all over the spectrum, as far as their origins were concerned.

Any Earthling other than Alliance members, peering into that lab would be astounded at the diversity of color, size and physical attributes of those assembled here in the awe-inspiring backdrop of the Swiss Alps, far away from any Earthly village. When you considered you had to take a 45-minute helicopter ride from the nearest village to get there, as there were no roads leading to the observatory, it was rather unlikely that that would happen, however.

"So now, we wait," Burt sent to Elizabeth. He hated waiting. It was his least favorite thing in the multiverse.

. . .

"Hurry! The show is about to start!" Mynn said excitedly to the rest, making little shooing motions at them to herd them into the gate office.

Jenny couldn't help but laugh. More than any of her three bodyguards, Mynn had been the most anxious about this, not wanting to miss a single thing. Jenny was about to take them all 'riding along' mentally to the "war games" Burt and the team at the Swiss observatory had put together for their new robot army.

Actually, Mynn had taken to calling it the "anti-army," as its entire purpose was to reduce potential casualties to as close to zero as possible. Up until now, in the history of war in nearly every culture in the multiverse, the entire purpose of war was to do as much damage as possible to the opposing forces. This experiment took every bit of technology they could harvest from among the Alliance member dimensions to put together a force that was designed to save the lives of both sides of the conflict, with the greatest emphasis on eliminating civilian casualties.

It never ceased to amaze Jenny how just looking at an issue from a completely different point of view could alter all the potential outcomes so significantly.

They entered the gate office and seated themselves, Chidwi on the back of Jenny's office chair, Tidbit in his comfy cat bed, and the three bodyguards nearby. Jenny noticed none of them except Tidbit and Chidwi appeared to be at ease. Each of the women she depended upon for her safety and security was perched at the edge of her seat in anticipation. Jenny herself had to admit she was also both anxious and excited to see what would happen next.

She leaned back into the office chair that had been designed by Alliance techs to be not only supportive but also comfortable and relaxing. This was where Jenny did a large part of her work for the Alliance. She placed both hands on her lap in a relaxed position and nodded to the girls, who responded by leaning back more comfortably in their own chairs and assuming a more relaxed position to allow themselves to be included in what Jenny would do next.

In her mind she thought of Burt and Elizabeth, bringing everyone in the gate office into her protective thoughts. Nearly immediately, they were no longer seated in the office. Standing in a tight grouping, they were now looking out over what appeared to be a sea of robots, Burt and Elizabeth standing before them with big grins on their faces.

"Glad you could join us," Burt said, his eyes soft and relaxed as he looked into Jenny's across the thousands of miles that separated them in the flesh.

"Happy to be here. Good to see you, Elizabeth. Are we ready?"

Elizabeth nodded happily. "We just got the 'all-clear' from the troopers who are now set in their various hiding places, and the battle techs just acknowledged that signal. We will see the bots begin to disperse any moment now."

And sure enough, she had hardly gotten the words out of her mouth when the first rank of bots rose into the air, followed rank on rank by over half of the assembled robots.

"The second half will wait and disperse only as needed. We are trying to determine the ratio of bot to potential enemy troops to see how many we will actually need to employ in combat."

Burt invoked a large transparent screen from his MDP. "We will be able to track much of the action via the screen. The battle tech commander will be switching viewpoints on the screen based on what the bots are actually seeing. One of the new advances is that this software allows the screen to combine several bots' perspectives into one scene. This gives us an overall view of the battleground but also allows the battle commander to switch to a more detailed or close-up view of what one bot may be experiencing."

Jenny couldn't help but be impressed. She remembered Sam telling her about how a director worked in the television control room where she had worked before revealing her true nature as Engoza. Switching from one camera viewpoint to another was done under the instruction of the director to the switcher. It required every person in the control room to be constantly on their toes to avoid switching to an unprepared or bad shot.

In this case, there was no switcher. It was entirely at the discretion of the battle commander, requiring him or her to only think what he wanted to look at and it was done. This particular innovation was a direct result of what Jenny had described of her mental excursions and how it worked for her.

This entire battle system was completely controlled by the thoughts of each of the participants. Orders were relayed via mindspeech from the overall Battle Commander and then implemented via mindspeech directly from the individual battle techs to their assigned robot. This was similar to real soldiers taking their orders from a general or sergeant without any risk to the human operator of the bot.

Amenia had been directly involved in this project through Tarafau, thanks to the insights she had gained by working with Jenny on her breakthroughs. Jenny wasn't sure how far this would go within the Alliance, but it was now true that the 'cat was out of the bag' where this particular talent was concerned.

The entire Alliance communications network had been reimagined, and the young women Jenny had initially trained with Amenia's help had gone on to become trainers themselves. They no longer needed to access this gift through Jenny's little communications office in her own mind village, but they had used the principles involved to become official communications specialists in this new secure way to transmit information.

None of them had known while Jenny had been exploring her own mental talents that it would lead to this. They still used the original Alliance communications network for mundane communications and any "red herrings" they wanted to toss in the direction of any potential Inseni spies; but for anything that remotely required any security, it was standard practice to use the mental network instead.

As the bots rose into the air, the view on the screen changed to show the dense forests surrounding the observatory. The building itself was built into the side of the granite mountain, but beyond the community that encircled the observatory, including some farmlands, pastures, and homes, were dense forests with no established paths within them.

This is where the Alliance troopers had chosen to do the first test of the bots in combat. The troopers had been armed with special virtual blasters that were a lot like the weapons used in a game of laser tag. They also wore sensors to indicate scored hits by the bot for a human. They couldn't inflict any actual damage, but hits would be registered by the bots; and a certain amount of virtual damage would indicate that the bot hit had been virtually destroyed or disabled, and it would return to the observatory.

The view now shifted to what was being seen from the back ranks. They could see the bots in the front moving towards the forest as they had been commanded. Beyond them, the deep blue sky was punctuated with a few fluffy white clouds, a beautiful contrast. They were flying away from the sun, so the bright light reflected from the backs of the bots ahead of them.

Suddenly every one of the bots faded from view.

"Did they actually disappear? Was this supposed to happen?" Jenny asked incredulously. "One minute they were there—"

Burt laughed delightedly. "Exactly what was supposed to happen. No. They are still there, not disappeared or transported somewhere else, simply camouflaged to take on the scene in front of them. For all intents and purposes, they are invisible.

"Now they will attempt to infiltrate the forest. The next steps will be a lot like laser tag. The troopers will get points for any bots they hit, and the same for the bots hitting the troopers. And take note, none of these bots have Nanoites in them. These bots were designed for combat. Second note, they have weapons that allow them to stun instead of kill, courtesy of Alliance dastardly alien tech," he concluded with what Jenny could only describe as an evil grin.

On the air screen, the forest continued to loom closer. Jenny noted that the bots were completely silent in their flight, no sounds of whirring or any engines one would normally associate with mechanical flight, such as an airplane or drone.

They reached the trees; and for only a moment, Jenny could see the outlines of a few of them as they transitioned in their camouflage from sky colors to the appearance of leaves and branches. If she looked really hard, she could discern the difference between them and the actual trees, but only barely. To someone not expecting them, they would be relatively invisible; and even for those who knew they were there, they would be very difficult to spot, especially when they moved so noiselessly and appeared to be very good at avoiding anything that might cause a rustle, such as a tree branch.

The view shifted again to an individual bot that had spotted a trooper. The troopers were also in camouflage gear designed for a forest environment. The trooper in question had a blaster in hand and was peering around himself intently. Suddenly, with no sound Jenny could discern, a light went off that had been placed on one shoulder of the uniform. The trooper immediately raised his hands in surrender and sat upon the ground.

"Bots 1, Troopers 0!" pronounced Burt triumphantly, his hands over his head like the signal for a touchdown in football. "Notice we have a scoreboard on the screen, so that even without being able to see each hit, we can see how we're doing."

Sure enough, in the lower right-hand corner of the screen was a running tally. And even as Burt said this, the toll rose to four troopers tagged and only one drone. The after report by the troopers from their point of view would be interesting. Jenny wondered if the score against a bot was intentional or just a trooper randomly firing into the air. It occurred to her that this could be a tactic ground troops might choose to use against the bots, so there was still a chance the bots could be downed.

The numbers continued to change on the screen, and the viewpoint shifted back and forth between individual bots or back from a farther viewpoint. "What happens if a bot is actually downed by the enemy; couldn't that be a security risk?" she asked. "A captured bot could give the enemy a lot more information than we'd like."

"Ah, good point," Bob conceded. Jenny was startled; she hadn't noticed he had arrived, since she was so focused on the action in front of her. "We did actually think of that as we conferred with Gariel. All the bots are equipped with a self-destruct mechanism that will explode the internal programming mechanism and fry all the circuits in the bot if ever they are downed by enemy fire. The only thing left will be a husk, with no clue as to how it operates."

Jenny nodded, continuing to marvel at the thought and energy that had gone into these inventions. She knew she could only begin to comprehend all the scientific principles that went into their creation, not to mention the imagination and just flat out hard work the scientists had to have put into it to come even close to this final product.

Over the next hour or so, nearly every trooper had been located and tagged, mostly due to body heat sensors in the robots, but only four out of the fifty bots that had been sent out had been compromised in any way. Communications from the troopers indicated that none of them were harmed, but they sheepishly had to admit that in an actual combat situation they would have been completely defeated.

It also brought up questions as to whether perhaps Bob and the rest of the scientists could come up with a blocking mechanism that would prevent the enemy from detecting the troopers based on body heat. After all, it was likely the troopers would be confronting enemy troops themselves, and they didn't want to be subject to this issue in real combat.

At some point, when all but a handful of the hundred troopers were tagged, the general called a halt and sent out a call for all troopers to return to headquarters to discuss the outcome and work on tactics from both sides as to what would happen next.

The bots rose from the forest in company, now visible and in perfect formation, and returned to the observatory as if they had just been out in the forest gathering mushrooms—not a scratch or a dent or anything to indicate any damage, even in the few bots who had actually been tagged by the troopers.

Bob was practically strutting as they all entered the observatory entryway to enthusiastic applause by all the participants. Jenny knew that at this point they would all retire to the dining hall for a celebration, and she sighed. Those feasts were always so much fun, and she was only basically there "in spirit." Ah, well, she knew that there would be banquets in the future; but for now, she bade them all farewell and left them to their discussions about tactics and what Burt called "sciency stuff." She had to get back to her part in all of this, and as the observatory faded from her view, she prepared her mind to report to Liliath.

Chapter 26: When a Plan Comes Together

"What do you mean, 'It's gone'? It was right here, just last night! I put it there myself!"

Regil wanted to cover her ears but knew it would just get her into more trouble. As the assistant to the commandant of this base, she was used to his rants, but this was beyond anything she had witnessed before. The huge Inseni captain was livid, the one huge eye in the middle of his forehead nearly bulging out of his skull, and he was nearly purple with rage.

"Get me the guard! He must have been asleep on duty again! I'll have his hide!"

Regil rushed to obey, especially if it meant she could get out of his sight and his reach, as he appeared to be ready to grab anything he could find and start throwing things.

The item in question had been his favorite club, embedded with spikes, with a leather encased grip and wrist strap. He generally used it for show when he went to review the troops, and today he had scheduled them for a huge showing, the entire brigade. He was about to announce a further incursion into the depths of the jungle that surrounded their current encampment. This planet had been given to his brigade because of his soldiers' reputation for strength and cunning, but the natives of the surrounding jungle had been significantly less malleable than those in the coastal areas.

Their constant raids into Inseni secured territory were a huge irritant and were hindering their dominance.

Now that they were disconnected from the main Inseni nation due to the recent disaster on the Inseni home world, Ingold had decided that they would make the most of the situation by establishing his very own dominion, basically becoming more than a simple commandant, but inevitably the ruler of this entire world.

He stalked around his makeshift office, established early on when they had first conquered this dimension. The club simply was nowhere to be found. It was highly symbolic of his authority, and someone was going to pay for its absence.

It wasn't the only thing that had gone missing lately. It seemed that there were weapons, supplies, and equipment that had been mysteriously disappearing over the past few days. So far, there had been no clue as to how this could happen. It certainly wasn't any of the natives, as they lived as far away from the encampment as they could and never voluntarily came into its confines.

He and his troops often visited the village closest to their little fort, but he preferred and trusted the stewards and servants he had brought with him, as opposed to the locals, who he considered primitives. They didn't understand the least bit of any of the equipment or even the simplest weapons.

They lived on vegetation, not even harvesting the abundant fish from the coastline waters. They spent their time in peaceful pursuits, farming and crafting and singing and dancing, of all things. There wasn't a single weapon among them.

Those in the jungle, however, had a different attitude. Although they never seemed to bother their pacific neighbors, they seemed to object strenuously to Ingold's troops' incursion onto their planet and weren't the least bit shy about hit-and-run raids, especially anytime he or his troops ventured beyond the edges of the forested areas.

He had discussed this at length with his adjutants and the sergeants over the troops during their mealtimes and whenever they met for strategy and tactics meetings.

He also knew he wasn't the only one coming up with things missing. Could it be that his own troops might be implicated? Could they be selling things to the enemy? He would have to order another diligent inspection of the barracks and other areas of the camp. He hadn't come this far in the ranks by assuming loyalty from any of his troops or their leaders.

Regil re-entered the room, the guard wide-eyed behind her.

Before Ingold could begin his tirade, the soldier began, "No one came anywhere near the area, Commandant, honest! I have not failed to watch."

Ingold held up one massive hand, and the corporal stopped abruptly. "Do I look like I am interested in your excuses?" he thundered. "Personal items have been taken, and this isn't the first time. You will be assigned to latrine duty for the next entire moon cycle, and the cost of the missing items will be deducted from your pay! I will not tolerate this kind of lax security in my troops. No excuses!" he continued with one finger pointed at the soldier. "I will not stand for it! Dismissed!"

The soldier gulped, nodded, and turned to leave. Ingold didn't even send another glance his way, turning now to Regil.

"I will inspect the troops now. Go about your duties and notify me if the club is found."

Regil's frightened nod faded from Jenny and Burt's eyes as they once again found themselves side by side with Bob and Merv, facing the Mookookie old ones.

"And that's just one of the hundreds of reports we have to sort through," Burt said, with a sigh of resignation. "Mind you, it looks like our plan is working, as far as it goes. I only wish I could export a few of my nanobot bite-'ems into the mess. Bob, could you see about that potential? It would be great to have our opponents dancing the itchy scratchy dance when we come across them, don't you think?"

Bob chuckled. "I'm sure glad you like me, Burt. You do have a bit of a mean streak, you know it?"

Burt cackled what he called his "mad scientist" laugh, and they all couldn't help but laugh with him.

"Okay," Jenny cut in when they had subsided. "We know that some of our strategies may be working to a certain extent, but it still comes down to this: How do we take this beyond massively irritating our opponents into corralling them and ridding the multiverse of their presence, and still stay within the strictures of doing the least amount of harm and not taking forever to free those who suffer under their regime?"

"You certainly know how to cut to the chase, my lady," Merv replied, with a courtly bow in Jenny's direction. "We do overaching have a few more preparations to make to give ourselves the best chance of success. The members of the Alliance are beginning to get restless, so to speak. Most of them, I would guess over 80 percent, still believe in what we're doing; but even among that group, they are hesitant to make this a long-term project. We keep getting inquiries as to our progress, and of course, Liliath is having to deal with all of that.

"My major concern is still security. None of this is going to work for us as we had hoped if the various components of the plan are leaked to the Inseni. Our major hope lies in the fact that our current research tells us there isn't a lot of communication or cooperation amongst our enemy at present. We cannot discern if there is an overarching force to be reckoned with, or if we are going to be dealing with a piecemeal situation."

Jenny shook her head. "So far, all the reports seem to indicate that the Inseni are a disjointed and disconnected lot and not very amenable to any input from any of their fellows outside their local jurisdictions. Each one of the generals or commandants of the various conquered planets seem to be taking the stance that now that Gall is out of the picture, they are their own boss, and as such, consider themselves local rulers of the conquered population."

"So, there has never been a hint of some kind of consortium or any other connection between the various conquered dimensions?" Bob asked, his mustache twitching in apparent agitation. "I am having a hard time believing that. Yes. I know Sam's massive temper tantrum disrupted the majority of the main governmental structure, but can we be sure of that? These various commanders appear to be acting independently, but how much of that was according to a plan already set in place by Gall in the first place?"

They all sat silently for a moment, taking that in.

"Well," Burt said, solemnly, "that is definitely a possibility, I suppose. I guess I keep thinking that any government on Earth that had gone through what Sam did on the main Inseni planet would be in such disarray that any kind of structure would have pretty much dissipated. But I keep forgetting that not all cultures think the same as we do. You'd think, with all the time I have spent as an Alliance agent, I'd have that figured out by now. Gracious, Bob, you sure know how to stir things up..."

Merv laughed. "That's one of the main reasons I brought him into the science team in the first place, Burt. He really knows how to turn things inside out and see them from an angle no one else considered before.

"So let's assume, for a moment, that Bob is exactly right. How do we figure out if there is anyone out there pulling the collective strings of the Inseni? Sam's actions may have seemed to knot them up, but did she do more than just snip a few? I've seen a weaver repair a broken thread before so you never knew it had ever been a problem. Maybe we can't see the whole tapestry yet?"

"Errg!" Burt exclaimed, an expression of pain blooming across his face. "Seriously, this feels so much like my mother's yarn basket. One day our cat got into it and had a blast while we were out. When we returned, the entire living room was draped in yarn, knotted and tangled, and the cat was sitting calmly in the middle of it, wearing dangling threads like a royal robe. You have no idea what it took to finally clean up the mess. And some of the yarn couldn't be saved, as it was so frayed and knotted that even my mother couldn't do anything but take her scissors to it," he finished dismally.

"Calm yourself," Merv said, shaking his head at Burt's vehement description of disaster. "We'll save what we can, which is all anyone can expect. When all is said and done, we can't save the multiverse from every little thing. We'll do our part, make no mistake about that; but pulling your hair out in frustration won't solve a thing, except to make you as bald as Tarafau. Let's take a step back and see as much of the big picture as we can."

Burt nodded and made a visible effort to calm himself. Jenny could understand his frustration, having also seen the despair of the people on Peril's planet. As she understood it, now, based on the reports they were receiving from the Mookookie agents out there, Peril's people actually had it pretty good compared to the other planets they now knew about.

She knew the Mookookie and the Nanoites were disgusted at what they were seeing and reporting back to this tiny council of hopeful rescuers. They held to their policies of no harm and no destruction, but she could also feel an urgent desire based on their reports to want to rescue the captives.

How did one balance these two contraries? On the one hand, no wish to impose their will on anyone and no desire to harm any living thing; on the other hand, a firm commitment to ensure the freedom of those who had been invaded by this inimical force. Jenny was sure she didn't know, but she also knew that they wouldn't quit until they figured it out.

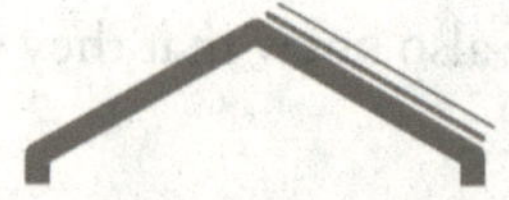

Chapter 27: What a Tangled Web

"Well?" Vena asked imperiously. "Did you do it? Or is this report just another round of excuses?"

"Mistress of All," Ga replied, her face nearly touching the floor before her. "We did it as you commanded. We captured a linkling, and it appears that Mi is truly resistant to its probing little mind."

"And Mi will pass their little test?"

"Indeed, we believe so, Great One. Mi has insinuated herself into the circle of companions currently being considered for the special training program, but she will need to pass all the tests, and it will take time."

"Time we have, at least for now. If they had decided on a battle strategy by now, we would be seeing an incursion; and our agents also tell us that the seeds we have planted amongst the various factions within the Alliance idiots are growing nicely. Even that despicable lizard, Liliath, has a fight on her hands directly from her own kin.

"We still have no hints as to how they wish to proceed. Their new way of communication mind to mind across dimensions is still the issue. I am hopeful that Mi will achieve our goal to infiltrate that network. She had better. Our next step, to break the Alliance, is very much in jeopardy otherwise."

Vena stretched languidly and stood, her royal robes swishing behind her as she left her servant still kneeling on the floor. "Call my Battle Commander and assemble the attack council in the War Room," she called behind her to the kneeling handmaid.

It was all so dreary, she thought, the little lives of the beings who surrounded her. She missed the times when this was all a challenge and not so tiresome. It was time she got directly involved again.

Her sniveling parents would have happily put her in a cage when she had begun to show signs of her aggressive and cruel nature. Not that this was any longer an issue. They were safely caged themselves in the lower levels of the castle. They had basic hygiene facilities and a bed, and they received the scraps from her table, as they were available, so they weren't quite starving. Very generous of herself, she was sure, considering their plans to confine her and prohibit her from taking her rightful place as the ultimate ruler of every dimension across space and time.

How dare they even begin to judge her? It had been obvious from her childhood that all things should be under her watchful eye. There was far too much leeway amongst the general populace for independent thinking, when it seemed to inevitably go against how she clearly saw things ought to be.

She sneered at the slave approaching her from the other end of the corridor, who instantly kneeled, staring properly at the floor until she passed, and then quickly got to her feet and almost ran along on whatever trivial errand she was about.

As she stalked down the wide mirrored hallway, she gloried in her striking appearance. Her velvety scarlet robes swished behind her, her black hair, streaked with silver, trailing down her back nearly to her hips. The single eye in her forehead was deep violet, and the usually wide black pupil was nearly a pinpoint as she allowed her fervent discontent to rise in her, making her pale face even whiter in the brightly lit corridor. She was certain this made her even more breathtakingly beautiful for all to see.

She knew her very presence struck awe into her subservient retainers. The fact that she was also incredibly beautiful and had authority beyond any other being as the ultimate ruler in her universe, certainly added to her power over all those who stood in the presence of her glorious manifestation. But the rule of only her own universe was a limitation she would not tolerate. It simply could not be.

As she entered the War Room, every being in the room snapped to attention, every eye on her, some with fervent adoration, some with trepidation, but all with reverent awe. She was, she knew, the center of rapt attention. No one would dare speak or move until she lent her generous permission.

"Be seated. We will be making some changes in the current plan. We have played the childish game of 'hide and find' with these Alliance dogs long enough. They will face the wrath and indignation of the true rulers of the multiverse. We now have a key to discover their conniving plans to disrupt our rightful and ultimate rule and domination of all beings to bring them into true order and control, to eliminate their need for unnecessary choices, and to allow them the privilege of serving their true masters.

No longer will chaos rule. With Gall disposed of and his factions scattered, there is no longer any reason to hide our intent or to keep any secrets. We will soon have what we need to infiltrate and cut short the plans by the so-called Dimensional Alliance to overrule our dominion. They will soon serve us and our purposes or be destroyed."

She looked pointedly into every eye of every one of her generals and adjutants individually, each one nodding solemnly in agreement, as if they would dare do otherwise.

"Now, there is an especially important target to consider. This being must be either convinced to join us or be destroyed. It is crucial to our plans, as it has great magical powers that may even rival my own. We cannot get to it directly at this point, as it is much too well guarded. We therefore must lure it out of hiding to a more vulnerable position. One of our tools is being put in place as we speak. In the meantime, you must make preparations to take immediate action once the trap has been sprung. Its magic is powerful, but it can be defeated.

Assemble your troops and prepare to give the orders I shall have written out for every unit across the multiverse that we currently control. You are dismissed."

They arose and left the room in dignified haste, each one bowing in turn to Vena with, "Great one, I obey."

She reclined smugly in the throne-like chair at the head of the long table, every seat now empty. She clapped her hands, and Ga appeared almost magically by her side, bowing deeply.

"Mistress? How may I serve?"

"Bring me the folder by my bed stand."

"Yes, Great One," she replied, and hurried off.

It was true, everything she had told her generals and adjutants. She was up against a magician of great strength and determination rivaling her own. Several times now it had escaped her grasp, but it would not escape again. She had no idea how it was accomplishing things she herself could not have imagined possible, but she was determined to learn and, if possible, duplicate those magics.

Ga came bustling in, not currently running, but Vena suspected that she had run the entire way to and from the bed chamber, as she was trying to suppress her panting breaths. She bowed and handed Vena the folder without comment.

Vena had seen through the eyes of one of her minions the face of the being that was standing in her way. Vena had projected the image to one of her court artisans who had created a fairly accurate painting of the creature. It was currently being reproduced for use by other minions who would be intrinsic to her plan.

She opened the folder and there it was. The two blue eyes... two? How disgusting was that? The two blue eyes looked up at her, and Vena felt her anger rise again. How could this little thing, this little creature, cause so much turmoil, interrupting her plans and creating so much havoc in what was inevitably to become her vast empire with no one to interfere or disrupt the order she intended to impose on every dimension she was able to reach via her portals? How could it actually keep her from obtaining the entire Dimensional Alliance network?

The linkling that perched on its shoulder was also an irritant, but with the capture of the linkling and the inoculation of that despicable yet talented Mi, she no longer concerned herself with that. It was enough that soon, if she could be patient, Vena would have the key to conquering the Dimensional Alliance once and for all.

She almost spit at the portrait. She would destroy it. She would erase it from existence. This would happen. She would see to it. And such a ludicrous name for this thing. She heard they called it *Jenny*.

The End

Watch for the next book in this epic science fiction fantasy trilogy: Tangles of Infinity

To write or not to write has never been the question...

I wrote my first 26-line poem at age 8, entitled "My Christmas ABCs". I then memorized it and performed it for the church Christmas party. This wasn't terribly surprising to the people who knew me. I started reading before Kindergarten and Dr. Seuss was one of my favorite authors, so rhyme came very naturally to me.

I have been writing all of my life, as long as she can remember. A lot of poetry, short stories and, of course, the usual school reports. I always got high grades on my writing assignments, even when I didn't in other classes.

Then, adulthood set in. Always a voracious reader, I dreamt of writing a novel, but after enlisting in the U.S. army, i got gloriously side-tracked with a wonderful husband and six amazing children. During that time, I still wrote: Musical plays for my kids at church and school, songs, poetry and even an

occasional newspaper article streamed from my pen.

I got involved in jobs that required clear concise writing and a lot of marketing copy. I put up her first website in 1996 and made my living on the internet for over 20 years, writing everything from blog posts to sales copy to scripts for online videos, not to mention copy for the websites I built for my

clients.

At age 64, at a time when I thought my adventures were over, I finally published the first novel in a nine book series. "The House on Infinity Loop" is the first book of the first of three trilogies of the Dimensional Alliance series.

To my readers: Never give up on your dream. It is never too late. There are many more adventures to come.

Also by Bonnie K.T. Dillabough

The Dimensional Alliance
Links to Infinity
Threads of Infinity

The Dimensional Alliance 2nd edition
The House on Infinity Loop
Infinity on Fire
Mirrors of Infinity
Ripples of Infinity
Chords of Infinity

Watch for more at https://dimensionalallianceheadquarters.com.